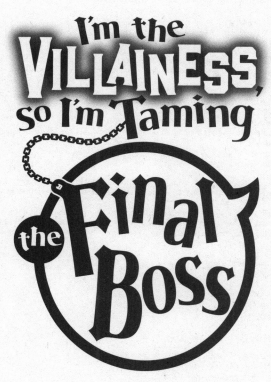

I'm the VILLAINESS, So I'm Taming the Final Boss

3

Sarasa Nagase

ILLUSTRATION BY
Mai Murasaki

YEN ON

New York

I'M THE VILLAINESS, SO I'M TAMING THE FINAL BOSS, Vol. 3
Sarasa Nagase

Translation by Taylor Engel
Cover art by Mai Murasaki

AKUYAKU REIJO NANODE LAST BOSS O KATTE MIMASHITA
©Sarasa Nagase 2018
First published in Japan in 2018 by KADOKAWA CORPORATION, Tokyo.
English translation rights arranged with KADOKAWA CORPORATION, Tokyo, through TUTTLE-MORI AGENCY, INC., Tokyo.

English translation © 2022 by Yen Press, LLC

Yen On
150 West 30th Street, 19th Floor
New York, NY 10001

Visit us at yenpress.com
facebook.com/yenpress
twitter.com/yenpress
yenpress.tumblr.com
instagram.com/yenpress

First Yen On Edition: June 2022
Edited by Yen On Editorial: Ivan Liang
Designed by Yen Press Design: Andy Swist

Yen On is an imprint of Yen Press, LLC.
The Yen On name and logo are trademarks of Yen Press, LLC.

Library of Congress Cataloging-in-Publication Data
Names: Nagase, Sarasa, author. | Murasaki, Mai, illustrator. | Engel, Taylor, translator.
Title: I'm the villainess, so I'm taming the final boss / Sarasa Nagase ;
    illustration by Mai Murasaki ; translation by Taylor Engel.
Other titles: Akuyaku reijou nanode last boss wo kattemimashita. English
Description: First Yen On edition. | New York, NY : Yen On, 2021
Identifiers: LCCN 2021030963 | ISBN 9781975334055 (v. 1 ; trade paperback) |
    ISBN 9781975334079 (v. 2 ; trade paperback) | ISBN 9781975334093 (v. 3 ; trade paperback)
Subjects: LCGFT: Fantasy fiction. | Light novels.
Classification: LCC PL873.5.A246 A7913 2021 | DDC 895.63/6—dc23
LC record available at https://lccn.loc.gov/2021030963

ISBNs: 978-1-9753-3409-3 (paperback)
        978-1-9753-3410-9 (ebook)

10 9 8 7 6 5 4 3 2 1

LSC-C

Printed in the United States of America

I'm the VILLAINESS, So I'm Taming the Final Boss

CONTENTS

Claude Jean Ellmeyer

Crown Prince of Imperial Ellmeyer.
The demon king and Aileen's fiancé.

Elefas Levi

A mage from the Levi tribe of
magic grand dukes. The final
boss of the *Regalia of Saints,
Demons, and Maidens 1* fan disc.

Aileen Lauren d'Autriche

A villainess who's remembered her past
life. However, her incomplete memories
are making it very hard for her to
avoid doom.

I'm the VILLAINESS, So I'm Taming the Final Boss

Character Introductions and Glossary

Pierre Jean Ellmeyer

The emperor of Imperial Ellmeyer.
Claude and Cedric's father.

Lara Jean Ellmeyer

The empress dowager of Imperial
Ellmeyer. Pierre's mother.

Cedric Jean Ellmeyer

The hero of the game. True to
pattern, he's broken off his
engagement and is now
bethrothed to Lilia.

Lilia Reinoise

The heroine of the game. Like Aileen,
she's actually reincarnated.

The *otome* game *Regalia of Saints, Demons, and Maidens 1* fan disc

The Levi tribe produced rare humans who possessed magic. These dangerous mages were destroyed by the righteous might of Imperial Ellmeyer—or that's the official story. The truth is that hostages were taken from the tragic tribe, and the rest were forced to serve as guards for the imperial family. As a mage from this tribe, on certain routes, Elefas destroys the empire. In addition, in "this world," the tribe was conquered because the current emperor wanted a large number of mages in order to control his son, the demon king.

Second Prince Cedric Jean Ellmeyer is walking down a gallery lined with the portraits of past emperors. Hearing approaching footsteps, he stops.

Sunlight streams in through the large, evenly spaced windows, but the corridor is broad and long, and shadows hug the walls. That said, only members of the imperial family are allowed into this part of the castle. Not even his friends or his beloved fiancée can set foot in this corridor, so there are very few people he might encounter here.

"Is that you, Cedric?"

The steady footsteps draw closer, then stop in the shadows, two windows ahead of him.

"...Brother. That's unusual. You never come here," he says ironically. He does his best to sound more animated than he feels.

These are the residential quarters of the imperial family, and only four people can pass through them: himself; his father, the emperor; his grandmother, the empress dowager; and this man, his older half brother. However, although his brother is crown prince again, he still doesn't live within these walls. Instead, he spends his time in the dilapidated castle in the forest.

That fact weighs heavily on their father. He worries that his oldest son may never forgive the family.

Ridiculous.

Cedric hates his father. The emperor hadn't been able to hide Cedric's older half brother completely or protect him. He always lamented, *"But he's so brilliant,"* and yet because the boy was the demon king, he said they had no choice. He simply let the empress dowager and those around him make the decisions and eventually cast his son aside. He told Cedric, *"Thank heavens you were born,"* and made excuses to abandon his eldest, then privately despaired over the fact that his second son wasn't as outstanding as the first. The man only wanted to play the role of a father.

The fool hasn't even noticed that his oldest son had abandoned him long before he could forsake anything.

"Have you finally decided to leave that tumbledown castle in the woods and move back here?"

"No, the empress dowager summoned me."

"Grandmother? Well, well. She may have picked up a new poison."

Cedric hates his grandmother as well.

"I will make you emperor. You needn't worry about a thing," she whispered, like a devil of temptation. Cedric knows it's only because she thinks he would make for a good puppet...and yet she's obsessed with his older brother, calling him *that odious woman's child*. Women's fights are endlessly ugly.

"My condolences. Do your best to not die, Brother."

"I'm sorry. I'm constantly making you worry, aren't I?"

"Worry? You're as laid-back as ever, I see. In case you've forgotten, we're fighting over the throne."

"But we aren't the ones who are fighting, are we?"

—And then there's Cedric's brother. His older half brother is...

He keeps calling him "Brother" and only realizing he's done it later. *"I'm sorry for forcing this onto you,"* his brother had said when he left him behind. Cedric had always known his brother came to see how he was doing every so often.

Why is his only relative who feels like family the demon king? Irritated, Cedric looks away, staring at the ground as he spits out, "No, you're wrong. We *are* fighting, and I'm going to be emperor."

"For your fiancée's sake?"

"That's right."

Everyone had forced him into the role of crown prince that had been destined for his brother. Still, he's always tried hard to be a good one in the hopes that they'll acknowledge him one day... even as his true self stagnates.

Lilia is the one who rescued him. If this is what she wants, then...

"You're trying to become emperor because that's what Aileen wants, too."

Aileen, Cedric's former fiancée, is obsessed with being empress. That's why she left him for his older brother. She can say she "admired" him, but if he didn't feel it, it means nothing.

Cedric bites his lip. His brother steps closer, and as the sunlight hits him, his unearthly, inhuman beauty only become more pronounced. His emotions can affect the surrounding weather, so he normally doesn't let his feelings show. To casual observers, it probably looks as if he has no heart at all.

However, a closer examination reveals what he's feeling. That hint of a gentle smile, for example.

"You really are stubborn. If you don't know what to do, you could just talk to me about it. I *am* your older brother."

"...Stop looking weirdly happy. You can't lord that over me forever."

"Let me give you a word of warning, then. When a man does whatever a woman tells him, she tires of him quickly."

He speaks as if he's seen through everything. When Cedric looks up, the shadow of a large palm blocks his vision. His brother pats his head once, lightly. Cedric's eyes widen, and then he slaps that hand away. He glares at him wordlessly, and this time, his brother flashes a smile anyone could see. "I'll be bringing Aileen to the next soiree. Don't cause any mischief."

Lilia's words skim through his mind.

"—*Are you sure you don't love Lady Aileen?*"

"Claude! Lilia's plotting something."

Claude has already gone three steps ahead of him by then, but he turns back.

"I'd be careful if I were you... That's all I can say." Unable to endure his brother's gaze, Cedric walks on rapidly. He grits his teeth, refusing to look back.

Just outside the imperial family's residential wing, his childhood friend Marcus is waiting for him. As Cedric emerges, Marcus asks, "How was your audience with the empress dowager?"

"She still says she'll back me as emperor. She's angry that Father returned the position of crown prince to my brother without consulting her; apparently, she's already finished laying the groundwork. She said she'll be giving Lilia a dress later on as well."

"Then there's nothing to worry about. Now the only influential nobles on the demon king's side are Duke d'Autriche and his family. That said, they are a serious problem..."

"If I'd married Aileen, I imagine my path to becoming emperor would be much easier than this."

"You don't mean you have some weird regrets after all this

time, right? Over Aileen of all people?" Marcus grimaces, but Cedric looks back at him coolly.

"I'm just stating a fact. Making an enemy of the d'Autriche family was a poor move."

"What are you talking about? We were both sick of cleaning up Aileen's messes, remember? She may be a very old friend, but there are limits. She said and did whatever she liked, without thinking of anyone else…"

He's absolutely right. Both he and Cedric had been fed up with that unrepentant arrogance. They'd also been concerned that Duke d'Autriche's already vast power would only grow.

However, it's true that there was a time when he thought, *Aileen's like a little sister to me, so what can I do?*

"I'm one thing, but if you let anyone else hear such careless remarks, they'll get the wrong idea for sure. More importantly, you'll make Lilia uneasy. Remember how she suspected you might like Aileen a little while ago?"

"…Yes, that's true."

"Pull yourself together," Marcus tells him and sets off. Apparently, Lilia and the others are waiting.

Lately, her entourage has grown. Even if Cedric is officially her fiancé, if he doesn't stay on top of things, someone may very well snatch her away before he even has time to blink. That's what Marcus is mainly worried about.

…Make Lilia uneasy?

When she asked him if he liked Aileen, at first, Cedric also wondered whether he'd made her nervous. That was why he responded with *"Why ask such a thing?"* His first instinct was to dispel her unease.

And yet Lilia appeared disappointed.

In that moment, her eyes seemed to say, *You boring man*. Then she laughed at him and dropped the subject.

When a man does whatever a woman tells him, she tires of him quickly.

Cedric slowly clenches his fists, keeping them out of sight. Then he looks at the face of his beloved fiancée.

"Welcome back, Cedric. Was the empress dowager well?" she asks with a smile.

As always, she's smiling derisively at the men who do nothing but obey her every word.

Nights spent in masks are...honeyed wine.

Aileen accurately recites the password from memory, and the stone door opens for her. High heels clicking, she enters the gloomy venue. The place is suffused with a sweet fragrance. As she looks around from behind her amethyst-studded mask, what she sees is even more questionable than she anticipated. Gold ingots piled on a table. Attractive slaves in birdcages. A tank in which nothing but unusual red eyes float. All the participants are smiling at one another from under their masks.

With enough money, nothing is out of reach for this establishment's patrons.

A place for dark dealings, packed with all the world's degeneracy.

"And here I wondered where you were taking us... An underground auction. Unbelievable." The tallest of her four guards, a youth with soft blond hair, grumbles behind his black mask. "Where in the world did you find out about this, sweet Ailey?"

"That's 'Lady Aileen,' Walt."

"Better than using real names in a place like this, Kyle."

Irked, the second youth falls silent. He seems to be of Eastern stock, with porcelain skin and black hair. Aileen put him in a white mask.

"Well, maybe so, but...still, a woman named Ailey?"

"It wouldn't have been a bad idea to come dressed as a boy,

now that you mention it. However, I'm supposed to be a widow with a retinue of young men at the moment."

"Before that, I've got a question, Ailey..."

"It'll have to wait, Auguste. A demon-snuff transaction is supposed to happen here tonight. I hear they'll be selling demons as well. Here, in the imperial capital, right under Master Claude's nose. How incredibly brazen of them."

Having found a corner behind a thick black curtain, Aileen turns to face her group. "If it comes down to it, Auguste, you'll make arrests as a member of the Holy Knights. I have Isaac and the others standing by outside. If we give Jasper some scandalous tidbits regarding the participating aristocrats, it should make everything else go smoother. Luc and Quartz will tend to any injured, and if I cannot be reached or become otherwise incapacitated, look to Isaac for orders. If things take a bad turn, flee through this wall. Denis has tampered with it and turned it into an exit."

"Oh... I see, everyone's in on this one... That's good, but what I meant was—"

"That concludes the explanation. With your skills, I really doubt there's any real danger, but don't be careless."

"Does Master Claude know about this?" James asks her, point-blank.

Aileen smiles, pretending she hasn't heard him. "All right, let's commence the operation."

"Does. Master Claude. Know. About this?"

"He couldn't possibly know, James. When she borrowed us from him, she said it was because she'd been invited to a certain lady's salon and she wanted a guard detail."

"If I recall, she also told Master Claude she couldn't take him along. Obviously a lie."

"When I borrowed you from Master Claude, I simply wasn't certain what would happen yet, that's all. Besides, the part about the salon was genuine. The ladies are no longer young, but they're still quite active. I have a standing invitation to drop by with some handsome young male guards in tow. Apparently, they love feasting their eyes on straight backs and well-toned chests and torsos. They requested Walt and Kyle by name..."

The two she's designated freeze up. Opening a red fan that matches her mask, Aileen uses it to hide her smile. "Of course, you two are Master Claude's precious guards. Even so, those ladies have a great deal of influence in high society, and I can't simply ignore their wishes. Oh, what to do...?"

"No, no, no, no, wait, you're saying no matter what happens to us, we won't be able to complain, right?!"

"Does that mean that if we don't want to be thrown to the wolves, we have to hold our tongues and cooperate?"

The only response she offers is a significant look. Walt's and Kyle's faces stiffen. Glancing at them rather sympathetically, Auguste lowers his voice. "Not telling the demon king is a bad idea, Ailey. You made him mad just a little while ago, remember?"

"Why, I don't know what you mean. Master Claude is always kind to me."

"This is ridiculous. All I have to do is let him know right now."

Being half demon, James is able to link to Claude's mind, although not as well as the demons can. Tipping him off would be a simple exercise. However, before his pale eyes turn red, a telltale sign of magic, Aileen adds another quiet comment. "The ladies were interested in you as well, James. They said something about wanting to see that beauty of yours twist in humiliation."

"......"

"Would you also like to participate, Auguste? The fresh-faced recruit of the Holy Knights seems to be the center of attention. At their age, the words *fresh-faced* seem particularly appealing, or so I've heard. They mentioned being especially taken with your rump, which they caught glimpses of while you were training."

"Okay, guys, let's give it our best! This operation's preferable to a salon of lusty matrons!" Auguste rallies the group, and everyone nods.

Fluttering her fan, Aileen sighs. "And they were so looking forward to you. How will I ever make it up to them?"

"What do we have to do, then?" James glares at her.

Aileen snaps her fan shut and calls to a passing waiter. "Where is the manager? I've brought merchandise I'd like to sell." Aileen hands the servant a tip—a jewel that she hid in the lining of her gown—and the masked waiter nods in understanding.

James looks perplexed. "Merchandise? You mean you actually have something on hand?"

"Yes, articles that are just the thing for a place like this."

"Huh?! You do, sweet Ailey?"

"It had better not be demon snuff."

"Two church-made augmented humans and a cambion."

The looks and utility of the church's "Nameless Priests," expertly dressed by Aileen in contrasting white and black outfits, have appeal that needs no introduction. Meanwhile, the half demon's inhuman beauty is enhanced by his formal ultramarine uniform, and his rarity only adds to his value.

While the other four stand frozen, Aileen signs the sales contract the waiter holds out to her. Then she smiles at them. "You've fetched a good price. Go on now. Do your jobs properly."

Though her retainers are screaming that she'll pay for this outrage, she's sure they'll come back to her safely.

Left alone with Aileen, Auguste murmurs, sounding stunned. "A-are you sure this is all right?"

"It's fine. Those three will do well. I've placed them where they are because I trust them."

Two of them are human but were raised by the church to be demon-killing weapons, while the other is a cambion who survived wretched years of being hunted by those humans. None of them has led a decent life. That means she can relax and let them take care of this.

"Auguste, you come with me. You've never been to this sort of place before, correct? Watch and learn how to conduct yourself. If you want to succeed in the Holy Knights, only knowing your way around in respectable establishments won't be enough."

"Hmm. All right... We're pretty close in age, but everyone else is a lot more experienced than I am, huh."

"Don't let it trouble you. Growing accustomed to places like this often happens in the span of a single night."

"How?"

In response to his innocent question, Aileen sets an index finger against deeply rouged lips and smiles. "You simply have to let a bad woman deceive you. You'll be more of a man overnight."

"In that case, I think it's already happened... Huh?" Without warning, Auguste stops in his tracks.

Aileen follows his gaze. "Did you see something?"

"...Well, I thought I'd spotted Serena. I suspect my eyes are playing tricks on me."

Auguste's diplomatic smile is erased by a scream.

When Aileen hears the words "A demon's loose!" she mentally

switches gears. "That must be James and the others. They work fast."

"No, I think they're probably just really mad that you sold them!"

"We'll take this opportunity to slip into the organizers' rooms. If we're lucky, we'll find a list of invited guests..." Lifting her skirts, Aileen takes off, threading her way through the confused crowd.

She's known the layout of the interior ever since information about the auction first reached her. The basement may be an auction venue, but the structure above it is a hotel. The rooms the organizers are using as meeting rooms are on the fourth floor. At that height, they can make do with the stairs—no need to use the elevator.

Security is thin; the guards seem to be busy sorting out the uproar. Aileen and Auguste duck behind cover every so often, but they're able to head straight for their destination.

"Auguste, watch the corridor."

"All ri— Ailey!"

Aileen registers the tip of the blade just as Auguste deflects it. Her brilliant Holy Knight has foiled their assailant. As the figure emerges from the shadows, Aileen is startled—and not just because the attacker is a woman.

"You're...Serena?!"

Without responding to Auguste, the girl turns to flee. Her face is veiled with thin silk gauze, and she's holding a dagger. She makes for the terrace, where white curtains flutter in the breeze. In her other hand, there's a document.

"After her, Auguste! She has something—!"

Suddenly, an arm reaches out of the wall and covers her mouth. Auguste turns back, striking at the throat of the individual who's restraining Aileen as he does so, but an invisible force knocks his blade away.

Was that magic?!

A black velvet hood brushes Aileen's cheek. She can't see the face inside it. However, judging from the size of the hand restraining her and the feel of the figure pressing against her back, her opponent is a man.

"Hush. If you make noise, the guards will return. If anyone learns that Duke d'Autriche's daughter is in a place like this, it probably won't end well."

As the young man's quiet, rather low voice tickles her ear, he removes her mask.

He knows me. How did he find out? I only decided to infiltrate a few hours ago—

"Don't be alarmed. I'm on your side. I simply wanted to keep you from treading on the carpet."

"...The carpet?" Auguste asks. His voice is sharp, and there's none of his usual friendliness in it.

The hooded man nods. "The carpet one pace to your left is enchanted. A magic item. As the bearer of the sacred sword, if you look closely, you should be able to see the spell."

With her mouth still covered, Aileen looks at the spot he's described. On her left, there's a carpet with an intricate design woven in gold thread that she would be able to touch with her toe if she takes a single step in its direction. At first glance, it appears to be a perfectly ordinary rug.

The stranger is right, though. When she stares at it, even in the dim room, she can see a vivid haze.

"If that carpet detects magic, it will use a spell to seal off this room. It's a trap to capture any thieves who use magic to break in.

The sacred sword is imbued with divine power, so it won't trigger the trap, but there's magic in your shadow."

He must mean the spell Claude cast. Aileen's shadow acts as a gateway for the demons.

"That fellow's weapon has also been enchanted. At any rate, it would have been dangerous to let that carpet detect you, so I intervened. I apologize for the abrupt discourtesy."

"......"

"If you understand that I am not your enemy, I'll release you. Do we understand each other?"

Aileen nods. As Auguste lowers his sword, the hooded man removes his hand. When she steps away from him, he kneels. "Once again. It's an honor to meet you, Lady Aileen Lauren d'Autriche."

The stranger bows his head. He's still wearing the black hood, and she can't make out his face. He seems to be very knowledgeable about magic, but there are no horns on his head or wings on his back. Most telling of all, the sacred sword within Aileen doesn't react.

He's human. Drawing a slow breath, Aileen answers him. "You seem to be well acquainted with me... You're a mage, aren't you?"

"Huh? A mage... You mean like a magician? Do those actually exist?"

Auguste is startled, and for good reason: At this point, there are almost no humans in this world who can use magic and spells. However, not only did this man emerge from the wall, but he also deflected Auguste's blade with some sort of invisible power, has eyes that can detect magic, and knows much about magic items. Taken together, there's but a single possible conclusion.

"At the very least, we seem to be conversing with one."

"You have the right of it. I realize it's terribly rude of me to ask, but I've come to request an audience with the demon king."

"With Master Claude?" Aileen's eyes widen, but then her ears catch hurried footsteps. There are several people in the corridor.

Noticing them as well, the hooded man rises to his feet. "It appears we won't be able to talk at our leisure here." He points at the door, and the lock falls, all by itself. Then he turns his palm toward it, and a sofa and heavy chest of drawers slide in front of it of their own accord.

Auguste is impressed. "That's incredible. It really is magic... Whenever I ask James to show me some, the only thing he does is break things."

"I could put our investigators to sleep, but there would be no end to that. I suggest we make our escape."

"We can't; I haven't found anything yet."

"The guest list is here."

He probably smiled just now. When she spots the document in the folds of his robe, Aileen smiles back at him. "Excellent. I take it I can buy it from you by putting in a word with Master Claude?"

"That would be a tremendous help. All right, Lady Aileen. This way."

He beckons her onto the terrace, and Aileen steps outside. Behind her, the voices on the other side of the door turn suspicious as they notice it's locked. It's only a matter of time before they kick their way inside.

There's a rope tied to the balustrade. Aileen let the woman who'd attacked her get away while she was distracted by the suspicious hooded mage; her would–be assassin must have made her escape this way.

I wonder if that really was Serena. This is the fourth floor... Where would she have gotten the ability to...?

Abruptly, she thinks better of it: The girl is the heroine of *that* game. It's far from impossible.

"Say, can't you just teleport us out of here, like the demon king does?"

"I'm afraid that's beyond me. It's an extremely advanced spell, and while I might be able to teleport myself, three of us would make for a heavy burden. That would only be a last resort in case of an emergency."

"Really? But the demon king does it like it's nothing."

"His magic far surpasses mine."

"Huh..." As usual, Auguste is easygoing even with people he's just met. "I guess the demon king really is the demon king... At the soiree the other evening, he said the roast beef was delicious and completely pigged out on it, but he actually is the demon king..."

"He is my Master Claude, after all. You mustn't assume he's like the average man. In any case, how will we be making our escape if not by teleporting?"

"I'll control the wind, so jump off, if you would."

He says something incredible as if it's a simple matter. However, the door to the room has begun to shake and rattle, and Aileen hears someone yell, "Bring an ax." It won't be long until they break through.

"It's all right. Go on, stand at the edge."

"O-okay. Ailey, here, take my hand. That dress must make things tough. The wind's strong, too."

"Y-yes... Oh, that's right; what is your name?" Placing one

hand in Auguste's, she turns back. Just then, a stronger gust of wind buffets the black hood, and it falls back, baring the mage's face.

His hair gleams softly, the color of moonlight. His eyes are the shade of red considered sinister by many of the people who inhabit this world, proof that their owner wields magic. Wrapped in that black hooded cloak, out in the wind, there's something dreamlike and melancholy about his smile.

However, when Aileen gasps, it isn't because his ephemeral appearance has moved her.

I—I remember this, but it—it can't be. Game art...?!

This shouldn't be happening. Again?

The man looks straight at Aileen, then lowers his intelligent eyes. "I should have introduced myself earlier. My name is Elefas Levi."

There's no mistake. She feels faint. *The final boss of the Game 1 fan disc!!*

"Ah! Ailey, look ou— Oh."

Aileen reels and nearly falls over backward, but someone catches her, holding her up. The jolt brings her back to her senses, and as she hastily tries to regain her balance, she sets a hand on the chest of her rescuer. It's only at this point that she realizes something's off.

She'd been falling away from the terrace. Into empty space.

In other words, the person who's caught her is floating in midair.

"If you wanted to go for a stroll through the sky, you could simply have asked me. You really aren't honest about these things, you know."

The sound of the voice coming from just above her head makes her stiffen. She knows that if she looks up now, death will be waiting for her.

"Or should I bring out the carriage? You're particularly fond of carriages that race through the night sky, aren't you?"

"M–Master...Claude..."

"There's something I must ask you first, though. You're quite clever, so I'm sure you already know what it is I want to ask."

The demon king shows no mercy. Setting a hand on Aileen's chin, he forces her head up. There's an unnerving smile on his thin lips.

"My darling Aileen. What have you been doing behind my back this time?"

Behind her, the final boss of the Game 1 fan disc. In front of her, the final boss of Game 1.

Aileen's world is positively brimming with final bosses.

This is the world of an *otome* game Aileen played in her previous life.

...If she explained that to someone honestly, and they believed her, the proper course of action would be to take them straight to a physician—that's how ludicrous the story is. And so with the notable exception of when she's talking to the one person whose memories are similar to her own, Aileen never mentions it.

In the first place, since I actually am living here, this is reality.

However, the game's plot still *holds true*, even in this reality. Since regaining her memories of her previous life, Aileen has had two direct experiences with this.

The title of the game that's plaguing her is *Regalia of Saints, Demons, and Maidens*. While its scenario and story were rather slipshod, its voice acting and art earned the series many fans. There were numbered games that made up the main story, and corresponding fan discs for each one. There were also ports and remakes, and Aileen has a vague memory that a spin-off release date had been approaching right around the time of her past life's death.

Aileen has been reincarnated as the villainess of the original game, the one that started it all. According to the game's timeline, her character should already be dead. However, Aileen has dodged that fate by romancing the cause of her death: the final boss of Game 1, Demon King Claude. Putting it that way makes it sound as if there's no love between them, but that wouldn't be accurate.

This is how things really stand...

"After giving careful consideration to diverse and sundry things, I've reached the conclusion that we no longer needed anything so boorish as words."

In the demon king's office, Claude has pushed Aileen down onto a full-length couch. He's wearing a gentle smile. Aileen has planted both hands on his chest and is pushing him back.

"M-Master Claude. I do think we need to talk things over if we're to achieve mutual understanding."

"It's all right. There are ways to deepen understanding without talking."

"Y-you're angry, aren't you?! Yes, I see! I was wrong. There simply wasn't time to tell you, Master Claude, and—"

"No time? James. What was it that you reported to me?"

"I expressed the opinion that we should inform you, but Lady Aileen ordered me to hold my tongue and threatened me."

"James, you traitor! So it was you who told Master Claude!"

Her anger gets the better of her, and she tries to sit up, but Claude holds her down. He isn't being rough with her; in fact, he's gentle from start to finish.

"I would like you to understand, physically, just how important you are to me."

...But his eyes aren't smiling.

"We— W-w-we aren't married yet! More importantly, it
would be far too improper in a place like this!"

"You were the one who refused when I invited you to the
bedroom earlier. That means it will have to be here."

"W-we are in public! Auguste and James and Walt and Kyle
and even Isaac are here! Consider your dignity as a leader!"

"All right. I'll have them give us some privacy."

"That's no good either, please wai— Eek!"

He's bitten her earlobe. Her ear promptly flushes red, and
Claude whispers into it. "Let's begin. First, I'll make it so you
can't go out in public."

Screaming internally, Aileen kicks and struggles, casting about
for a way to cool her beloved's anger. "I-I'll let you rest your head
on my lap, Master Claude!"

"Shall I extinguish the lights? Or should we keep them on?"

"A-and on top of that, I'll give you a good-bye kiss!"

"So we'll be keeping them lit, hmm? I like it when you're
bold, too."

"That's still not enough?! I-in that case, why don't we steal off
for a picnic in disguise? You like going about incognito, don't you,
Master Claude? I did refuse the other day because I was busy..."

"You know, you're right. I'd be more than happy to do this
outdoors."

"No, that's not— A-all right, I'll set aside a day and do nothing but gaze at you, Master Claude!"

Claude already has his teeth around the ribbon over Aileen's
chest, but finally, he pauses. Capitalizing on this opening, Aileen

hastily slips out from under him. The ribbon comes undone, but she can't afford to bother with it and lose her chance to turn this around. "I'll look at you, and only you, all day long. Work has kept me from leisure recently, after all."

"......"

Claude gets up, sweeping back his glossy black hair. He seems to be thinking hard. Aileen keeps talking fast and desperately. "I won't work or do anything else that day; I'll simply stay by your side, Master Claude. I won't so much as glance at anything else."

"—And if you do?"

"What?" The moment she stops, Claude turns toward her, so Aileen clenches her fists. "I–if I do anything else, as a penalty, I'll give you a kiss, Master Claude! On the cheek, or the forehead—anywhere but the lips!"

"...Can you promise that?"

"I promise! And I'll keep my word."

"Very well, then." Her relief is short-lived; Claude is wearing a deep smile. A shudder runs down Aileen's spine. "I imagine you'll be quite fetching as you avert your eyes in embarrassment, kissing me on command. I'm looking forward to it very, very much. Even if you cry or scream, I won't let you escape."

"Checkmate...," she hears Isaac mutter, but she decides not to give that bridge too much thought until the day she has to cross it.

Telling herself it's enough that she's been forgiven, she hastily reties her ribbon, then stands very straight. "That aside, Master Claude, I have a report."

"You've done something else? Depending on what it is, we may resume right where we left off."

"No, I haven't done a thing! I was only asked to facilitate an audience with you. Just to confirm, you aren't already acquainted...

correct?" Aileen takes another look at the youth in the black hood who's standing in the center of the office.

Recrossing his legs, Claude follows Aileen's gaze. "We've never met... You've picked up another unusual one. A mage, hmm? What is your name?"

"I am Elefas Levi, Your Highness, Crown Prince Claude Jean Ellmeyer."

Although he's been forcibly teleported from the underground auction to the demon king's office, Elefas bows calmly and respectfully. Even when Aileen and Claude were being noisy, he made no attempt to speak until granted permission. Then there's that lovely bow. He behaves as though he's used to serving some noble personage.

"Elefas Levi. A mage. You're descended from the Levi tribe of magic grand dukes?"

"I no longer have the status to claim that title. At present, I simply serve Imperial Ellmeyer." Elefas's eyes are downcast, and his attitude is clearly self-deprecating.

Aileen resumes her seat beside Claude, cocking her head slightly. *The Levi tribe's history is practically what it was in the game, then.*

They were a rare tribe of humans with an affinity for magic. However, in Imperial Ellmeyer, magic was closely associated with demons. There were some who believed that those who could use magic had gained their powers by laying with demons. That was why historically, humans with magic powers had been treated like demons: cursed as monsters and ostracized from society.

Even under those circumstances, until twenty years ago, the Levi tribe had maintained their own small country under the rule of a magic grand duke. However, they had declared war in an attempt to expand their territory and lost. Their sovereign territory was broken up, and the tribe scattered. One could learn that much by studying this world's history.

The problem was what came after. Thought to possess dangerous magic, the people of the Levi tribe were pressed into clandestine service as mages who protected the imperial family. Their children and elders were taken as hostages, ensuring their obedience. Even within the empire, this was known only to a scant handful of people who were close to the imperial family. Aileen's knowledge about it chiefly comes from her foreknowledge of the game.

After all, the official story is that a just empire destroyed a country of dangerous mages... Even though if I recall correctly, it was the Ellmeyer Empire that made unreasonable demands and cornered them, forcing the Levi people into a war of desperation.

The game had covered that history, so it's probably safe to assume it as fact. The Levi tribe had fallen neatly into Imperial Ellmeyer's trap, been branded as "dangerous," and subjugated. Even now, simply claiming to be from the Levi tribe is enough to get stones thrown at you.

This extremely inhumane treatment is based on the fact that the emperor wanted a great many biddable mages to control the demon king, who was still very young at the time. Aileen learned as much while eavesdropping on a conversation in her father's study between her eldest brother and her father, the prime minister. However, the Levi tribe proved to be incapable of controlling the demon king. In the end, they were simply relegated to being slaves under the imperial family's direct control.

"As you are the crown prince, Your Highness, I believe you know of us. Am I correct?"

"Yes. You're the tribe that was sacrificed when my father attempted to deal with me as a child."

Elefas bites his lip.

Claude narrows his eyes, guessing Elefas's wish before he can kneel. "You pledge to serve me faithfully, so as soon as I become emperor, you want me to grant the Levi tribe citizenship— Is that it? Or do you want your country restored to you?"

"! Yes, exactly. We beg you to save us...!"

"That will depend on how well you work." Claude's brief response all but acknowledges Elefas as his retainer already. Elefas's eyes widen.

The rapid decision startles Aileen as well. True, Claude does need human allies. However, he's only just met Elefas, and he doesn't know his character. That's a problem.

Isaac, who's been watching from across the room, speaks up. "Demon King, what are your grounds for believing that guy can be trusted?"

"I have none."

"Oh, you don't, huh? In that case, I'm against this. The Levi lost a war. They probably resent us."

"Revenge is a contest. If he tries to challenge me at it, that means he has admirable spirit, and that he's capable of intrigue. If he possesses outstanding talent, wouldn't it be best to acquire him?"

He has a point. Aileen blinks. *True, Elefas is the final boss of the Game 1 fan disc... On certain routes, he did succeed in destroying the empire. Put another way, that's solid proof that he's brilliant.*

Her knowledge is vague because she never played the fan disc that thoroughly. Aileen—or rather, the person she'd been in her previous life—had been a stickler for canon material. She didn't play the remakes or ports of games she liked, and the only ones she had gone through multiple times were the originals. She didn't actively seek out fan discs. She read the spoilers, and if they looked like they'd be her thing, she'd tried them. Even then, most of the time, she only played far enough to see one or two endings with the character she'd been after, then lost interest.

As a result, although Aileen has a general grasp of the fan disc packages, spoilers, and game art, she doesn't know the details.

I only played the Cedric route on the fan disc. That means I know Elefas was doing various things behind the scenes for the sake of his revenge, but on that route, they were kept very vague...

In the first place, in the game, both she and Claude would have been dead by now, but they aren't. The game scenario and reality already contradict each other. Deciding that thinking about it is probably pointless, Aileen takes another look at Elefas.

Although his entrance had been rather bizarre, he helped Aileen and requested an audience. He must have looked into their internal affairs a decent amount. His intelligence-gathering abilities seem to be solid, and from the fact that he's followed the proper procedures, he's skilled at maneuvering as well.

Most of all, she wants to focus on reality, not the game. A young man who wants to save his oppressed tribe... What reason could there be to refuse offering him aid? Especially if Aileen's beloved is the cause of it.

Yes, that's sure to be on Claude's mind. Even after he gave up his right to the throne, he's been concerned about people who tend to slip through the cracks and often goes out of his way to help them. There's no way he'll abandon people who've been turned into second-class citizens because of him. Even if they do betray him, she's sure he'll try to save them anyway.

Love and respect fill Aileen's breast. What a splendid man she's fallen for this second time around!

"Even so, the mess in Mirchetta only just calmed down. You're being too optimistic."

"Isaac. We are trying to convince demons and humans to coexist, you know. It's only natural to save humans who've been exploited and mistreated for their association with demons, isn't it?" Rising to her feet, Aileen looks straight at Claude. "I am in full agreement, Master Claude. I'll devote all my energy to this cause!"

"...Just a moment ago, I believe you were saying the exact opposite. Are we ignoring that?"

"I am grateful for the thought, but, Lady Aileen... To tell the truth, serving Master Claude isn't the will of the entire tribe. I came hoping that I might be allowed to serve him in secret, even if no others joined me."

"That's an admirable mindset. Master Claude still has few allies. If you'd come to us after he had many, our opinion of you wouldn't have risen as easily, and your tribe would not be given favorable treatment."

"Quite true," Elefas agrees with a wry smile. He isn't hiding the fact that he's calculating; that's another point in his favor.

"However, that alone would not be enough to let you truly grasp Master Claude's greatness. To that end, I will teach you all about how wonderful he is!"

"...Um, yes, of course. I'll be looking forward to that."

"Demon King, remember what we talked about earlier? Reins."

"Yes, that's right. Let's adjourn on that note for tonight. Aileen."

She's been thinking about what she can do, and it delays her reaction.

He drops one light kiss on her eyelid, whispering gently. "It's time for bed. Good night, my love."

She hears his fingers snap beside her ear and then experiences a brief moment of motion.

The next thing she knows, Aileen has fallen onto the bed in her own room.

"—Honestly, Master Claude! Teleporting me in the middle of a conversation!"

She tries to get angry at him, but it's the middle of the night. As someone who stole out of the house in secret, she appreciates this particular method. Besides, with *my love* being the last words he said to her, she can't muster any real ire.

Rachel, her lady-in-waiting, had helped to conceal her covert outing under the cover of darkness. Calling her, Aileen removes her makeup. Rachel prepares a quick hot bath and then Aileen changes into her nightclothes and climbs into bed.

Once the lights are out and she's lying down, a pleasant drowsiness comes quickly.

That's a great help, though. The final boss is on our side right from the beginning this time.

It had taken significant effort to woo Claude. It had also been very difficult to pull James, the final boss of Game 2, into her camp. However, all they'll need to do this time around is fulfill Elefas's expectations, and they'll avoid the sobering situation that occurs in the game—the fall of the Ellmeyer Empire. Viewed in that light, this is awfully nice and easy.

The issue is the question of what Elefas actually decides to do. Since Claude is still alive, though, she can't imagine the man will be capable of very much. The demon king is the strongest by such a wide margin that he's perilously close to destroying the game balance. In any case, during the Game 1 fan disc, Claude was—

—*Hmm? Wait, Master Claude was...in that one?!*

Aileen bolts up in bed.

She just remembered a certain piece of game art. It's the scene that came to mind when she saw Elefas earlier.

Unless she's recalling incorrectly, at that point in the game, he had some sort of spell ready.

"Almond! Come here, please! Or Ribbon, or Beelzebuth!" As she gets out of bed, Aileen is already shouting. However, in the moonlight, her shadow makes no sound, and nothing changes.

Her heart thumps once. It must be coincidence. An accident—or at least, that's what she hopes. She has to make sure. Aileen opens the window. Since Elefas has appeared, the events of the game could start at any moment.

"Lady Aileen, did you just call someon—? Wh-what's the matter?!"

Aileen has set a foot on the edge of the terrace and is about to leap into a nearby tree. The sight seems to shock Rachel.

"I'm going to Master Claude! Take care of things here, if you would!"

"What, again?! At this hour...!"

"Aileen, Aileen!"

An enormous crow comes flying toward her out of the full moon. At the sound of his voice, Aileen looks up. "Almond...! What's the matter? Don't tell me something's happened to Master Claude!"

"The demon king—gone!" Almond seems flustered as well; he keeps flapping his wings, without descending to the edge of the terrace, and he speaks in a mad rush. "The demon king isn't anywhere!! No response! Demon king! Demon king!"

"A-Almond, calm down."

"Find the demon king! Aileen! The forest barrier's gone!"

That barrier is something Claude created with his own magic to protect the demons. It marks him as the demon king.

It can't be... No, Master Claude!

"Aileen. I'm sorry. It's the middle of the night, but I'm coming in. It's an emergency."

"M-Master!"

Rudolph, Duke d'Autriche, has entered his daughter's bedroom without knocking. Rachel hastily backs up a step, and on the terrace, Aileen turns around.

Her father is beaming—a sure sign that she's about to find herself facing great difficulties.

Aileen has the feeling she knows what Rudolph is going to tell her; she hugs Almond close. Almond is quiet as well.

This can't be happening.

Just a few hours ago, he'd called her *"my love."*

"A man we have stationed at the castle has sent a report: Master Claude has collapsed."

"Demon king!"

"Almond, my boy, his life is in no danger. However, he seems to have lost his memory—"

But love is always lost in a moment. Both the first time, and the second as well.

"What do you mean, you can't let me see Prince Claude?!"

"Aileen, you are in the presence of His Imperial Majesty. Behave yourself."

The one admonishing Aileen is her father—or perhaps, she should refer to him as the prime minister here. At any rate, she was in the process of rising from her knees, but at Rudolph's warning, she hastily plants them on the floor again. Her lowered eyes are fixed on a red carpet. Straight down it and up a short flight of stairs, the emperor is seated on a magnificent throne.

Emperor Pierre Jean Ellmeyer. Although he is Claude and Cedric's biological father, his face doesn't resemble either of theirs. However, his stern features and dignity befit the ruler of the vast Ellmeyer Empire.

It's Rudolph who arranged for her to have a direct audience with the emperor. Either that, or perhaps, the emperor possesses something like compassion as well.

"Lady d'Autriche. We would like to take your position into consideration."

"In that case...!"

"However, the matter has already been settled. Our son, Crown Prince Claude, has lost both his memories and his magic. He is no longer the demon king. This is a perfect chance for him to truly become emperor."

Aileen bites her lip hard.

Master Claude is brilliant, after all. If he had been an ordinary human instead of the demon king, his claim to the throne would've never been disputed in the first place. But...!

But he loves the demons. He does everything he can to protect them. Even when the humans, and his own family, cut him off, he didn't bear a grudge. Instead, he chose to live peacefully with the demons. The fact that he is that sort of person is why Aileen fell in love with him.

"We will separate him from the demons and allow him to recuperate. He's gained another chance to live his life as a human. Do you object to that?"

"Then what are the demons supposed to do? They adore Master Claude and have always protected him."

"Do you propose to make Claude their king again? You are too partial toward the demons."

"I—I don't intend to side exclusively with the demons! I'm merely pointing out the fact that Master Claude is and has been their king."

"That may be true, but what of it? Are you suggesting we should return our son to them?"

Aileen swallows her instinctive anger at the merciless remark. *Calm down, calm down...! For now, seeing Master Claude comes first.*

In the small hours of the previous night, Crown Prince Claude Jean Ellmeyer was found unconscious in the imperial family's residential wing. He had been stabbed in the abdomen. The weapon had not been identified, but the wound was shallow, and his life was in no danger. However, when Claude opened his eyes, he couldn't even remember his own name.

This is all Aileen has learned from Rudolph.

"I'll go to the imperial castle to ask what's happened. Stay calm and listen to James and Master Keith," she'd told Almond, then sent him home to relay the message. In an emergency like this one, she's grateful to have people she can rely on. She'd asked Rachel to summon Isaac and the rest of the group. Then she'd pleaded with Rudolph and managed to secure permission for an imperial audience first thing in the morning. Everyone is waiting for her report.

She can't go back and tell them she's learned nothing.

Or rather, she does know something—but only in terms of the game.

"Your Majesty, may I speak? I have a question, as a father."

"What is it, Rudolph?"

"You don't want to risk turning Crown Prince Claude back into the demon king by stimulating his memories through contact with my daughter and the demons. Therefore, you will not allow my daughter to meet with His Highness without your permission— I understand that. However, what will you do regarding their engagement?"

With a gasp, Aileen looks up. Her betrothal to Claude has political significance. Cedric has already caused the d'Autriche duchy to lose face with his peremptory dissolution of their engagement. Breaking a second engagement could very well make the duchy their enemy.

The emperor must be aware of this. He sighs. "We don't intend to cancel it immediately... We will give the utmost consideration to the moment and our reasons."

"Wait, you mean that you *do* intend to eventually dissolve our engagement?!"

"Aileen. Don't make me repeat myself. You are in the presence of His Majesty." Rudolph cautions her more mildly than the emperor, but his tone is intimidating.

The emperor nods emphatically, as if he's satisfied with his prime minister's handling of the matter. "We understand your feelings on the matter. However, Claude has no memories. As a parent, we would like to give him the opportunity to reconsider his options. If he has regained his humanity, no doubt he will be highly sought after."

He speaks as if being the demon king meant Aileen had been his only option.

Not only that, but Master Claude is supposed to "reconsider" while I'm not allowed to see him?! He's absolutely planning to dissolve the engagement!

Rudolph seems to give it a little thought. "It isn't good for the crown prince to be without a fiancée, though. We'll have to remedy that without delay."

"In that case, Father, I could simply keep the position!"

"Aileen. I have no intention of spoiling you."

Under his daughter's murderous glare, he blushes happily. She really wishes he wouldn't. *I'm going to tell my brothers about this, I swear it… And Mother, too! Although, I get the feeling Father would enjoy that as well!*

Or should she go to Almond with her gripes and have him pluck her father's head bald?

"Do you have a specific proposal? If you'd like, I could…"

"There is no need for that, Prime Minister d'Autriche. I have a plan." The voice is like a little bell. Light footsteps and a robe of sumptuous quality glide across the marble floor. The emperor's eyes widen. "Mother! You're feeling better?"

"I'm quite well today, Pierre. It's good to meet you. You are Aileen, correct?"

As the woman makes her way toward the throne, she nods to Aileen, and Aileen hastily bows her head. "H-how do you do, Your Majesty?"

"Heh, what an adorable young lady. I'm jealous."

She wants to say, *You must be joking*, but manages not to.

I'd heard the rumors, but… So this is Lara Jean Ellmeyer, the empress dowager!

The woman is the emperor's biological mother, but although she's past sixty, she possesses the countenance and smile of a young girl. There's no exaggerating how much she seems to be the very image of youthful maidenhood.

Skin as fair as porcelain, without a single wrinkle or stain. Plump, charming lips. With every step she takes, her glossy hair ripples like water. Perhaps because it was chosen to suit her Eastern features, her dress is plain. However, the finest silk, combined with intricate embroidery and lace, perfectly accentuates her slender limbs.

On light feet, the empress dowager climbs the steps to the throne, although only the emperor is permitted to sit there. She looks down over the others with a face that's more vivacious than her son's, or even Aileen's. "I plan to host a ball in one month's time. The invitations have already been sent. No doubt all the young ladies in the empire will attend. It should be a fine opportunity to choose a wife for my dear grandson, don't you think?"

"Well, well! How thoroughly you've prepared. Really, Your Majesty, I have nothing but admiration for your political talents. Perhaps it isn't a coincidence that no invitation was sent to my house?"

"Oh, that was merely an error. However, receiving an invitation at this late date would be nothing but troublesome, would it not, Prime Minister?"

The wily old fox and the vixen smile at each other mildly until the emperor clears his throat, interrupting them. "Then it would appear our problem is solved. We thank you for your service, Aileen Lauren d'Autriche. No doubt it was fate that you restored him to his position as crown prince."

"Please wait, Your Majesty! I am still Prince Claude's fiancée!"

"Whom he doesn't remember and has effectively never met." There's a smile on the empress dowager's rouged lips. "Both Pierre and I will fuss over the boy to our hearts' content, enough to make up for all the intervening years. Cedric and Lilia are devoting themselves to his care, too. They seem to be getting along quite well. Even if they are half brothers, it is reassuring when members of the imperial family are close. You have nothing to worry about."

"At least let me meet with him! I haven't been allowed to see for myself whether Prince Claude is all right, or whether he's truly lost his memories. And yet you've—"

"Girl, if you claim to love that child, shouldn't you step aside? This is unseemly."

"Grandmother! Don't say such cruel things to Lady Aileen!"

Suddenly, the door to the audience chamber opens, and two figures appear. Lara's eyes widen. Aileen also turns, then forgets herself and audibly clicks her tongue.

"Why, Lilia. And Cedric, even. What is it?"

"When I heard that Lady Aileen was here, I just couldn't help myself...!"

"Please pardon our intrusion, Your Majesty, Grandmother— Lilia insisted."

Leaving Cedric behind, Lilia runs thoughtlessly up to the throne. Rudolph watches her coldly; however, since no one objects, he says nothing. Aileen doesn't make a fuss about her lack of courtesy, either. Only the emperor frowns.

"Lilia Reinoise. Withdraw. You must not come up here."

"No, I must speak. Grandmother, Lady Aileen was the fiancée of Claude, *my brother-in-law*. You can't just force her to leave him—the poor thing! At least let them meet."

Aileen's eyebrows come down as far as they'll go. *What is the woman plotting?!*

As Lilia implores her, Lara tilts her head slightly. "We mustn't."

"Oh, please don't say that. Just a glimpse, even."

"She's right, Grandmother," Cedric says as he comes up beside Aileen. Startled, she scrutinizes his profile. "Dissolving his engagement the moment he loses his memories wouldn't look good. After all, this woman and my brother were famously close. We'll end up inviting groundless suspicion upon ourselves."

"Yes! At least invite Lady Aileen to the ball. People will think we're shunning her otherwise."

Never mind what others think, as that's absolutely 100 percent the case, but apparently, appearances always matter. First, the emperor falls to thought. Then Lara narrows her eyes and gives her decision. "All right. I shall invite her to my ball. However, that will be the end of it. If the girl attempts to meet Claude at any other time, her head will be struck from her shoulders as punishment for ignoring an imperial edict. Of course, since that would also be a failure to control their daughter, the d'Autriche family will not escape unscathed, either." The smile in Lara's eyes is that of a woman waiting for prey to fall into her trap. "I wonder what you'll be able to manage at a single ball. I do hope you won't embarrass yourself."

"Oh, Grandmother, don't worry about that." Lilia, who's been clinging to Lara, turns to Aileen. A smile appears on her face. She looks down on her, as if she's enjoying herself. "Lady Aileen is the protagonist, you see. She'd never let a *scenario* like this defeat her. Would you, now?"

"*I am the player.*" Words from a night filled with the choking scent of roses come back to her.

...I see. So that's what this is.

Unbidden, a smile comes to Aileen's face.

In the Game 1 fan disc, although Demon King Claude should have been dead, he made another appearance as a potential love interest. He had actually survived but had lost all his magic and his memories, and he appeared before the heroine as an ordinary human.

The heroine knew Claude was once the demon king, and she worried about him. Claude couldn't even remember his own name, and as the heroine helped him, he fell in love with her. When it seemed as if he might succumb to his role of demon king once more, their love saved him—that's the general outline of the Claude route on the fan disc.

In this version, Claude—the final boss of the first game—can be romanced without having to unlock the route. And of course, the heroine is Lilia Reinoise, the heroine of Game 1. A girl who, like Aileen, retains memories of her past life. The very same girl who's currently looking down on Aileen from the dais.

Rising to her feet, Aileen returns Lilia's gaze squarely. The game is already underway.

She's made up her mind. Really, she'd almost like to thank her.

"Yes, Lady Lilia. Let me inform you in advance that this will not happen twice."

"Ha-ha, yes, that's right. That's the spirit, Lady Aileen. You mustn't slink away with your tail between your legs." The corners of Lilia's lips rise. Those are the eyes of someone who's just acquired a new toy.

Aileen lowers her own eyes, then puts on a smile that befits the daughter of a duke. "I gladly accept your invitation to the ball.

Please don't worry; I won't cause any trouble for you, Empress Dowager."

"I certainly hope not."

"There is also something I would like to tell His Majesty the emperor." She takes the risk of speaking to him. Setting a hand over her heart, she flashes a lovely smile. "I will keep the demons under control, so please refrain from launching any campaigns against them."

"…What do you mean?"

"It is a natural measure, intended to avoid incurring Prince Claude's wrath once his memories return. There's no need to be concerned. After all, this task naturally falls to the demon king's wife."

Don't mess with the demons. I won't allow you to dismiss me out of hand, either. Fear what will follow when Claude regains his memories, and the demon king returns.

Apparently, her threat has gotten through. As the emperor responds, his voice is bitter. "You are not yet our son's wife."

"My, that's quite true. I fear I've spoken a bit hastily."

"What impudence. Do you want me to crush you, child?" Discarding her innocent girlish pretense, Lara smiles.

Aileen beams in return. "You mean the empress dowager, celebrated flower of high society, would personally involve herself in my affairs? I'd be honored. Now then, Your Majesties, if you'll excuse me."

"Lady Aileen."

As she's leaving, in a voice as sweet as a songbird's, Lilia calls to her.

Make it fun for me.

Lilia only mouths the words silently. Aileen locks eyes with her, then turns on her heel.

Her footsteps are light. Both her spirits and her mood are bright and breezy.

Ha! If this is reality, how terribly cruel it is. Poor Lady Aileen.

Forgotten by her true love, with her second broken engagement looming—and all for the ridiculous reason that that's how the game's scenario went. Even so, Aileen is facing the situation without shying away, and Lilia thinks she's magnificent. Just imagining how she might manage to turn the tables sends an electric thrill through her.

This is probably what it's like to feel truly alive.

"Are you sure about not banishing Aileen?" Marcus asks, frowning. He's been waiting for them outside the audience chamber.

Lilia knits her eyebrows together. "She and Prince Claude were engaged, and this turn of events is far too awful. She should at least be able to see him and come to terms with her emotions, shouldn't she?"

"...You're a kind girl, Lilia. However, we've let the chance to isolate the d'Autriches slip through our fingers. Lester's bound to be angry."

At the mention of the surprisingly irascible strategist character, Lilia looks troubled. "Oh dear. But you're my accomplice in this, Marcus. Remember, you brought me here."

"That's... Well, I suppose that's...true..."

"Hee-hee. Then let's all get scolded together. Right, Cedric?"

His reaction is just a little delayed. Lilia's fiancé, who's done as she told him to and recommended that Aileen be allowed to attend the ball, hastily puts on a smile. "Um, yes... That's right."

"What's the matter, Cedric? Is something worrying you?"

"No, er... We don't even know who attacked my brother. I'm a little concerned..."

His evasiveness makes the pieces fall into place for Lilia. *He's worried that his brilliant brother may steal me away, hmm? What a petty man.*

However, it's very important that she stay Cedric's fiancée. On his route, she'll become empress, which facilitates the closest possible thing to a harem route. Besides, the rank of second prince's fiancée is really convenient in terms of playing the game.

"True... It's fine, though. You and all the others are here for me, Cedric." When she immediately whips out the best answer, Marcus smiles wryly, while Cedric's expression softens. Behind her pasted-on smile, she sighs. Compared with Aileen, these characters are so unbelievably dull.

Lady Aileen really is my favorite character right now. Oh, how splendid!

And a character who's vital to enjoying the game that's just begun is here, in the depths of this room.

"...Lilia. You're back?" The man who's sitting up in bed turns to her, closing his book.

Without even thinking about it, Lilia breaks into a smile. It's probably sincere. "Prince Claude. Is it all right for you to be up?"

"Yes. Where's Cedric?"

"Oh, he said he needed to talk to the others. I think he'll

stop by later. He was worried about you." She opens the window, letting the wind blow in. It stirs the white curtains and his black hair. "How are you feeling? Have you managed to remember anything?"

Softly, Claude lowers his long eyelashes. His eyes are black. There's no red in them now. "No. I'm sorry... I don't know. I can't remember anything... I must be causing you so much trouble."

"That's all right, Prince Claude. We're family. There's no need to hurry."

"Family..."

"I'll protect you. I won't let them make you the demon king again, not ever."

She hugs his head close and feels Claude's fingertips hesitantly touch her back—which is one of the hallmark signs of an iconic scene in the game.

"Thank you, Lilia. I may have lost my memories, but I was lucky to meet you two."

She feels like bursting into raucous laughter, but she controls it. Still holding Claude's head, she limits herself to a smile.

She's not about to get careless, though. She'll trigger all the pertinent game events accurately, efficiently, and carefully, ensuring that Claude falls for her.

Lady Aileen is the protagonist, after all. I'll have to corner her and make her suffer properly.

"And the villainess married the demon king, and they lived happily ever after." —If that were the end, it would be boring. Nobody wants that.

"That must be the place."

Once she's spotted the mansion hidden in the dense trees, Aileen tosses the binoculars to Elefas. Catching them neatly, he peers through them. "Yes... That mansion is definitely protected by a sacred barrier. I'm impressed you found it."

"Our air force is outstanding."

A mansion hidden in a valley some distance away from the imperial castle had been abruptly enveloped by holy power. Almond and the others discovered this clear abnormality as they flew around the capital.

The building's modest appearance and its concealed location in the forest are due to the fact that it was built as a place for the imperial family to hide during an emergency. It's probably connected to the castle at one point or another. There's a small pier inside a nearby cavern. Although she can't see it, there may even be a boat inside.

"I don't know where they got it, but if their goal is to keep the demons from coming near, that barrier will definitely do the trick. Sacred power doesn't work on humans, though. Even if it isn't possible to find the entrance from the castle, it's quite easy to infiltrate it from outside. I do believe they've underestimated me."

"Perhaps it's because, as a rule, no young lady of good upbringing would think of jumping off this cliff?" Lowering the binoculars, Elefas looks down the sheer precipice and smiles. The wind whistles up from the valley. A fall from this height will mean certain death. "In addition, I doubt they will have expected you to dress as a man," Elefas suggests with a straight face.

Aileen looks down at herself. Her hair is hidden under a wig, and she's wearing the uniform apprentice knights wear at the palace. She's lightly equipped, but she is carrying a sword.

"Well, I hear they've stationed a large number of knights to guard Master Claude. Given what we know, if I want to blend in, isn't this the best thing to wear? Oh, and call me Ailey."

"That isn't the problem... In the first place, if they find out you've met him, you'll be executed. I'd think you'd at least hesitate a bit."

"I explained that to you yesterday. If all I do is sit here wringing my hands, my fate will be unchanged either way. Master Claude isn't so easy that he'd fall head over heels for me at a ball simply because I prettied myself up a bit!"

"I believe Isaac very clearly stated you weren't allowed to say that."

"He meant in front of James and the others. You're the only one who's here now."

"Hey, cut that out, you're gonna kill the duck squad." She didn't really understand what Isaac had meant by that even now, but because he said it, she's remembered something else.

When Beelzebuth heard what had happened during her audience with the emperor, he raged, grieved, and burst into tears. James stayed outwardly calm, but he wandered about, unable to hide his internal consternation. They've grown emotionally unstable. Even so, because she's sworn to them that she'll find Claude, the demons are still behaving themselves.

There's no telling how long that will last, though. In fact, some demons have already gone missing. There's no telling what they may do, particularly the ones with hot tempers. If they attack humans in an attempt to reclaim Claude, they'll give the opposition an excuse to retaliate. Aileen is certain she has to do something before that happens.

"All right, let's go. Cast the wind spell, please. I'll turn the sacred sword into a wall to get us through the barrier."

"Are you sure about this? If you fail in your jump, you could very well die. More than anything, if you're discovered, you'll be executed for disobeying the emperor. It's quite likely that it won't just be you, Lady Aileen, but all your allies as well who—"

"Don't tell me you're having second thoughts about taking our side now that Master Claude isn't here."

Beelzebuth and James are keeping the demons in check, and she's set Walt and Kyle to guard the castle in the forest, so that they can respond at once if anything happens. Jasper and Keith are gathering intelligence through their separate networks. Auguste is reporting to the Holy Knights for duty as usual, so that they'll find out immediately if any demons get violent. The rest seem to be carrying out Isaac's requests, so it's safe to leave them to it.

Of that group, Elefas is the only one Aileen chose to bring. It isn't just because he's still new and she's concerned he might not feel at home with the others yet.

I have to make sure Elefas is firmly on our side. As the final boss of the fan disc, he was plotting to make Master Claude the demon king again. He may have some sort of hint regarding his amnesia...

Besides, Elefas is very suspicious. As a matter of fact, Isaac and James actively suspect him. They wonder if it's really a coincidence that Claude lost his memories right after Elefas appeared.

They think he might be a spy for the emperor or another hostile party.

In other words, Aileen has to conquer both Claude, the amnesiac final boss of Game 1; and Elefas, final boss of the fan disc; and win either their heart or their loyalty.

Of course, her romantic target is Claude and no one else, so when she's interacting with Elefas, she conducts herself as the wife of his liege lord.

"In that case, hurry and make up your mind. I trust you, you know."

"...Newcomer as I am?"

"Yes. After all, Master Claude decided to trust you; it's only natural."

Elefas is wearing an odd expression, neither scowl nor smile. Pointing an index finger straight at that face, Aileen beams at him. "I won't let you get away now. If I'm executed, come and lose your head with me."

Elefas is silent. Aileen can't read what he's thinking. However, as a leader, she cannot afford to waver.

Master Claude would have kept Elefas with him even if he betrayed him.

Since Claude isn't here, Aileen is the one who has to pull that off.

Finally, slowly, Elefas bows his head. "As you wish."

"All right. Then let's go."

"Lady Aileen, if you please." Smoothly, he extends a hand to her. When she looks at him blankly, he answers with a gentle smile. "I'll protect you. Should anything happen to you, I'll get dragged into it."

"That's a splendid way to look at it."

She takes his hand, fixes her eyes on the mansion, and steps off the cliff.

Elefas quietly chants something that sounds like a spell, and the wind slows their fall.

In the blink of an eye, the mansion is very close. Aileen calls silently. *Sacred sword.*

Her chest grows faintly warm. As she wills it, a thin membrane forms around her and Elefas, who's holding her hand. The membrane is the same density as the barrier that protects the hidden mansion, and it doesn't burst or repel them. They slip right through.

"I expected nothing less. You use the sacred sword so well, one would never think it was stolen."

"That's not true. When it doesn't do what I tell it, I threaten to snap it in— Ah!"

As if to say its job is done, the sacred sword's protection suddenly vanishes. Since they're close to the ground, Elefas has relaxed the power of his magic, so the timing overall is rather unfortunate.

"Hey, sacred sword—!"

"Lady Aileen!"

Aileen's cloak has caught on a tree branch, and with her full weight suspended from it, it rips loudly. On reflex, Aileen covers her wig, which means she's in no position to break her fall properly. Elefas catches her from behind, and they both hit the ground on their backsides.

"Ow, ow-ow-ow... Elefas, are you all right?"

"Y-yes. What about you, Lady Aileen? Are you injured?"

"I'm fine. Y-you know, lately, I get the feeling the sacred sword's developing a mind of its own. I've seen it arbitrarily materialize to defend the heroine before, but...!"

Did calling it the cursed sword warp its personality somehow? Or is it unhappy that Lilia isn't its owner anymore? Either way, it's got some nerve.

"Heroine?"

"Don't worry about it. Never mind that, let's hurry inside."

"...What's all the noise about?"

Aileen has just set her hands on the lawn when that voice makes her expression stiffen. *P-P-P-Prince Cedric!* She's just seen her former fiancé's bright-blond hair enter the garden. She kneels hastily, and Elefas follows suit.

Since I'm dressed as a boy, I doubt he'll see through my disguise, but I'll have to make a good excuse, or else—

"What are you doing here, Aileen?"

After one stunned moment, she speaks. Her voice cracks. "Wh-what are you talking about, sir?"

"I'm talking about you. You're parading yourself dressed as a man again? And you call yourself a duke's daughter?"

He's seen right through her. Not only that, but it also took him just a single glance. Is that one of the perks of being a child-hood friend?

It's fine; the situation isn't unsalvageable. All I have to do is silence him permanently!

She'll show him no mercy. But just as she's considering doing something heartless to her former fiancé...

"I assume you're here to see my brother. Come on."

"Huh?" Aileen, who's already balled her fist to punch him, looks up in open confusion. Cedric shoots her a derisive glance, then turns on his heel and strides off.

"What should we do?"

"...We'll have to go with him. If Master Cedric starts to make noise, knock him out ruthlessly."

Elefas gives a small nod.

Getting to her feet, Aileen picks up her torn cloak and follows Cedric, keeping an appropriate distance between them. If she'd said she wasn't curious about what her former beloved was thinking, she would have been lying.

However, more than that, she wants to see Claude's face, even if only for a moment.

Isaac, who's gazing out a window in a quiet corridor of the forest castle, turns at the sound of his name. "What, Duck Ranger Blue?"

"Who's a Duck Ranger, and who's Blue?! Wipe that damnable costume from your memory right this instant... Where's Aileen?"

"Off to see the demon king. She took that Elefas mage guy along as a guard."

At the name *Elefas*, James frowns. "I see... Is that all right?"

"We'll just have to pin our hopes on Aileen's ability to turn everyone into her lapdogs. So what's up? I know that's not why you called me over."

James is a little too proud, but he's coolheaded and intellectual. He sighs but switches topics with good grace. In that sense, he's really easy to work with. "I thought I would let you know... about the moment the demon king ceased to be the demon king."

"...It's something Aileen shouldn't hear?"

"Yes. All the demons share that emotion. Whether they take it as an order will depend on the individual demon, but I don't know what that means in practice, and I'm hesitant to tell that woman about it. I told Auguste, Walt, and Kyle a moment ago. Keith as well."

As information sharing goes, that seems the appropriate thing to do. The fact that he's the only person on Aileen's side who James is telling is a smart move, too.

"I see. So? What happened?"

"Just before the demon king vanished, there was a shock that startled me awake. It was his scream." James pauses for the space of a breath, then goes on, sounding troubled. "When he cried out, he said, 'Aileen.'"

"...Huh?"

"He kept calling her name. Like he was desperately trying to hold on to it."

Aileen, Aileen, Aileen.

As Isaac imagines that calling voice, he stops knowing what sort of expression he should be wearing.

"The demon king likes Aileen way too much... Seriously, who does that?"

"Yes, it exhausts me as well, but at the very end...he said, 'Protect Aileen.'"

If they interpret that as an order from their king, the demons will protect Aileen. To the death. However, for Claude's sake, Aileen is trying to protect the demons as well.

"Argh, what a pain in the ass..."

"Isn't it just? If the humans harm Aileen, the demons may

obey the demon king's orders and attack them. And Aileen will naturally do her best to stop them."

"A huge pain in the ass! Oh, did you maybe talk this over with Pink, Yellow, and Black? Figure out what to do about the emperor's men and that mage." At present, those are the only people who may physically hurt Aileen. That means they'll need humans to protect her, so that the demons don't get riled up.

James seems to share Isaac's concern; he nods. "That's right. Make good use of Walt and Kyle. There can't be many humans or demons capable of defeating those two. I've gone over it with Auguste as well, so I think he'll maneuver skillfully. Although, he seems to have a matter of his own to investigate..."

"Oh, the woman who was at the auction?"

"We don't know whether she has anything to do with this whole mess, but Auguste is concerned, and no doubt it's better to look into it. The woman did have demon snuff, after all. Besides, the emperor and the empress dowager will probably start putting pressure on him before long. He should gather information while he can."

Isaac couldn't agree more. The more time passes, the harder it'll become to move freely.

"So we're racing against time... By the way, what move do you think the emperor's men will make?"

"They'll either find or create proof of a violation of that imperial edict. Then they'll watch for the best time to use it to destroy the d'Autriches. Conversely, no matter what we do now, they're bound to ignore it until the ball."

"Yeah. I wish we'd had a better plan than having her go see him, but..."

"If they don't meet, we'll never get anywhere." Aileen isn't going to rely on a miracle like love at first sight at the ball. Isaac doesn't think there's much chance of that happening either way.

"Our only hope of winning is if Master Claude regains his memories, or if he chooses Aileen even without them. Until then, we'll just have to do what we can."

"In the end, no matter what that mage is up to, it won't change what we do, huh?" Isaac asks.

James lowers his voice. "Since the king has placed his trust in the mage, assume the demons won't doubt him in the slightest. Considering Aileen's personality, I imagine she'll trust him completely as well."

"Yeaaaah, she totally will. Having at least one other guy who doubts him is better than nothing, I guess. I'm real glad you're half human."

"...That's something I never thought I'd hear." James smiles very faintly. Then his expression tenses again. "Listen, telling Aileen is pointless, so I'm telling you instead: If anything happens, cut the demons loose. If the demon king's absence continues, a day will come when we won't be able to manage them."

"...Well, yeah, we'll do that if we have to. Should you be the one saying it, though?"

"It's extremely annoying, but the demon in me has accepted the demon king's request to protect Aileen. I can't go against it."

Isaac doesn't say anything insensitive like *You know that's not why*.

"Besides, Master Claude fought hard to keep his memories. I don't know how they did it, but someone has robbed the demon king of both his memories and his magic. Keep that in mind."

"Parenthetically, could a mage do that?"

"No matter how brilliant the mage, there's no way they would be able to strip those things from the demon king. If they had the sacred sword, there might be a chance, but Aileen has that."

It's quite apparent by now that debating who's done it and how is a waste of time. Isaac nods, and James turns on his heel.

...*Oh, but this is one of those* nasty hunches are always right *things, isn't it? Maybe I'll have Denis pick up the pace.*

Scratching the back of his neck, he heads down the hall. Then he bumps into Rachel, who's carrying a cosmetics box. They're around each other all the time, but Rachel gets flustered whenever she sees Isaac, and because he can't help but watch for it, he always makes eye contact. And once their eyes meet, he has to say hello.

"Hey there. Did Aileen take off already?"

"Y-yes. Dressed as a boy..."

"What, again? Man, she hasn't changed. Always dives right in with no hesitation, never worrying about a thing... What?"

Rachel watches him steadily, without blinking. Then she smiles. There isn't a trace of her usual confusion. "It's nothing. I'm just glad I managed to conceal Lady Aileen's dark circles so well."

He gulps. She gazes back at him mildly.

"If you can't even notice when a woman close to you has changed her makeup, you'll never manage to beat Master Claude."

Rachel gives a charming curtsy, then leaves.

Isaac has the overwhelming feeling that he's been completely outplayed, and it hits him.

"Uh, I've never even considered trying to compete with the demon king... Why put it like that, huh?"

He can't ask her, *What, didn't you like me?* That would make it sound like he's sulking. Instead, casually, he kicks the wall of the corridor. He hits the wrong spot, and it hurts way more than he expected, so he ends up writhing in agony, but that's still better than admitting her words got to him.

As accommodations for a member of the imperial family, the second-floor room they're shown to is rather plain. It has only minimal chests and shelves, and the wallpaper is a calm moss green. However, it's properly clean and neat, and above all, it's quiet. No doubt it's perfect for a convalescent.

"This is the shared drawing room. The room on the left is where I nap, and the one down at the end is my brother's bedroom."

There's only one door. In other words, to enter Claude's bed-chamber, visitors either have to get in from the terrace or pass through this room, which Cedric also uses.

There's no telling whether Cedric has noticed Aileen plan-ning out infiltration routes; he sits down on a couch in the draw-ing room, kicking his legs out casually. "I'll be right here. You do whatever you want."

"What on earth are you playing at? Why show me all the way here?" Aileen has removed her wig, and she sweeps her long hair back, glaring at Cedric. "Are you helping me because you think Master Claude might steal Lady Lilia from you? I'm grateful, but that's dismally petty."

She openly states the most likely possibility she can think of, trying to goad him, but Cedric doesn't rise to the bait. He just picks up a nearby book and opens it, responding impassively. "It's nothing to do with you. Hurry up and go. I'm not going to tell you when they stop by to check on him."

"...Elefas, wait here. If anything happens, call me."

"All right."

Not being able to read Cedric's intentions is unsettling, but she doesn't have time to waste. Leaving Elefas behind, Aileen grasps the knob of the door at the end. She takes a deep breath, then turns it.

The room is spacious, with white curtains that drift in the breeze. On the canopied bed in its center, she sees black hair.

"...Master Claude!"

It's as if she hasn't seen him in years.

Claude is asleep, his upper body raised slightly by a pile of bulky pillows. She rushes over to him, then timidly puts a hand to his cheek. It's warm. He's breathing peacefully.

He's alive...!

Her eyes almost tear up, and for the first time, Aileen realizes just how uneasy she's been. His hand is lying on top of the coverlet. She takes it gently, nuzzling her cheek into his palm.

Thank goodness. I'm so glad... As long as he's alive, nothing else matters.

Apparently, the part about his wound being shallow is true, too. He doesn't seem to be in pain. His sleep is quiet and serene. There's an open book lying by his pillow. He may have fallen asleep while reading.

Wanting to be closer to him, she leans over the bed, careful not to make a sound. Then Claude's fingertips stir against her cheek.

"...Master Claude?"

Has she awakened him? She sees his long lashes quiver. She feels an overwhelming urge to cling to him, but she fights it back, putting on the loveliest smile she can manage. When he sees her, she wants to be the most beautiful thing in his world.

Slowly, Claude's eyes open. They're black.

Aileen stares, and Claude's thin lips tremble. His voice is hoarse from sleep, but still oh so sweet.

"...Lilia...?"

She must make him hers and take him home immediately. Yes, even if she has to tie him up and spirit him away.

When he opens his eyes, he finds that an unfamiliar person, of ambiguous gender and dressed in a knight's uniform, is currently straddling him.

"Good morning, Master Claude."

It's a woman's voice. Claude blinks, then speaks with sleep-dry lips. "...What are you—? Why are you tying me up?!"

The woman is busily binding his wrists with rope. Claude is confused, and the woman gives him a faint smile. "It's all right. There's no need to be frightened. Please rest easy."

"No, something's wrong here! This is definitely wrong! Who are you anyway?!"

"Master Claude. Are you familiar with the concept of a woman flinging herself at you?"

"I'm asking who are— Flinging herself...?"

It can't be. Is his virtue in danger? Claude swallows hard. The strange woman beams as if she's enjoying herself immensely. For some reason, she takes out a cookie. An odd chill runs down his spine. How strange. He recognizes this.

"I'm glad I brought these just in case. You don't have any magic right now, and no poison-neutralizing abilities, correct? I'm told you'd built up a tolerance for toxins to begin with, which means that potions tend not to work on you, but that's all right. Luc made it more potent. Come, Master Claude. Say *aaaah*."

"…L-let's talk this over before one of us does something we'll regret."

"Oh, but it was you who said we didn't need words, Master Claude!"

He seems to have incurred her wrath, but he has absolutely no idea why. Still smiling, she bears down on him, her eyes blazing with anger. In a dim corner of his mind, he understands that this woman knows his past self, but she's dangerously close to forcing an obviously suspect cookie into his mouth, and this definitely isn't the time.

"Gracious, you'd run away?"

"W-wait, I don't understand the situation, but let's not do anything hasty…!"

"Don't be so timid. Accept your fate!"

He's twisted away, taking evasive action, but the woman is trying to pin him down. She's still smiling and couldn't be more frightening if she tried. Claude is genuinely scared.

However, she isn't that strong. She seems to have bound him in a hurry, and fortunately, while he's been kicking and struggling on the bed, the knot has come loose. Using one of his newly freed hands to hold the woman's head down on the coverlet, Claude twists her arm up behind her.

From the fact that he's managed to do this without trouble, he must have some sort of martial training.

"Who in the world are you?!"

He's panting, shoulders heaving; he tells himself to calm down. Then with a jolt, he realizes that the woman's back is trembling. She seems to be crying.

I know I'm not holding her down that hard...

Maybe he's hurt her somehow. Or else—handicapped by his missing memories, has he made some sort of mistake? Guilt wells up inside him, and he eases his grip. In that moment, the woman nimbly flips over. He grabs her right wrist just before she shoves the cookie into his mouth. She *tsks* softly in irritation.

She doesn't seem the least bit apologetic, and a feeling somewhere between anger and amazement explodes in Claude. "Were you faking those tears?!"

"Oh, please, you're the one who jumped to conclusions!"

She kept her left hand hidden, and now she uses it to thrust another cookie at him. Calmly, Claude catches her wrist. Apparently, he really does know martial arts.

"Seriously, who are you...?!"

"Why don't you examine your own heart on the matter?"

"I'm not acquainted with any female perverts...I don't think."

"Female perverts? I'd rather not hear that from someone with a face that makes him a walking display of public indecency."

"What sort of face would that even be?!"

"...Your eyes aren't red anymore, are they?"

They're still locked together on the bed, glaring daggers at each other. Then without warning, she lets her shoulders fall. "So you really don't remember me..."

Claude is wary of another trap, but the woman's comment sends a stir through his heart.

Who is she? I don't know; I don't remember.

Not that silky blond hair, or those intense, shining eyes like blue jewels—

"But if you don't, there's no help for it! Very well. In that case, please marry me."

—or this bizarre way of thinking, which is wrong and twisted in so many places.

His opponent is smiling with her arms spread wide. Feeling a fatigue that's more mental than physical, Claude plants both hands on the bed, letting his head droop. "...How did we get from that to this?"

"Simply agree, and I guarantee you a comfortable life and a blissful future. If you want to be happy, muster your courage and take that leap of faith."

"Are you some new sort of missionary? I may have amnesia, but I'm not fool enough to bargain with someone whose name I don't know. Introduce yourself already."

"That's quite sensible. I beg your pardon. In my excitement, I forgot myself."

She nimbly leaps off the bed and, still in her royal guard's uniform, executes a flawless curtsy. "My name is Aileen Lauren d'Autriche."

"......?!"

Claude looks terribly taken aback. As if mocking his reaction, Aileen flashes him an elegant smile. "I'm your fiancée, Master Claude."

"This demented pervert, of all people, is my fiancée?!"

Aileen's eyebrows twitch. Claude puts a hand to his mouth, struggling with a sudden bout of dizziness.

He doesn't want to believe it. No wonder they speak of her as if she's a dangerous character. Realizing he mustn't get involved with her, he impulsively reaches for the bell to call for help—but she confiscates it.

"How boorish of you, Master Claude. Here you are, alone with your fiancée, and you'd summon someone else?"

"I-I'm very sorry, but I don't intend to get involved with you."

"How can you be so cold?"

"I won't become the demon king again. Do you have any idea just how great a burden having someone like that for a crown prince has been on the empire, on the people, on my family—?"

He's been told he was once the demon king. He has no memory of it, but he's heard from his grandmother that it tore his family apart. That's only natural. As far as he's concerned, they were lucky that the nation had managed to get by without plunging into chaos.

This woman he has no memories with, fond or otherwise, a fiancée in name only, is watching him closely. Is it guilt that makes him quietly avert his gaze from her clear sapphire eyes?

"Lilia and the others saved me. I don't want to make their efforts come to nothing."

"Master Claude…"

"If you care for me at all, please agree to dissolve our engagement—"

He's trying to settle things peacefully, but she interrupts by stabbing a sword into the bed, right in front of him.

"……"

"I'll pretend I didn't hear that. Master Claude, you are currently, as they say, ill. I won't abandon you. Even though, if I didn't love you, I would have cut you down on the spot just now."

She's smiling, but it doesn't sound like a joke, and she's scary. No, there's something more important to address.

"Did you just say...you love me?"

"Yes, I did. Not only do you have amnesia, but someone appears to have filled your head with a great deal of presuppositions. However, I do love you. If I didn't, I wouldn't be risking my life to see you."

"Your life?"

"My, are you unaware? If they find out we've met, my head will have to say good-bye to my shoulders. There's an imperial edict that says I mustn't see you, and I've disobeyed it."

It takes a moment, but then it sinks in. He's shocked. "Y-you mean if they find you, they'll execute you?! Go home!"

Even if their engagement is already scheduled to be broken, her death would weigh heavily on his conscience. Claude panics. Aileen watches him blankly for a moment. Then she breaks into carefree laughter.

"Th-this isn't the time to laugh!"

"They won't kill me so easily. I'm sure they're watching and waiting for the proper time to do it. That won't be a major concern for a while."

"How can you be so calm about this?! Listen, don't come near me again. I don't know what our relationship was before, but even for me, it's...it's a nuisance!"

"...So you're still as kind as ever." Smoothly, as if it's the natural thing to do, Aileen slips her arms around him. "I'm glad you're safe. Memories don't matter one bit. As long as you're alive, I can win you over as often as I must."

A pleasant fragrance tickles his nostrils. That silky blond hair. Those slim shoulders. She isn't strong enough to hold him tightly, and she seems all in all incredibly fragile. Unconsciously, he touches her shoulders—then comes to his senses with a jolt.

"L-let go."

He shoves her away from him, covering his mouth with a hand. Embarrassment wells up inside him. "L-ladies shouldn't carelessly embrace men like that."

"Pardon?"

"I—I mean, even if you do love me, doing shameless things before marriage is unconscionable."

Abruptly, she puts a hand on his forehead, checking his temperature. When he frowns, she tilts her head. "...You don't have a fever. Your face is red, though. Are you delirious?"

"Th-that's because you thoughtlessly clung to me. Have you no shame?!"

Even when he glares at her, Aileen looks rather stunned, as if she's seen some peculiar animal. With a gasp, it hits him. "D-don't tell me... Did I do shameless things to you before, when I was—?!"

He had been the demon king, after all. However, Aileen shakes her head, slowly. "N-no... We hadn't even kissed properly yet, but..."

"I—I see... Good. If I had done something, breaking off our engagement really would have been irresponsible."

Just as he's feeling relieved, her hands clamp onto his shoulders. When he looks up, she's right in front of his nose, wearing an absolutely fiendish expression. "Th-that's right! A demon king who pretended to be cruel without equal but was lonely, sad, starved for affection, and actually pure of heart—I remember! That was the scenario! So if you eliminate all the demon king–esque parts, this is what's left. How careless of me. What have I done...?!"

He wants to ask her what she's talking about, but the woman's appalling gaze overawes him, and his lips won't move.

"The initiative will be mine! I want to take you home with me right this minute!"

"N-no! It's c-clear that you won't listen to reason, and I mustn't let you take the initiative! Leave right now! I'll call some-one, I mean it!"

"Oh, but if you do, my head and body will be forced to part ways. You don't mind?"

"Why am I the one getting threatened?!"

The woman simply refuses to listen. She hugs him again, and he swallows a shriek at the sudden soft sensation. "I—I asked you to stop that!"

"Whatever will I do? This is so fun! Oh, come now, don't run away. Your body may remember me even if your mind doesn't. After all, the old Master Claude couldn't possibly have loved me more."

"Y-you just said we hadn't done anything! I don't have any experience with that!"

"What a brazen comment. Take a good look at your own face in the mirror when you say that."

"And I have to ask again, what does my face have to do with this?!"

"I'm terribly sorry to interrupt your fun, but, Lady Aileen, it appears it's nearly time for the guards to come by on patrol."

The sudden voice makes him jump. A young man in a black hooded cloak is standing in the doorway, smiling wryly. "Also, you shouldn't make such forceful advances. I feel sorry for Master Claude."

This must be a companion who led her here. One who pities him.

"I suppose there's no help for it. It's a shame, but that will have to be all for today, Master Claude. I'll come again."

"Please don't come back ever."

"I will, though."

She's absolutely going to return. Even if it means risking execution. The idea makes him shudder.

"Oh, that's right. Excuse me a moment."

"Huh? —Ow! What are you doing?!"

She's abruptly yanked two or three hairs from the side of his head. The woman smiles into his startled face.

"They're a souvenir. I'll take very good care of them."

He's too afraid to ask what they're a souvenir for.

"All right, I'll take my leave. But, Master Claude, one last thing: You mustn't cheat on me."

"Cheat on you?"

"No doubt they've recommended a new fiancée. Even though you have me."

"Are you daft?" Aileen blinks at him. There's something childlike about the gesture, and he pointedly glares at her so that he won't accidentally think she's cute. "Right now, I have my hands full figuring out whether I'll be able to get by as crown prince. I don't have any time or energy to spare for that sort of—?!"

She's pressed her lips to his cheek with an audible *smack*. Claude blushes bright red, and his mouth gapes uselessly before he finally squeezes out the words. "Wh-what are you doing...?"

"That is precisely what I love about you. I'll capture your heart again, I swear it. As often as I must. Remember that, if nothing else."

With a triumphant smile, the woman pokes his chest lightly with her index finger. Then she turns on her heel. "I'll come see you again. Wait for me."

As she makes for the terrace with her servant in tow, her figure looks oddly gallant. Perhaps it's the knight's uniform. As he watches, dazed, she casually leaps off the terrace.

This is the second floor, but Claude is already too exhausted to think too deeply about things like that. He slumps, his head drooping. "What...? Who is she? That's my fiancée...?!"

If he falls in love without fail, again and again, wouldn't that make it simply fate?

No, that couldn't happen. Absolutely not. Even if she really does l-love me, that utter lack of modesty...

Oh, but when her lips touched his cheek, they seemed soft and sweet. The thought occurs to him absently—and then Claude turns bright red again, yanks the covers over his head, and curls up in a ball on the bed.

He must still be unwell. That has to be it.

"And so here you are: Master Claude's hair! Treasure it."

"Ohhh... Sire... It really is the demon king's hair!"

"Demon king! Demon king!"

Moved to tears, Beelzebuth holds the black hairs high, and the weeping demons prostrate themselves around him. As she watches them, Aileen relaxes, sipping tea. The couch in Claude's office is very comfortable.

"Perhaps that will placate the demons for a little while... James, you aren't going to join in?"

"I categorically refuse. Hey, that's enough. Knock it off already."

James is scowling so hard that the wrinkles on his forehead couldn't get any deeper. The demons have formed a ring around the hair and begun to dance, and he goes over to break it up. However, from the fact that he's telling them he'll put the hair away somewhere safe, he may be happy after all.

"He really isn't honest about these things. Rachel, can I trouble you for something sweet?"

"Yes, I'll bring it right away. Here's some lemon for your tea as well. I'm sure you're tired."

"I am... Still, I'm relieved. If Master Claude is like that, all I have to do is fabricate a fait accompli, and he'll be mine!"

"You could stand to be a little nicer to the demon king, you know!" Isaac yells at her from across the room.

Aileen looks at him blankly. "What are you saying? Preserving our engagement takes priority. I can nurture our love after I've captured him."

"Whatever you do, don't say that to the demon king, all right?! No matter what!!"

"Now, now, Master Isaac. She's always been like that. Hasn't she, Beelzebuth?"

"The king! Keith, the king is here! A shard of him is here with us! You should come and revere him, too."

"I'll refrain, thank you... Well, I think it's a good thing that Lady Aileen is being herself."

"Uh... Even if it's normal for her, ordinarily, that would turn you right off. Guys are unexpectedly delicate, you know," Walt comments from a short distance away.

For some reason, Kyle is hanging his head, pale-faced. "If that were me... If I were going to fall, I think it would be off a cliff."

"How rude. I simply confessed my feelings to Master Claude. I'll keep on pushing and pushing and pushing until I've shoved him right off that cliff, and then I'll put a lid on him so he can never climb back up!"

"Now seems like a good time to say this, so I'm gonna take the opportunity, but you know that's where you went wrong with Prince Cedric, right?! Learn your lesson and grow a little! Factor in a guy's love of the chase and hold back a little!"

"But if I ever pull back, it's because I no longer need that man."

Silence falls. Rachel claps her hands lightly, agreeing innocently. "Oh, yes. When they start chasing you after you've lost interest, it's just unpleasant."

"Isn't it? Why they chase us in the first place is a mystery. What's going on inside their minds?"

"Fine. That one was our fault."

After watching Isaac's surrender, Aileen turns to Elefas. "More importantly, Elefas, were you eavesdropping? Don't tell me Master Cedric was as well."

"I wouldn't call it eavesdropping. You were very noisy, so we happened to hear you."

"I see. And how did Master Cedric look?"

"As if he was fighting a headache."

Gazes that seem to say *I bet* converge on her, but Aileen unabashedly ignores them. "I wonder what he was thinking, letting me go like that."

"Well... Case in point? Maybe he started wanting to chase you. He's probably got some lingering feelings for you."

Aileen sets her cup down on its saucer with a *clatter* and drops her forehead into her hands, muttering, "I'd like to cut him down!"

"Yes, it does make you want to cut him down."

"Sweet Ailey and Rachel, your eyes are dead serious. That's scary!"

"N-never mind that, shouldn't we think about what we're going to do next?!"

Shuddering, Walt and Kyle both shout their responses.

With a sigh, Aileen pulls herself together. "The crux of the matter is this: How am I going to get Master Claude to eat these cookies?"

"You're not even gonna try winning him over the regular way, huh? I feel bad for the demon king..."

"It's all right, Master Isaac. Milord's chastity essentially doesn't exist."

"That's pretty heartless, Keith!!"

"Hey, most everybody's here. Got a minute? Your uncle's got a report to make." Behind Walt and Kyle, Jasper pokes his head in through the door. With everyone's attention on him, he opens his notebook, launching right into the report. "Rumor has it that His Highness the crown prince is going to be inspecting the third layer soon."

"An inspection? ...I wonder if it's a performance for the townspeople. But at a time like this?"

"It's probably because it's 'a time like this.' Prince Cedric and Lady Lilia will be with him, so I'd wager it's meant to show the solidarity of the imperial family. Basically, it's a whole production to reassure for the populace and act as a check on other nations."

The fact that Claude has lost his magic has been officially announced already, at the same time as the upcoming ball. They've reported his amnesia as well, and she's heard that people have been worried about the crown prince's well-being.

It's no wonder Master Claude is concerned. Even though his amnesia must already be making him anxious...

Still, there's no doubt he'll try to relieve the people's uneasiness before his own.

As he offers Jasper tea, Keith cocks his head. "I haven't heard a word about that. Is it not an official inspection?"

"They were originally going to do it on the sly, incognito and all that. Lady Lilia planned it herself, apparently. She said he should see the country he'd be ruling."

Aileen knit her eyebrows together in a frown. Inspections are all well and good, but they aren't following proper protocol. *As always, she has no common sense... No, that's not true. After all, this is something she's doing* now.

The thing is, there's a similar event in the game. During that event, some sort of event flag is tripped. It's probably safe to assume that's the reason behind this.

She doesn't know what the flag is, but she can guess. In the fan disc, thanks to Elefas, the shadow of Claude's damnable memories as the demon king is constantly hanging over him.

Aileen glances at the mage. "Elefas. If you were to attempt to restore Master Claude's memories, how would you go about it?"

The question is a complete non sequitur, and Elefas blinks. However, he puts a finger to his lips and thinks about it. "That's...a good question. First, I might bring him into contact with something that would remind him of the past."

"But I met him, and it didn't work... That hurt a little, if I'm being perfectly honest."

"If I may be so bold, speaking from my perspective as a mage, I believe that's only to be expected. You have the sacred sword, Lady Aileen, and so your affinity with Master Claude's memories is poor."

Aileen hasn't even considered this, and hearing it startles her. Isaac and the others are also listening intently.

"From the fact that Master Claude's memories disappeared along with his magic, we should assume that his magic and memories are linked. However, the sacred sword—so-called holy power—negates magic. It would be difficult to use it to restore it."

"In other words, you mean it isn't likely to act as a stimulus that'll return Master Claude's memories to him?"

"That's right. In theory, encountering the demons should rouse his magic, making them a better stimulus."

In other words, the event during the inspection is likely to be demon related.

"However, if Master Claude's vast magic is the ocean, then the demons' magic is the equivalent of grains of sand. Since the stimulus will be no stronger than throwing sand into the ocean, there may not be much point..."

"No, that was quite useful. Thank you, Elefas."

"Uh, speaking of demons, I've got one other item here." Jasper flips through his notebook. "We're starting to get scattered reports of demon sightings even around the second layer. It doesn't sound like they're causing any trouble, and there's a gag order in effect to keep the demon king from getting riled up about the news, but the mood there isn't stellar."

They're probably demons who've left the forest in search of Claude. Aileen sighs. "Perhaps I should have plucked more of Master Claude's hair for them."

"Here's hoping they don't snap and storm the castle to retake the demon king," Walt mutters, propping his chin on his hand.

Kyle grumbles to himself, too. "In the first place, as Master Claude is now, will the demons even recognize him as their king? Excluding the lot that were rejoicing over his hair..."

"They most definitely will." James has returned. He's put the hair in a small container for safekeeping, and Beelzebuth and the other demons are following it around restlessly. "To the demons, it doesn't feel as if Master Claude has vanished. It's more as if they've suddenly lost contact with him. That means they'll instantly know he's the king if they meet him, even if his memories and magic are gone. Right, Bel?"

"? Even without magic, the king is the king."

"So if the demon king gave you some sort of order now, you'd still obey it without question?" Isaac asks.

Beelzebuth throws out his chest. "Of course."

Aileen feels like sighing. If the emperor's faction finds out about that, they'll have a disaster on their hands. It would only take a word from Claude to make the demons cheerfully commit mass suicide. Unless they make the emperor think that Claude is no longer the demon king, and that the demons won't take orders from him, there'll undoubtedly be trouble.

Of course, that's a double-edged sword. It will necessarily mean letting them think the demons are dangerous and an active threat.

How far will they be able to restrain them? Typically, for high-ranking demons, Beelzebuth and James are able to control the others to some extent, but their authority isn't absolute like Claude's. Aileen's sacred sword is also a factor, but that's meant to kill demons. She doesn't want to use it unless she has to.

However, she gets the feeling that the day when she'll have to may not be far off.

"Well, that does it for my reports. Oh, right—Isaac, Luc, and Quartz said to tell you they've prepared what you asked for. Also, Denis sent this. He said it's blueprints."

"Speaking of that, Isaac, what have you been doing? I hear you're bringing a variety of things into the castle."

"Oh, this and that, just in case. And? What's our next move?" Isaac prompts.

Aileen sets her index finger against her lips, thinking. "...I'll infiltrate Master Claude's inspection. Something's bound to happen."

"'Bound to'? How do you know?"

"Because the demons may go after Master Claude, perhaps?"

Considering the current state of affairs and Elefas's suggestion of an effective way to restore Claude's memories, that seems like the biggest possibility. She's said it mischievously, but Isaac stops asking questions and starts thinking, his face serious.

"Yeah, I could see that happening. Right now, the demon king's in a mansion that's protected by sacred power, right? But during the inspection, he'll leave that protection behind to be out and about. As far as the demons are concerned, it's the perfect chance."

"Even if that's true, there's no way you'll be able to sneak into the inspection, sweet Ailey."

"If you violate an imperial edict in front of the general public, you really won't be able to talk your way out of it."

"Elefas, can't you use magic to erase me from the memories of people who see me?"

"Unfortunately, I cannot. If I could, I'd tinker with the demon king's memories directly."

Her rather dicey question has been answered in kind. Isaac and James glare at him, scowling, but Aileen is unconcerned. She simply thinks, *He's very good.*

"To begin with, I'll disguise myself as an apprentice knight and throw them off my scent that way. Then I'll make sure I have his cooperation."

"Whose cooperation?"

"Oh, who else?"

There's no one who'd accept Aileen's recklessness but her beloved fiancé.

"And so! Master Claude, if you happen to spy me during the inspection next week, shield me by insisting it isn't me. All right?"

"I will not! I wondered what you were up to when you came bursting in from the terrace out of nowhere... Do you genuinely understand that you'll be executed if they find out you're seeing me?!"

She does, of course. That goes without question. However, as soon as she appeared on the terrace, Claude hastily let her into the room. That kindness makes her feel all warm and fuzzy inside, and so she clings to him in spite of herself.

"I do understand, Master Claude. It's been three days since we last met. I see you're able to be up and about now."

"A-as I said before, don't cling to me— What are you, even?!"

"Your fiancée."

"They're breaking that off!"

"Well, before they do, I'll make it so your body can't live without me."

She gives him a smile, and he tears her away from him. Then with a scowl that puts deep wrinkles in his forehead, Claude sits down on a distant couch and begins paging through documents.

Apparently, he's elected to ignore her. She wonders if it's strange that makes her heart beat faster. Aileen ultimately decides it's only natural. Even his cold profile is a precious treasure.

"Master Claude, I've brought an apple pie today."

"I don't want it. There's no telling what's in it."

"What are you reading?"

"It's nothing to do with you."

"Are you working? In that case, I'll make some tea that will go with the pie."

"Don't you ever give up...?!"

"Not until you choose me as your fiancée at the ball, Master Claude."

Claude caves first, slumping with one hand to his forehead. Setting the basket with the apple pie on a little side table, Aileen sits down beside him. He gets up, moves away, and sits down again, so she promptly closes the distance. He relocates to an armchair; she seats herself on the arm. Seeing Claude bury his face in his hands, giving up, she grins.

"Hee-hee-hee. This is fun, isn't it? Just like old times."

"I'm not enjoying this at all!"

"This is my first proper unrequited love. It isn't bad."

Claude glances at her, but he immediately decides the better of it and looks down at the documents he's holding instead.

And so Aileen peers at them as well.

"That's your handwriting, Master Claude. Is this…a proposal for judicial reform?"

"You can tell?"

"Yes… That's an interesting idea. Rejecting laws with inappropriate content, even if all appropriate procedures are followed… Are you targeting the tax system?"

From the way his eyes widen, she knows she's correct. As if she's worn him down, Claude speaks. "…Grandmother and Father brought me materials on the empire; they said they were for my studies as crown prince. I read through them, and…tax collection is supposedly regulated by law, but those laws are far too imbalanced. The standards were drafted carelessly as well; too much is left to the discretion of individual jurisdictions, and the amounts collected are currently the same whether the economy is doing well or doing poorly."

"That's quite true, but the aristocracy will oppose any change to the status quo. Particularly the great nobles who side with the emperor. If they end up at a disadvantage under a new tax regime, they're sure to be angry."

She's implying that's exactly why the law is this way to begin with. However, Claude doesn't let that trouble him. "That's why I'll start with a judicial reform, so that they won't pick up on it right away. It's important to do things in the proper order. I skimmed materials on the territories as well, and the gap between rich and poor is far too great. If nothing is done, it's going to be a problem someday."

He's absolutely correct. However, Aileen is sure the emperor didn't give Claude these documents because he wanted his son to think about things like that. The miscalculation makes her chuckle to herself.

It serves them right for underestimating Master Claude's brilliance simply because he's lost his memory. But...

Extraordinary talent can also attract ire—that's the way of the world. On top of that, even if he isn't aware of it, Claude is a bird in a cage right now. He has far too little power.

"...When will you be showing this to the emperor?"

"Why does that matter to you? Does the d'Autriche duchy have an uneasy conscience? If I recall, your oldest brother is the acting lord of your domain."

"Goodness, my brother isn't that foolish. That isn't what I meant."

"In the first place, I'm not asking for your opinion. I'm free to propose this whenever I like." With that, Claude hides the set of documents from her.

...There's no help for it. Hopefully, Father will cleverly protect— He won't, will he?

On the contrary, he might actively throw Claude to the wolves. After all, her father has taken a great liking to him. She can see him putting the idea that Claude is dangerous into the emperor's head, fanning internal division and isolating Claude, then having the d'Autriche duchy extend a helping hand to him.

"...Master Claude. If possible, stay well away from my father."

"Where did that come from? You don't have to tell me that; I wouldn't purposefully rub him the wrong way when I'm planning to break off my engagement to you. Never mind that, you should go home—"

Outside the room, they hear a door open and shut. Claude freezes. Then he grabs Aileen's arm, quickly scans the room, opens a wardrobe with glass windows in its top half, and bundles her into it.

"Don't come out."

His intense eyes won't take no for an answer. Aileen nods obediently. He promptly shuts the doors, and the inside of the wardrobe goes dark.

Claude's jackets and robes are hanging in there. They're in the way, and it's cramped, but not to the point where she can't move. Rising to her knees, Aileen quietly peeks into the room. Through the thin lace curtains over the glass windows, she sees that Claude has let Cedric and Lilia in.

"How are you feeling, Prince Claude?"

"I'm quite well now, Lilia. And you're here, too, Cedric? I know you're busy."

"Yes, there's been a change to the inspection route, so we came to tell you."

"I'll make us some tea first. I've baked cookies! —Oh? What's this basket?"

It's the basket of apple pie Aileen brought. Claude snatches it from her very, very quickly, hiding it behind his back. "I—I asked the servants to get it for us."

"You should have asked me… Oh dear, what will we do with the cookies? You don't want them?"

"N-no, you went to all that trouble. Let's have those instead. Is it all right to leave the tea to you?"

"But of course!" Lilia tells him with a smile and gets right to work. Claude heaves a long, deep sigh and shuffles the basket of apple pie off to a corner.

How cute to act like this even after he told me he didn't want my pie.

She spiked it with various things, so his wariness is only natural, but she isn't amused.

Perhaps I shall kick the door. Prince Cedric already knows about me anyway, and I'm sure Lady Lilia won't try to end the game until the ball— but it would irk me to go out of my way to inform them of my presence.

"By the way, Prince Claude? You haven't seen Lady Aileen, have you?"

No, she has the feeling she already knows. Not that she's going to come out if called.

"Of course not, Lilia. I wouldn't do anything that would trouble you or Cedric."

"I'm glad. Be careful, though. Lady Aileen always has been one to use every trick in the book."

"Yes... You're right..."

Claude appears to be agreeing wholeheartedly, but she decides to believe that he's acting.

"She's right? Have you remembered something, Brother?"

"N-no...? To hear the two of you talk, it seemed as if that must be the case. That's all."

This amnesiac Claude is a bad liar. It's cute, so she'll forgive him, but Cedric is concerning. From the look of it, he hasn't even told Claude he's the one who led her here.

In addition, she gets the feeling he's looking her way. He can't have guessed that she's in the wardrobe, can he? These perks of being her childhood friend have been a downright nuisance lately. She isn't the least bit happy about it.

"Oh, good heavens. That makes it sound as if I've been speaking ill of Lady Aileen to you, Prince Claude. I didn't mean to. Um, Lady Aileen is an incredible young noblewoman."

"I know, Lilia. You're only supporting me since I can't remember on my own."

"But I...I'm frightened. We've finally become good friends, Prince Claude, but if you become the demon king again..."

That's the heroine of an *otome* game for you; her words, the angle of her face, the way the tears filling her eyes don't fall—it's picture-perfect. Aileen would love to take a page from her book. Claude frowns, looking troubled. Cedric thumps him on the shoulder.

"Lilia, it's fine. Look, the tea you've made for us is getting cold."

"Oh... You're right. Goodness, listen to me. I really do need to get ahold of myself, don't I?" From Lilia's smile, it's patently clear that she's trying to stifle her unease.

It can't be... Is this the holding back Isaac was talking about? But if I tried the same thing, it would only earn me suspicious looks... I wonder what the difference is.

Aileen simply doesn't get it. While she's puzzling over it in the wardrobe, the others begin their teatime.

"Hmm? These documents... Prince Claude, did you draft these?!"

"Oh, yes. Cedric is currently carrying out the crown prince's duties in my place, you know. I thought that if I could at least make some sort of proposal... It's still in the rough stages, though."

"No, that's not true! This is amazing! I'm sure the empress dowager and His Majesty the emperor will be delighted."

"I hope so, but..."

"Let me see those later as well, Brother. By the way, demons have been making frequent appearances in the capital, so security for the inspection has been heightened. As an additional measure, they've changed the route."

"Demons..." At Claude's murmur, Aileen strains her eyes. As he listens to Cedric, Claude's gaze is downcast, and his expression is a little melancholy.

"There was talk of sending the Holy Knights along, but the captain is currently away on an expedition. Even if that weren't the case, he's Duke d'Autriche's second son, and there's someone under Aileen's influence in the brigade. There's a good possibility that we'd have an information leak on our hands. As a result, we're pulling together a detail using the apprentice knights, and we'll have them provide security for the inspection."

"You mean apprentices who haven't had any serious training? If demons do turn up, they'll be in danger."

"Oh, it's all right. Since they hope to join the knights, they've learned swordsmanship, and the veterans will take command if anything major happens. Besides, when demons appear in the capital, they're only little ones." At that point, the corners of Lilia's lips rise ever so slightly. The fact doesn't escape Aileen.

I knew it! A demon really will appear during the inspection! A big one, at that.

She wants more information. Impassively, Cedric continues his explanation. "Just in case, the emperor has given us permission to call upon the Holy Knights if the need arises, so there's no cause for concern. We'll have Marcus and other knights stationed at all the important points as well."

"Marcus is very strong, Prince Claude! Don't worry."

"I see... I'll leave it in his hands, then."

This from an individual who had once thrashed the man in question without so much as glancing at him. Ignorance is cruel... Although, even if he had regained his memories, Claude wouldn't have remembered that.

It's all right, Marcus. I haven't forgotten how wretched you looked! Fighting back tears, she continues listening to their conversation.

The route won't be settled until the day of the inspection, but the major sites have already been determined. The one Aileen pays particular attention to is a large park in the center of the third layer. It has a big fountain where children play, and a plaza where lots of street theaters and pie vendors ply their trades. The forest that surrounds it contains a popular date spot that's frequented even by nobles who go in disguise. Aileen hasn't overlooked the fact that Lilia speaks excitedly about wanting to stop by there no matter what.

That's a crowded place. If something's going to happen there, I'll have to come up with appropriate countermeasures with Isaac and the rest. With Master Claude gone, we mustn't let the demons harm any humans!

The tea party continues peacefully. The part about Lilia and Cedric treating Claude kindly seems to be true. It's no wonder he's grateful to them. If Aileen has the potential to destroy this relationship, it's only natural that he'd treat her with distaste.

Of course, that doesn't mean she plans to back down. She doesn't, but— She sighs, hugging her knees.

"All right, Prince Claude, I'll come again this evening. Let's dine together." Lilia rises to her feet; a maid has called her away. Apparently, she has a fitting for the dress she'll be wearing during the inspection.

"Yes, I'll be waiting. Cedric, don't you need to go as well?"

"I'll take it easy here a bit longer."

"You too, Cedric; good luck in your duties! Oh, that's right— Prince Claude, you haven't had any of the cookies yet. You don't like this kind?"

"...No, that isn't it."

"Then have just one and tell me what you think! Here, say *aaaaah.*"

"What in—?!" A cry escapes Aileen. They don't seem to have noticed, but she stares fiercely at the scene through the wardrobe's window.

However, although Lilia has leaned in toward him, Claude grasps her wrist, stopping her. "Lilia, Cedric's right here. It wouldn't be good to give him the wrong idea."

Claude has refused kindly and with great care. Aileen sighs with relief. Just for a moment—a mere instant—Lilia narrows her eyes appraisingly, but she promptly smiles. "You'll be my brother-in-law someday, Prince Claude. Cedric wouldn't get mad over a thing like this. Would you, Cedric?"

"...Lilia, my brother is spoken for. If you pester him, he'll dislike you."

"Goodness, we can't have that, ha-ha! All right, then you have it, Cedric. Say *aaaah.*"

Lilia shifts her attack to Cedric. Aileen narrows her eyes. *Her methods are the same as ever... How dare she do that to another woman's fiancé.*

Cedric had refused as well, at first. However, he understood that what Lilia did was based in her affection and innocence, tolerantly accepted it, and finally began to say it was cute.

Aileen accused him of being absurd, but he didn't love her; no matter how sound her arguments had been, they held no weight for him.

No doubt that's the case here as well. After all, right now, Claude doesn't love Aileen, either.

...Oh, so this is what unrequited love feels like.

A smile comes to her lips. Lilia leaves the room, and she

sees Cedric turn to face Claude. "Brother, I'm sorry Lilia was so demandi—"

She slams a foot into the wardrobe door, and it swings right open. As she boldly emerges, both Claude and Cedric nearly fumble their teacups.

"Y-y-you— I told you to stay inside..."

"There's no need to hide. Prince Cedric has already noticed anyway."

"What? Is that true, Cedric?"

"Of course not. I recognized that basket, that's all."

Aileen doesn't join their conversation. Instead, she picks up a cookie from the table and pops it into her mouth. As the other two exchange looks, she chews, then swallows. "I'd expect no less of Lady Lilia. It's delicious, Master Claude."

"I—I see."

"—I'll take my leave now."

It wouldn't be good to stay here longer. Retrieving the apple-pie basket from the corner it's been relegated to, she forces it on Cedric.

"Wh-what is this? Why are you giving it to me? It's for my brother, isn't it?"

"Waste must be disposed of in a proper receptacle."

"What waste are—? Wait, did you just call me a waste bin?!"

"Master Claude."

Claude is still seated, and he looks up at Aileen suspiciously. Belatedly, the fact that his eyes aren't red makes her want to sob and cling to him, but she controls herself, intentionally putting on a smile. "Next time, I'll bring cookies that will make you fall in love with me at the first bite!"

"Don't bother! As I keep telling you, don't come at all!"

"Let's meet at the inspection, then."

"Wait, do you seriously intend to be there?! Hey!"

She hears him try to stop her, but he doesn't go so far as to jump off the terrace after her. Aileen sighs. Elefas, who's been waiting in the shade of the trees below the terrace this whole time, calls to her. "Leaving already? Did you learn anything?"

"I learned that unrequited love hurts."

"That's quite, er... Forgive me for being presumptuous, but I believe showing Master Claude this particular expression would do the trick. Men are weak to women's tears."

"Never. I don't intend to win him over by crying."

"I've begun to want to make you cry."

Aileen plans on seeing a love like that sky of falling stars again, so until then...

"...I had heard that a fair number of people want to make you cry, Lady Aileen. I believe I now understand why."

"Who said a thing like that? I'll smite them."

"Aileen! Emergency! Fight! A fight!" They've walked away from the mansion, and the moment they're outside the barrier, as if he's been waiting for them, Almond yells.

Aileen frowns. Catching the incoming crow demon in her arms, she questions him. "Fight? At a time like this... Don't tell me it's the demons."

"No! Auguste, at the castle! He brought a woman!"

Aileen and Elefas exchange looks. In front of them, Almond puffs out his chest and adds, "Defeat draws near!"

The demon king's castle is enveloped by the forest that encircles the northern half of the capital, where the imperial palace sits at its center. While the castle used to be terribly run-down, Denis has repaired and remodeled it with the help of the demons over the past year. He's even begun building additions to it, and now it's a comfortable place that's equipped with guest rooms.

At the moment, one of those guest rooms is—unusually—filled with the violent shouts of a quarreling couple.

"Never mind that! I'm telling you, give back what you took from me!"

"But it's demon snuff! I can't let you keep this!"

"Why do I have to abide by your decision, Auguste?!"

"Serena, this is what got you attacked by the church's agents. Do you understand that? If I hadn't been passing by and saved you, who knows what would have happened?"

"Passing by? Ha! You were tailing me."

"W-well…"

"You follow me around, confiscate my possessions while I'm unconscious, and call it 'saving' me? Is that supposed to be a joke?"

Serena is winning this argument, and Auguste's face is turning red, then white, then back again. James, Walt, and Kyle are all present, but they're merely spectators. Similarly, Aileen has knocked, but no one's noticed her standing in the doorway. She turns to Rachel, who took care of Serena until she woke up. "Have they been like this the whole time?"

"Yes. She won't tell us about her situation."

"Well, considering her position, I imagine that's only natural."

"You were at that underground auction the other day, weren't you, Serena? What are you plotting this time? And more importantly, where did you learn to use a sword like that?!"

"I've been taking my anger out on a cushion every day, and it came to me naturally."

"What are you even talking about?!"

Auguste clutches at his head, but it makes sense to Aileen.

Serena Gilbert—the girl who's currently glaring at Auguste—is the heroine of *Regalia of Saints, Demons, and Maidens 2*. In other words, she's the protagonist. The *Regalia of Saints, Demons, and Maidens* series incorporates parameters. In order to successfully romance a target, the right choices need to be made, and the protagonist must also have the proper masteries.

In Game 2, on the routes for Walt and Kyle, boosting the parameters for athleticism and agility led to an ending where Serena lived alongside those two as a fellow Nameless Priest. In other words, her latent abilities were good enough to let her stand side by side with the church's augmented humans.

So she was punching cushions and slashing them apart with swords, and before she knew it, she gained formidable skill with a sword?

She might be a servant now, but once a heroine, always a heroine. No matter how improbable it sounds, her combat skills have blossomed.

"In any case, there's no point in turning James into a demon now—what's that look for?"

"I couldn't care less about that anymore. Honestly, why do

men always think women never change? Are you dreaming or something? Ugh."

"Wha—?"

"I never thought the day would come when we'd share an opinion, Serena Gilbert."

When she speaks, Serena finally notices her. The superficial, condescending smile Serena wore before is gone. As she spits out her words, she doesn't try to hide her hatred. "You're the last person I wanted to see."

"Goodness, what could I have possibly done to merit such hatred from you? This is only our second meeting."

"I like that! You set me up as Ashtart, a criminal, then forced me into life as a servant. You can't expect me to feel obliged to you for rescuing me."

"Serena! You did half demolish Misha Academy; that's a fact. And you tried to make James, Walt, and Kyle fight! I still haven't forgiven you for that, but Ailey—"

"Auguste." When Aileen checks him, Auguste grudgingly falls silent. Reading the room, Walt takes Auguste's arm and walks him over to the wall. Kyle lectures him on something, and James looks away petulantly, making retorts about bits of it.

The four of them seem very close, and Serena snorts. "They've got a regular boys' club going over there, don't they? Idiots."

"Don't be so prickly. It wasn't all bad for you, either, and you know it. Count Gilbert's family had exploited you left and right, and they were ruined by the end of everything. On top of that, you didn't have to marry a nouveau riche man who was more than twenty-five years older than you just after graduation. Isn't that thanks to me?"

From their spot by the wall, Auguste and the others give them shocked looks. The only ones who don't turn a hair are Rachel, who's heard about it from Aileen, and Serena herself.

"You really did do your homework, didn't you? So what? Am I supposed to be grateful? That's not even funny, I'm—" A faint shadow falls over Serena's confident smile. However, the corners of her lips promptly rise. "...I'll take my leave, if you don't mind. I have work to do. The precious servant's work you gave me."

"Is your current master Prince Cedric?" It's a surprise attack, but Serena doesn't respond. However, she doesn't look perplexed, either. That's enough for Aileen to know even without hearing the answer. "I'm right, then. Lady Lilia's the only one I've told about how you came to be a servant. Her personality being what it is, she was bound to give some pretext and ask her friends to get you away from her. I imagine that's why you were targeted by the church, isn't it?"

Serena doesn't respond. Aileen walks in front of her, seats herself in a chair, and crosses her legs. "But you're still at the imperial castle. In other words, you've secured the protection of someone with the power to keep you there. I'd wager you were at that auction because you'd infiltrated the venue on their orders."

"......"

"That individual is aware of your circumstances and is attempting to use you. They also have a rank and a future promising enough that you, calculating as you are, find them worth serving. I couldn't think of anyone besides Prince Cedric who would fit that description. After all, I knew he was planning something unsavory again."

He's using Serena for the same reasons he let Aileen go. She's sure of it.

"He's the lowest cur there is, but he isn't a fool. Did he

insinuate something and arouse your interest? Perhaps that if you
helped him, he'd make you his favorite mistress?"

"You do know him well, don't you? Just what I'd expect from
his former fiancée."

Aileen had made that remark intending nothing more than
simple provocation, and she's rather appalled by the fact that she
was correct. "Don't tell me you decided to serve him based on
that."

"I can, and I did. What's wrong with that?"

"Uh...his mistress? Serena, do you know what that means?!"
Auguste, who's been standing there stunned, forgets he's been
warned and speaks up.

Serena gives him a cold glance. "Yes, I do. So what?"

"P-Prince Cedric already has a fiancée. There's no way he told
you that because he loves you. He's probably just trying to use you
because you're convenient!"

"It's still better than being a servant."

"Wh-why?! That's a respectable job! It may be hard work, but
even so."

"I was my family's servant for ages, and now I'm a servant
to the imperial family. And then what? I marry and become the
servant of a man with no future? You're telling me to spend my
whole life serving people? Don't even joke about that."

Auguste wilts under Serena's sharp glare, but he keeps arguing
in a mumble. "I-if you did the normal thing, found somebody you
liked, and got together with them, I bet you'd be happy…"

"You're as naive as ever. The lowest maidservants in the castle
marry because they have to, in order to survive. Men can climb
the ladder to become valets or knights, but women are servants for
life; the daughters of nobles are sent to court to learn etiquette,

and they're always set above us. We're all desperate. We have to marry someone with an income while we're still young, and anyone will do. Even a gate guard who gets drunk and throws things at us."

"……"

"We don't have the luxury of marrying for love. We just weigh our options and choose the man who's best to obey. That's the only thing I've done. This talk of romance is ridiculous. In the first place, men only see women as domestic help or outlets for their lust. And in turn, we only see them as piggy banks."

"Serena. You're absolutely correct about the troubles of the maidservants at the imperial castle, but I'd like you to refrain from making my subordinates doubt all women, if you don't mind? What if you render them unable to marry?"

It isn't just Auguste. James, Walt, and even Kyle look stunned.

"I can see why you would try this approach. As Prince Cedric's mistress, you'd never want for money, and if you gave birth to a prince, you'd have a chance at becoming empress. As you are now, it's certainly a bet worth taking."

"Thank you for your understanding. May I go now?"

"However, Prince Cedric may use you and cast you aside. You've taken steps to guard against that, haven't you? I don't suppose you'd tell me what they are."

Such as the fact that she's still secretly in possession of demon snuff, for example. Aileen puts out a feeler, but Serena laughs it off. "Do you think I'll answer that?"

"No. But I do think we could be friends, don't you?"

"Absolutely not."

She'd been fairly serious about that proposal, but Serena

summarily rejects it. Shrugging, Aileen issues an order. "Auguste, return her possessions."

"Huh...? A-are you sure? I mean, this is..."

"It's her lifeline, I would imagine. However, I will be confiscating the demon snuff, as my fee for having saved you."

"...What? You can't think you've put me in your debt over that."

"Perish the thought. I'm merely curious how much you can manage on your own, and I've begun wanting to support you." Rising to her feet, Aileen slowly dons a smile. "Should you ever feel inclined to sell me information, let Auguste or Rachel know. I assure you I'll give you what you want."

"Ha, as if! You know nothing about me."

"I do, though. When Prince Cedric said he'd make you his mistress, the truth is that you saw red, didn't you?"

With that, Aileen whispers the reward the other girl seeks in her ear. She watches until Serena's eyes widen, then turns on her heel. "Auguste, escort her to the castle."

"Huh? ...Um, but I..."

"No one needs that. I'll go back alone." Serena snatches her things from Auguste.

Unexpectedly, Rachel speaks up. "Lady Aileen. May I see Lady Serena out?"

"Of course, Rachel. You were classmates, after all. I'm sure you have much to talk about."

"...So she's a guard. I see. Do as you please." Serena walks out, and Rachel follows her.

After their footsteps have receded, Walt speaks up brightly, as if to dispel the stagnant mood. "Well, Serena's gotten pretty intense, hasn't she? Although, I suppose that's what she was really like all along."

"I've been on the verge of developing a distrust of women for a while now. There was the matter of Ailey, too..."

"I...didn't know. I had no idea she was being forced to marry once she graduated," Auguste murmurs, his eyes lowered.

Quietly, Kyle admonishes him. "Everyone has their own circumstances. If you let yourself get wrapped up in every last one, there'll be no end to it, Auguste."

"Y-yes, you're right, but... The thing is, I always wondered why she tried so hard to make practically everybody like her. Inwardly, I made fun of her for it. I thought, *You can tell she isn't really interested in me just by watching her.* But when I think maybe she was just desperate, it feels... And now she's the second prince's mistress?"

Exchanging glances, Walt and Kyle fall silent. Before Aileen can say anything, James speaks up. "The sentimentality does nothing for me, but is it all right that the church is after her? Won't Rachel get dragged into that?"

"...Huh? Oh, you're right! I-I'll go!" Auguste abruptly whips his head up, and then he rushes out of the room. It's happened before she can blink.

Walt whistles. "James, you're actually pretty nice to Auguste."

"I merely stated the facts. If he wants to apologize, he should just do it. Although, I doubt it's going to mean anything in the long run."

"I don't think Serena Gilbert will exactly hate it, either. She used to be infatuated with him."

"...You three, prepare to console Auguste." The trio is ready and eager to cheer their friend on, but there's a distant look in Aileen's eyes. "He's almost certain to come back shattered."

Just as she's about to round a corner in the corridor, Rachel pulls on her arm.

"Wh-what are you doing?!"

"There's a medicine chest in this room. Lady Serena, you've sprained your left leg, haven't you?"

Serena is startled, and as a result, Rachel manages to pull her into the room with minimal resistance.

Briskly sitting her down on a sofa, Rachel turns on a light and brings some bandages and ointment. Bending over, she gently slips Serena's shoe off, revealing her ankle. "I knew it. It's swollen. This ointment is effective for pain from sprains or bruises when there's swelling. It's going to feel a little cold, but bear with it. It will pass quickly."

".......!"

"There, all done. Wait just a little while, until it dries." Rachel puts the lid back on the ointment.

Serena props an elbow on the armrest, putting her chin in her hand. "I'm surprised you noticed I was injured."

"You were favoring that side as you walked. I think Lady Aileen noticed as well."

"Hmph. Is it all right for you to treat it when your mistress pretended not to see it?"

"Lady Aileen didn't propose treating it because it was clear you'd refuse. Making up for what she isn't able to do is my job."

"That slavish disposition is revolting."

"You flatter me."

The conversation is stiff, but curiously, it isn't unpleasant. Her conversation with Aileen was the same way. "You lot don't sympathize with me, do you?"

"Of course we don't. You brought this on yourself." The extreme bluntness of the remark makes Serena laugh in spite of herself. In the meantime, Rachel swiftly bandages her leg.

"You do manage to get along with that ill-natured mistress of yours, after all. You're quite nasty yourself."

"Not as nasty as you are, Lady Serena."

"What is this 'Lady' business? Sarcasm?"

"Some of it is, but you are also Lady Aileen's guest." Finishing her first aid, Rachel rises to her feet, looking down at Serena. "Of course, once you are no longer a guest, I'll just call you Serena. Do your best to let me address you as 'Lady' forever."

"Once I'm Prince Cedric's mistress, I'll have you call me 'Lady' in perpetuity. My condolences."

"That's all right. I'll call you 'Lady' out of respect for your brazenness in stealing Lady Lilia's lover after you worshipped her so as the Maid of the Sacred Sword. I'm amazed you can do a thing like that."

"When my life is on the line, it's only natural, isn't it? Besides, that woman has a sweet face, but she's a complete enigma."

Serena had seen a troubled-looking Lilia discussing her with her henchmen once. It was after Claude Jean Ellmeyer had dropped her into the dung heap; she'd been on her way to borrow Lilia's perfume to mask the smell. The frightening part was the way the people around Lilia naturally decided to dispose of Serena, just as Lilia wanted, even though she never explicitly told them to. That, and the way Lilia greeted her with a calm smile when she stopped by to borrow the perfume.

That woman doesn't think of me as human.

That's common among people with power, but Serena has the feeling this goes beyond that, and that truly frightens her. She suspects Lilia doesn't even treat Cedric and the others as human.

The one person she does consider human is Aileen Lauren d'Autriche. In that sense, being Aileen's guest isn't a bad idea... Although, the male former student council members who hang around her are irritating.

"And you'd go after the fiancé of someone like that? You're playing a dangerous game."

"So what? It's not as if I have anything to lose anymore." She rises to her feet. With her ankle firmly stabilized, it's easier to move. Thanks to the ointment, she doesn't feel much pain, either. "I'm not going to thank you. You owe me anyway."

"I do?"

"The Princess Lily White selection. You told me that losing was embarrassing, remember?" Rachel frowns, watching Serena. Back then, Serena had been the one gazing into Rachel's face. "Don't get the wrong idea. I haven't lost to you."

"......"

"If it hadn't been for that woman, I would have been Princess Lily White. So you owe me, understand?" Serena snorts.

In response, Rachel sighs. "So you won't apologize for pushing me down the stairs."

"What, did you want me to?"

"No. It was quite the experience—you may have this." She holds out the jar of ointment.

Serena takes it but cocks her head, puzzled. "Why?"

"It's a modest parting gift for you, who fights alone. Best of luck."

Not bad. Serena laughs, slipping the object she's been given into her pocket. "You don't have to go any farther with me. I'm leaving."

"That won't do. We can't have you wandering around without permission."

"I'm not obligated to listen to you."

"Serena! And Rachel, you're here, too. Good, I'm glad I found you." Just as she opens the door, Auguste comes running up. Apparently, he's been chasing them. "I'll escort you back after all. I'm the one who brought you here, and anyway, I think I owe you an apology. I won't forgive you for what you did to James, but I didn't know about your situation, and, um."

"Are you going to tell me you're sorry for secretly ridiculing me for being a desperate man hunter?" Although she didn't particularly mean it to be, her voice is cold. He looks startled, and his good-natured face freezes up. This irritates her even more.

"I won't forgive you, but look at me being considerate, aren't I kind? Is that what this is?"

"N-no, it's not like that! I just realized you were dealing with other things, too... I mean, there's no way I could agree with your methods, either at the academy or with Prince Cedric! What do you mean, you want to be his mistress?! Why does it have to be like that? You know there are other ways!"

"True. If I'd known you were going to join the Holy Knights,

I would have worn my best face around you. Then you would have pitied me and at least made me your lover."

How patronizing. Because he feels sorry for her. Because although he doesn't like her or anything of the sort, he wants to help her.

What a cheap sense of justice. So typical of men.

Auguste is standing there, stunned and wide-eyed. Serena laughs in his face.

"You're so very kind—never talk to me again. You disgust me."

"……"

Auguste is speechless. Leaving him behind, Serena turns on her heel. She's gotten her revenge, but it hasn't improved her mood at all; she's still irritated. She walks faster, and Rachel trots to catch up with her.

"Um, Auguste…"

"*He meant no harm*? I know. He's only making fun of me."

"—But you didn't take advantage of him."

"Well, I'm going to be the second prince's mistress, you know." She has no reason to take advantage. Serena gives a rather empty smile. "He may be a Holy Knight, but he's still a fresh recruit. As long as he allies himself with Aileen Lauren d'Autriche, he has no prospects of advancement, and I don't have time to waste on him."

"You never know."

"No, I know. They'll crush all of you soon. The emperor has his eye on you. That other one— What was his name, Isaac? There's no telling how much longer he'll be able to stay as he is. It won't be long before they start putting pressure on his family's company."

"…Even so, Isaac won't abandon Lady Aileen."

She thought Rachel might lose her composure, but she's

impassive. Serena isn't happy about that. "What? So you believe in him? Why don't you give a little more thought to how you'll fare in the coming days?"

"If he were the type who'd betray Lady Aileen at that point, I'd have it much easier." Rachel's eyes waver just a little. That's all, though. Even so, for some reason, Serena's irritation smoothly recedes.

Perhaps it's sympathy. She makes a remark she didn't plan to say. "...I'd recommend running immediately, before you're conveniently used and discarded. Like me."

Rachel doesn't respond. Serena doesn't feel the need to say anything else, either.

As Aileen had predicted, Auguste comes back a wreck. Aileen has heard the gist of the conversation from Rachel, and she feels like applauding Serena for not taking advantage of him.

Auguste grumbles to James and the others—"That wasn't what I meant"—but he's probably learned by now that it's irresponsible to be concerned for Serena in a half-hearted way. He's depressed, and James and the others comfort him, trying to cheer him up. Thinking this will be educational for them as well, she decides to leave them to it.

I wonder how this will go. Although really, I'm in no position to be concerned about others at the moment.

She's just the tiniest bit reluctant to see Claude as he is now.

However, even as she mulls over things like that, she doesn't want anyone to realize it.

Besides, awkwardly, even if her love is unrequited, the mere sight of his face makes her happy.

"These are the men who will be guarding Your Highness's carriage. Raise your heads, all of you."

Not to mention the moment when he sees her, and that beautiful face twists.

The official who's just finished the preinspection review introduces the apprentice knights briefly by name. In the meantime, Claude is clearly disconcerted. His reaction is absolutely adorable.

"This is Ailey Calois. Although he's a novice, if anything happens, he is the one who will take command of the unit and secure your escape, Prince Claude."

"Command?! D-don't tell me sh—he's the captain!"

"He's an apprentice, but he's skilled enough to knock out a member of the Holy Knights. He was specially selected in recognition of that fact."

"H-he knocked someone out?!"

"I hear he shows great promise."

"Great what now?!"

Claude is looking from the official to Aileen and back, echoing the man's words. Beside him, Cedric has a hand pressed to his forehead as if he's fighting a headache. She doesn't like that, but because Claude is so cute, she decides to let it slide.

"Of course, since they are apprentices, they are simply in charge of keeping watch and acting as your guides. In actual combat, rest assured that someone from the Holy Knights will take command."

"I—I...see... N-no, that isn't the problem..."

"It's almost time. Ailey Calois, escort His Highness to the carriage. The rest of you, prepare for departure."

Aileen stands, responding to her name, and smiles at Claude. "This way, Your Highness. I'll show you the—"

"First, come over here!" He grabs her arm and drags her away. As the rest of the group exchange puzzled looks, Claude takes Aileen from the square into a passageway. After looking around to make sure they're alone, he plants his hands on the wall and slumps. "What are you doing?! Are they really going to execute you if we meet?!"

"If you keep our engagement, Master Claude, I won't be executed."

"So you're here to threaten me?! Look, go home, right this minute. I don't want anything more to do with you!"

"......"

A pause opens up. This isn't normal, and Claude notices; he blinks at her. "...Why aren't you arguing?"

"There's nothing more to say. If a demon should appear and abduct you, Master Claude, they'll make me out to be the kidnapper."

"That's not what I meant... Uh... You aren't acting the way you usually... Did something happen?"

"—Were you worried about me just now?"

Claude falters. However, it's clear that he's concerned about Aileen from the look in his eyes, and that alone is enough to send her spirits soaring. "My... My, my, my! I'm on your mind, aren't I, Master Claude?!"

"Th-that's not true, I only thought you weren't acting like yourself— Don't come near me, don't embrace me, I'm not worried about you at all!"

"You don't have to put up a bold front, you know. You could simply be honest and say you love me."

"Where does this endless optimism of yours come from?! Never mind, just get away from—"

"Lady Aileen. If you embrace Master Claude while dressed as a boy, you'll start baseless rumors." Elefas abruptly materializes out of thin air. Claude, who's been desperately trying to free himself from Aileen, does a shocked double take.

"Oh, yes," Aileen says, putting some distance between herself and Claude. "You're right. I'll be careful, Elefas."

"Wha... Wha—? He just— Where did he...?"

"He is my guard, Master Claude. He's concealing himself with magic." Elefas bows to Claude. Smiling brightly, Aileen goes on. "Since he is here, don't trouble yourself about me. Of course, I will protect you, Master Claude! Please don't worry about that."

"Aren't you getting something wrong?! Ordinarily, as the man, I'm the one who should protect you, aren't I?!"

"I will protect Lady Aileen, so don't let that concern you."

Claude looks Elefas straight in the face. Elefas accepts his gaze with a smile. The two of them fall silent, and Aileen cocks her head, perplexed. Claude's expression is hard. "You...were there the other day, too. Are you her retainer?"

"Not technically. However, she persuaded me by telling me that, in the event that we died, we would do so together."

He's probably insinuating that he's supposed to be Claude's retainer. The way he puts it is unexpectedly confrontational, and Aileen is already exasperated. "What's the point of telling Master Claude a thing like that as he is now? Stand down, Elefas."

"Understood. However, if something happens, Lady Aileen,

call me at once." Elefas whispers the words softly in her ear, then vanishes.

Claude's eyes stay fixed on the spot where Elefas had been. His expression is rather odd. "...Is he really just a retainer?"

"I'm not sure one could say 'just.' He is human, but he's a mage, which makes him unusual."

"That isn't what I meant..."

"Brother, there's no use belaboring the point. That's just the sort of woman she is." Somewhere in there, Cedric has appeared in the passageway. Apparently, he ran after them. As usual, just seeing him makes her angry, and her anger makes her eager for a fight.

"Hurry up and return to your post. Or did you want me to unmask you here and now?"

"Go ahead and try it. I truly will plunge you into hell this time. Did you think I knew nothing about Serena Gilbert?"

Cedric turns pale. Aileen snorts contemptuously. Bluffs are important.

Claude blinks at them both, perplexed. "Serena? What's this about?"

"Oh, I'm sorry, Master Claude. Just look at me, talking to a waste bin."

"You— Why do you insist on calling me that?!"

"A talking waste bin. That's quite unusual."

"...So you can't tell me, hmm? You two are close, aren't you?"

""Huh?"" She's accidentally spoken in unison with Cedric.

Claude turns his back so that she can't see his face. "I'm sure it's inconvenient for you if I'm here. I'll be going."

"...What? Wait, please, Master Claude. I'll go, too."

"No need. Stay away from me."

He turns her down flatly, and she stops in her tracks. Part of what's stopped her may be that his cold gaze is just the way it was when his eyes were red.

No matter what happens, Claude is Claude. That realization makes her happy, but she has no idea what's offended him. She sets a hand on the hilt of her sword. Cedric heaves a sigh.

"...Ridiculo— Hey, don't just slash at me out of nowhere!"

"I don't quite understand exactly what went wrong, but for now, could you just stop breathing for a moment?"

"You haven't changed a bit! No wonder my brother's uneasy."

"Master Claude is?"

Cedric snorts, then turns and leaves, following Claude.

Unexpectedly, Elefas appears in the now-deserted passage. "You know, you may have a chance with Master Claude."

"What on earth are you talking about? Forget 'chances,' Master Claude is my fiancé."

"...Are you speaking seriously?"

"Never mind that, how goes the operation? All according to plan?"

Elefas blinks at her before he answers. "Yes. As planned, the Oberon Trading Firm has reserved both the park and the route up to that point. The only people present are employees and d'Autriche family servants disguised as ordinary citizens. The plaza itself is deserted. In addition, we've learned who is in charge of this inspection. It's Lester Craine, a young man who is already a high government official. He appears to have planned the inspection route as well."

The name has come up abruptly, and Aileen dredges her

memory for it. *Lester Craine is a love interest from Game 1, isn't he? He's a bespectacled-upperclassman type, a calm, levelheaded strategist... I'm impressed she managed to secure him.*

As an upperclassman, he graduated ahead of the rest, so there was only a short window to romance him. Even in the game, it had been hard to get him on the first playthrough. And Lilia has managed to make him hers after graduation. No wonder she considers herself the player over Aileen or anyone else for that matter.

She remembers his pale, light features from the game art. Lester is the oldest son of Marquis Craine; very conscious of being an elite, he's an ambitious type with no qualms about using people. In the game, the d'Autriche family was ruined along with Aileen, and so he became the youngest prime minister in the history of the empire.

In reality, the d'Autriches are doing just fine, and Aileen's oldest brother is the next favored candidate for prime minister. However, Lester probably hasn't lost either his skills or his ambition.

...And now he's working as Lilia's strategist.

Resheathing her sword, Aileen turns to face Elefas. "Report this all to Isaac."

"Now? Besides, with nothing but a name, I doubt he can take any solid steps against him."

"If he's a high government official, Jasper will have information on him, and Master Keith may be acquainted with him. That alone will be enough to tell us what sort of person he is. We can leave the rest to Isaac. My subordinates are capable; they'll bring us the best possible results."

"You do trust them, don't you?"

"Yes, and you as well."

Elefas's eyes widen slightly. Then he gives a wry smile. "I'm honored. However, Lady Aileen, what about your guard?"

"I don't need one. Since I have the sacred sword, no one is stronger against demons than I am. Prioritize guarding Master Claude."

As Aileen sets off, Elefas bows and says, "As you wish."

"We're running behind schedule, Your Highness. I'm not fond of having my plans interfered with."

Claude pauses in the act of climbing into the carriage. The rather neurotic-looking man who's spoken to him pushes his glasses up and continues sarcastically, "Of course, I wouldn't design a plan that would be in trouble if this or that didn't go just right, but if the inspection comes to nothing, Lilia will be sad."

"...You're right, Lester. I'm sorry."

"I'm only doing this because she requested it. Follow my instructions and refrain from doing anything careless, if you would. I hear you still haven't chosen a new fiancée from the candidates the empress dowager recommended to you?"

"I'm sorry. I just haven't felt like it."

"Hurry and choose, if you would. Do you think you have a great deal of options as you are now? You're just deadweight, capable of nothing— Ah, I misspoke. I beg your pardon, Your Highness."

Lester's apology is insincere. Several in the procession exchange glances, snickering like the sycophants they are.

Involuntarily, Claude clenches his fists. As things stand, he has no achievements to his name. Still, does that mean he has to stay silent while they mock him to his face? He doesn't know. He has neither the memories nor the power to determine what is true and what is false.

Everyone seems to be laughing at his expense far too much. Since he's not the demon king, he's just a burden, nothing to fear. Even that woman is hiding things from him. She says she'll protect him. As the demon king, he probably had the power to turn these people to dust, and yet—

Startled, Claude blinks... *What was I just thinking?*

With a shudder, he climbs into the carriage as if he's running away. No one worries about it. Alone in the cramped vehicle, he squeezes his eyes shut and presses his forehead against the window.

He mustn't think about what it would be like if he were the demon king. That's a past he mustn't look back on.

I have to make her go away.

Being concerned about her and wanting to know more about her will direct him toward his past. Before long, he may begin wanting to remember. That lingering regret could destroy the world.

The carriage creaks, and Claude opens his eyes. Lilia has climbed in.

"...Where's Cedric?"

"It sounds as if he's not feeling well. He said he'll retire to the castle and rest today."

Has something happened with Aileen? The thought flickers through his mind, but he promptly shakes his head, banishing it. He turns to Lilia, who's sitting across from him. "Are you sure you don't need to stay with him?"

"Yes, he asked me to go with you, Prince Claude."

"I don't think it looks good for a man and woman who aren't engaged to be alone together."

"Oh, that's all right, you and I are going to be related by marriage! Lester said it was fine as well!"

The name makes him frown, but just then, the carriage sets off with a *clatter*. At this point, Claude has no way to stop it.

"I'm looking forward to this, aren't you?!"

"...Yes, I am."

Sighing, he glances out the window. There are an unusual number of crows loitering. It strikes him as odd, but then the sight of Aileen on horseback leaps out at him, and he pulls the curtain over the little window.

"They sell delicious pies in the plaza. Let's buy one to take back for Cedric."

"...Yes, let's do that."

"...Prince Claude. Um... Are you bored? Being here with just me, I mean."

Apparently, she's noticed his absentminded responses. He recrosses his legs, speaking as kindly as possible. "No, that's not it. I feel bad that you've had to be so careful and considerate around me. And then there's the upcoming ball... I've been told to choose a fiancée, but I don't understand any of this. I can't be relied upon, and I'm ashamed of it."

"What are you saying?" Lilia's face is earnest. Claude's balled fists are braced against his knees, and she lays her hands on top of them. Leaning closer to his frowning face, she speaks gently. "You're fine as you are. Even if you don't force yourself to do anything, you're important."

The words should be kind ones, an affirmation that this version of him is the right one. However, they wound his pride terribly, and before he knows what he's doing, Claude swats her hands away. *I've done it now*, he thinks, but the carriage that's been provided for their undercover inspection is an uncomfortable one, and it shakes and clatters. Lilia seems to have interpreted his motion as part of the instability, and she moves her hands to his cheeks, soothing him. "It's all right. There's no need to fret. Even at the ball— I know, why not dance with me? After that, you can just slip away and skip the rest if you like."

"Cedric would be angry. At balls, you're supposed to dance with whoever is closest to your heart—" Claude is beginning to lecture her on common sense, but the carriage jolts, interrupting him. Perhaps entering the third layer means the road has grown rougher... But the horses whinny, screams go up, and the carriage tilts. Lilia shrieks and clings to him. Supporting her, Claude kicks the door of the slanting carriage open. Wind rushes in, sweeping his hair back. Lilia screams.

"I-i-it can't be! We're floating?!"

"Lilia, calm down. What on earth...?"

The ground rumbles with regular, heavy thuds, and with each thud, the world rocks. As he tries to comfort Lilia, Claude leans out. Then he's struck dumb.

Before him, there's nothing but sky, and below him, there's a demon. The monster is as big as a house; it's picked up their carriage and is running with it. Crows are flying around it.

"What...in the...?"

"Go back, go back! You can't!"

The words come from the crows who are flying alongside them. In other words, they're demons. He's surrounded by demons.

Lilia's trembling; she clings to him. "P-Prince Claude...! I'm frightened!"

"Stop right there, demon! Stop, I said! Return Master Claude!"

With a gasp, Claude looks in the direction of the voice. Behind the running demon, Aileen has caught up with them on horseback.

"You mustn't! You can't do this, not now! Behave yourself and listen!"

"Yes! That's right! Do what you're told! Back to the forest!"

"King," calls the one-eyed monster that's running with the carriage. Claude looks over, and their eyes meet. Then in a voice that's far clumsier than the rest, the demon speaks. "I save. I protect king."

It's talking about him. Without thinking, he presses a hand to his chest. When it sees the gesture, the demon faces forward. "Not give to humans. King is sad."

"—Almond, herd this one to the plaza! We'll capture them there!"

"Understood! Unit One, deploy left wing!"

"Unit Two, stay behind. Right wing, follow me!"

"Get humans to shelter! Fenrir Unit, move the humans away!"

The flock of crows moves with shocking precision. Suddenly, Claude realizes that there are almost no humans in the running demon's path. *Did she anticipate this situation and issue orders ahead of time...?!*

Aileen's wig has come off, and her long hair streams behind her galloping steed. Then she drops the reins, rising to her feet and lifting both her hands. Those hands are shining.

That's the sacred sword.

As if the light has frightened it, the demon speeds up. She's driving it onward.

Beautiful.

The thought seems out of place. Is he thinking about that light, or about her? Either way, since he's looking at it, he registers the artificial, reflected light. Arrowheads. As if they've been lying in wait, the knights who've been hiding in the shadows form ranks, aiming arrows their way. A disagreeable, bespectacled smile comes to mind; is it just an illusion?

"No, don't, don't shoot! Lilia and I are fine—!"

But nobody listens to orders from a figurehead crown prince.

Countless arrows speed toward the hulking creature.

As arrows are loosed at the demon from both sides, Aileen *tsk*s. Apparently, Isaac's prediction has come true in a nasty way. Now they'll have to protect the demons from the humans as well.

"Walt, Kyle! Don't let that demon get hurt!"

"Yes, ma'am. Wouldn't want the demon king getting mad at us later! Kyle, you go left!"

"On it."

The two of them have kept up with the racing horse as if it's nothing, and now they launch themselves off the roofs, plunging into the rain of arrows. In the midst of it all, the demon bravely keeps running, carrying the carriage all the while. The cyclops came running the moment Claude left the sacred barrier. They're very large, but probably not very bright.

Even so, the demon's here, expressly to save Claude from the humans' clutches.

Have its feelings gotten through to Claude? With the sacred sword shining in her hands, Aileen looks up at him. From here, he's only the size of a pea. She can see Lilia clinging to him.

"......"

"Lady Aileen, we'll reach the spot Isaac designated soon. Walt and Kyle seem to have their hands full at the moment; what should we do? ...Lady Aileen?"

Elefas has flown up beside her horse, and the sound of his voice brings back to herself with a start. "My hands were just about to slip and make me destroy that carriage... Are Beelzebuth and the others in the plaza?"

"They're restlessly and eagerly awaiting their turn."

Is that going to be all right? Aileen frowns, then sighs. There's no time to hesitate. "Argh, fine. I'll do it. Elefas, catch me!"

"Huh? Wha—? Wait!" Aileen has leaped from the horse's back, and Elefas hastily catches her in his arms. "You really are reckless, aren't you?!"

"Never mind that, take us up! If I hit the demon with the sacred sword's full power, I'll kill them!"

Still looking rather appalled, Elefas wraps an arm around Aileen's waist and takes them high into the air.

The knights are still loosing arrows at the demon. Aileen draws a deep breath. At this distance, the demon will get away with nothing worse than a bruise or three.

"You're in the way! Everyone move!"

She lets the sacred sword's power fall from the sky. It flies as straight as lightning, striking the demon's back. The cyclops collapses into the plaza—but the impact knocks the carriage out of their hand.

"—Oh."

Aileen turns pale. Still holding her, Elefas draws a circle with his index finger. The wind blows, and the carriage with Claude and Lilia in it bounds up lightly.

"...Th-thank you, Elefas."

"I'm glad I could be of use."

His tone is as polite as ever, but his voice is a little cold.

In Elefas's arms, Aileen descends to the plaza, with its prone demon and floating carriage. The first one to come over is Beelzebuth. "Aileen. The demon's already unconscious... What about my turn?"

"Look forward to next time, please."

"But I was going to save the king and look amazing!"

From the fact that he's able to crumple to his knees and lament, he's still got plenty of energy left.

"Never mind that, let's hurry and take the demon back to the forest. Where are the others?"

"Here, we're here. Shall I give this big fellow an injection just in case?" Luc, who's emerged from the bushes, jabs something into the unconscious demon's foot.

James, who was in charge of protecting him and the others, turns pale. "Wh...what was in that syringe?"

"It's fine, our friend here will wake up in due time. It's not like the stuff made for the demon king."

"What would happen with the stuff for the demon king?!"

"Well, if past results are anything to go by, this guy would wake up...even though that isn't supposed to happen..."

"Excuse me! Give me a hand, please! We have to get the monster on this trolley and haul them off." Denis and the demons have brought an enormous handcart from the back of the plaza, and everyone swarms it.

Elefas looks impressed. "They're quite skilled."

"This? This is nothing. Enough, let Master Claude and that other one down."

Thanks to Elefas's magic, the carriage is still floating. Beelzebuth, James, and the other demons all turn around at once and line up behind Aileen, fidgeting restlessly. She wants to tell them to get back to work already, but it isn't going to happen. This is their reunion with their beloved demon king.

"So after this, I just have to escort the demon king and Lady Lilia back to the castle, right?"

"Yes. If we say the Holy Knights took them into protective custody, no matter how fishy it seems, it will be satisfactory under a cursory examination."

Auguste has come to the plaza in his Holy Knights uniform, as instructed. Straightening his collar, he stands in front of the carriage, which has completed its slow descent to the plaza.

"Um, are you all right, Demon King? Sorry, I mean, Crown Prince Claude?"

There's no response. "The carriage was handled quite roughly," Elefas murmurs. "They may be injured."

"What?!" Aileen turns pale again.

Behind her, a dismayed stir runs through the gathered demons. However, before they can start making noise about it, the carriage door opens, and a hand emerges. The figure they're eagerly awaiting steps out; his face is hidden by his long black hair. He pulls an unconscious Lilia from the carriage, cradling her in his arms. Laying her down on the flagstones, he lowers himself to sit beside her. Slowly, he looks up. His eyes aren't red. Even so, the demon king is beautiful, right down to the furrows in his brow. His lips move. "...Muh..."

"'Muh'?"

"Motion sick..."

Claude leans back against the carriage unsteadily, and the demons start to panic.

"Demon king! Demon king!"

"Sire, sire, are you all right? Don't die, my king!"

"Quit crying, don't yell, you're annoying. He's just sick from bouncing around in the carriage. Hey, don't you have anything for motion sickness?"

"Ah, yes, here you go."

James, the only one who's kept his cool, grabs the medicine from Luc. Then as if he's made up his mind about something, he steps forward.

When she sees this, for the first time, Aileen notices something.

For all the noise the demons are making, not one of them has tried to approach Claude. It's as if they know he'll reject them. They're keeping their distance, holding their breath anxiously. Only James advances slowly.

As if he's sensed him, Claude looks up—and his eyes go wide.

"K-king... King... I save...!"

Behind them, the demon has gotten up. Aileen turns around, but by then, the demon has already mustered their last reserves of strength, stomped the trolley flat, and broken into a run. Their mind still seems muddled; they misjudges the distance, stumbles, and falls. The impact makes Lilia's unconscious body roll right in front of the cyclops.

She really can't have the girl getting killed by a demon. Seeing that the monster is about to bring a massive palm down on Lilia, Aileen clicks her tongue and launches herself forward, but just then—

"No! Don't kill her!"

—at Claude's order, the demon freezes. Scrambling to his feet, Claude runs over and pulls Lilia into his arms, glaring at the demon.

"Don't hurt people. Get back."

Timidly, the demon lowers the raised hand. They murmur, looking at Claude as if in total bewilderment.

"...Then who? What human not needed? What is king's wish...?"

"—What are you talking about?"

Is it her imagination? For a moment, Claude's eyes seem to wander, as if he's frightened. Following his gaze, the demon turns around, glancing around before settling on Aileen. "You?"

"What?"

"The one who cause king trouble."

Demons reflect the demon king's feelings, just as they are.

"You in king's way. Disappear."

Meaning these words are Claude's own.

I...?

The demon charges at her. Aileen's eyes are wide-open. She can't move. Even though there are all sorts of things she should be doing.

I'm a woman he doesn't need?

Because he's lost his memories. Because he doesn't love her anymore. Because her love is unrequited.

"Ailey! What are you doing, stupid?! Move!"

What good will moving do? He hasn't even called her name.

"Walt, Kyle! It doesn't matter, kill the demon!"

"...You mustn't. Don't do it." Even so, that is what she says. She wants to be kind to the demons, even the one who's attacking her. "Master Claude will be sad."

"You fool." A moment later, a low voice speaks, and the demon sinks to the ground. "Misinterpreting an order out of longing for the king..."

"Beelzebuth..."

With his long hair streaming in the wind, she can see glimpses of the demon king's beauty in Beelzebuth's silhouette. He glances at Aileen with his red eyes, then promptly looks away.

"I will take this one away from here...sire." Turning to face Claude, Beelzebuth kneels. "Your wish is our command. If you say you do not need us, then we will leave your sight."

Claude gazes back at him. He's still holding Lilia. Rising to his feet, Beelzebuth turns his back without showing any regret. Then he and the other demons return to their work, preparing to transport the unconscious demon back to the forest.

...Beelzebuth is incredible.

Even when told he isn't needed, he doesn't grieve. He merely does his best. That is love.

"...Honestly, Master Claude. To think you're so obsessed with me that you'd attempt to have a demon dispose of me!"

"You aren't...on my mind, or anything like..."

Go on, smile. Just as you always do. You managed it even when Cedric forced you to watch him break your engagement.

Claude gulps, but Aileen doesn't notice. Her eyes find Lilia, cradled in his arms. Her love is unrequited. She knows that. This is misplaced. And yet—her hand flies up.

A dry, sharp sound echoes.

Claude is stunned, pressing one hand to his struck cheek. Even when he's utterly confused, his face is still lovely, which is incredibly infuriating.

"If I'm so very much in your way, then yes, I'll disappear for you. I won't even go to the ball!"

When she's angry, she tends to plunge ahead recklessly.

However, she can't take back what she's said. Glaring at Claude, Aileen retreats slowly, then turns on her heel.

Birds are flying through the blue sky.

Claude gazes vacantly at the expansive view from a chair on the terrace.

Immediately after the inspection, they moved him from the hidden mansion to the imperial castle. Since he had been abducted by a demon but had returned unharmed, Lester had deduced that the demons would still listen to his orders. To test that theory, no sacred barrier has been cast here. They gave a variety of plausibly official reasons for it, but in essence, he's serving as bait.

However, he doesn't have the energy to even get angry about his treatment.

The tea on the little side table went cold long ago. He can't muster any interest in the portraits of young noblewomen he'll need to choose from at the ball, though the event is only three days away.

He settles deeper into the chair. It should be a first-rate piece of craftsmanship, but he just can't get comfortable. Thinking it might be his posture, he tries resting his chin on his hand, but that makes him remember the pain that ran through his cheek.

He sighs. At first, he tried to forget it, but he's given that up as a lost cause. It's probably due in part to the fact that, as promised, her visits have stopped entirely.

Well, that isn't a bad thing. If she'd been executed for seeing me, I would've been racked with guilt.

However, secretly, seeing her cheerfully risking her life to come see him had given him a feeling of superiority and self-worth. And that thought makes him sigh again.

"Could I possibly be in possession of hazardous thoughts...?"

"That's hardly news. I don't think you need to worry about it."

The voice comes from the terrace he's been gazing at absently, and he straightens up involuntarily. However, neither of the two figures that have alighted there look like a woman. The voice was different as well.

Disappointed, Claude narrows his eyes. He doesn't summon anyone, though. He recognizes one of his visitors.

He's a demon. A week ago, when that other demon had gotten up again, he put it back down with one blow. Then he promptly vanished, as Claude had wished. If he recalls, his name is—

"You're Beelzebuth, aren't you?"

"! Sire, my name... You called my name...!"

"Who's with you? Sorry, but I don't remember anything. Introduce yourself."

"I am Keith, milord. I came because I thought you'd be moping right about now."

"...'Milord'? No, before that, who's moping?"

"Oh, that's no good." No sooner has he spoken than the bespectacled man starts fiddling with Claude's chair. "The angle's wrong. In terms of cushions, I believe this one will suit your preferences better."

"Huh? Who said you could—?"

"There, that should do it. Please have a seat."

Frowning, he sits down again...and is startled by how perfectly it fits his frame. He lets himself sink into the chair, relaxing and crossing his legs. It feels as if this is something he's always done.

"The tea's no good, either. I'm glad I brought some with me. I'll dispose of this and make your usual." Keith bustles around, putting the space in order. The demon Beelzebuth walks into his room and begins rifling through the bookshelf. Strangely, it doesn't bother him.

Is it because the chair is comfortable? Or because he recognizes the fragrance of the tea that wafts over to him on the breeze?

"What's wrong with this bookshelf? It has none of your favorite books, sire."

"...I was told this used to be my room."

"Oh, it's definitely the one you lived in when you were small."

"Did you know me then?"

"Yes. Beelzebuth over there knows you very well, too. That means you don't need to be concerned about the fact that you rejected the demons."

That last comment rattles Claude. Right in front of him, Keith quietly continues making him a fresh cup of tea. "They're used to it. It happened long ago as well, Master Claude. There was a time when you wanted to be acknowledged by the humans as crown prince, so you made the demons stay away from you. They always came to save you, though, and it eventually won you over. You really are weak to those who show you affection."

"...Am I?"

"Yes, you are. You're terribly shy, however. Even with that conspicuous face."

He can't be sure, but he has the feeling this is accurate. He accepts the tea in silence and takes a sip. It's delicious.

"And? Are you going to break off your engagement to Lady Aileen?"

He very nearly spits out his tea. As he chokes and sputters, Keith heaves a rather artificial sigh. "If you are, that's fine, but saying you didn't need her was going too far. I don't recall raising you to wound women needlessly."

"Wha...? Wait, you've got it wrong. I didn't say anything of the sort. She's too pushy, and I didn't want her getting any closer to me, that's all!"

"I imagine not. No doubt Lady Aileen was on your mind far too often for comfort, and you didn't want her to keep twisting you around her little finger. Then the demon picked up on that, but in an obviously distorted way."

He's seen through Claude so completely that it's frightening. On a more fundamental level, the fact that they're having a normal conversation at all is weird. However, there's no pressure in Keith's voice. "No one feels just one thing at a time, though. That's probably why Beelzebuth saved Lady Aileen. Right now, the other demons are desperately trying to ingratiate themselves with her."

"Y-you can't be implying that those are my feelings."

"Then are you claiming it doesn't concern you at all, milord?"

The question makes him fall silent. If he said he didn't care, he'd be lying. It hadn't been fair of her to slap him, and he'd still rather not be involved with her. However, back then, she was...

"...She was crying."

The words spill out of him. To somebody he's just met— No, he realizes that they haven't just met. He can't remember, and he doesn't know for sure. Still, the words keep coming. It's because the chair is comfortable.

"When I saw that, I was...happy..." That tough, stubborn woman had been wounded so deeply that her eyes filled with tears, and *his current self* had been the one to do it. The knowledge had delighted him before he even thought about the reason. He sighs, hanging his head. "Is there something wrong with me?"

"No, that's just like you. I'm deeply moved. Aren't you, Beelzebuth?"

"? Nothing you do is ever wrong, sire."

"Really? ...Doesn't it seem like something a demon king would do?"

"It's fine, that's just how you were built. It has nothing to do with the demon king. I mean, really, you've just proved that it doesn't."

Is that how it is? Somehow, he feels convinced.

"So I've always been like this? I see... I'm not the demon king now, at any rate."

"Exactly... However, that isn't the problem. Considering the state they're in, Lady Aileen's companions might genuinely attempt to assassinate you."

The conversation has suddenly turned dangerous, and Claude freezes up.

"You see," Keith continues, "right now, milord, you have no magic and no allies. You've also rejected the demons, telling them you won't become their king again. You'll be in checkmate before long."

"Checkmate?"

"Yes. And so you'll more likely than not need my help soon. I came because I thought I might be able to assist you in some way. Your guards are concerned, too."

"Guards... Did I have guards?"

"Yes. Lady Aileen brought them, but you were the one who trained them, so they can be trusted. Have a care, though. At the moment, all of Lady Aileen's minions are your enemies."

"...Wait a minute. 'Minions' as in plural? How many does she have?"

From the way Keith has spoken, it sounds as if there may be quite a lot. He's starting to get a bad feeling about this.

"You saw them in the plaza, remember? Everyone besides the demons, and more on top of that."

"A-all those people?! And there are still more?! Just how many...? Don't tell me every one of them is a man!"

"Well, most of them." Keith is smiling wryly. It's far too much, and he feels dizzy.

"She was my fiancée, wasn't she?! Is that sort of thing allowed?"

"What will you do, milord? She says she won't attend the ball. If this goes on, you'll be jilted before you can break off the engagement."

The man speaks as if he's teasing him, and Claude props his chin on his hand. Glancing at his face, Keith goes on. "Sulking won't help. As I taught you, those under you can't act unless you issue orders properly."

"......"

"You actually do know, don't you? That you've been fed lies. That you're being used."

Claude narrows his eyes, glaring at his perceptive attendant. Somewhere along the way, his wariness has vanished completely. "So what? If they're deceiving me, it means my memory loss was planned as well. In that case, I can't defy them carelessly. I don't have any of this magic you speak of. I'm no longer the demon king—"

His nostrils catch the scent of something burning; a chest has burst into flames. Keith, who's picked up on the cause before Claude does, yells, "What are you doing, Bel?!"

"There was poison in the chest, so I got rid of it. The wretched humans persist in targeting the king."

If he recalls, the now-blazing chest was a get-well present from some noble or other. He isn't surprised. From the moment the decision was made to move him into the castle, he knew there would be attempts on his life. However, this is a very brazen attempt. Either they had inside help or someone conveniently looked the other way.

Or were they testing the demons to see whether they'd come to save me?

He's being tested one way or the other. Given his precarious circumstances, he had intended to do his best to live up to their expectations.

However, the time for that may be over.

"Still, just setting it on fire? Think a little before you act, would you? You never think!"

"What do I care? All dangers to my king must be eliminated."

"...Bel. Put the fire out right now."

Claude doesn't realize it's an order until after he's given it. The handsome demon isn't bewildered; he simply bows, and that's all it takes. The fire—which has already spread to the wall—vanishes.

The demon obeyed without question.

"Command me, sire."

Not only that, but as if he's read Claude's mind, the demon also kneels. Keith shrugs, then kneels beside him.

It would be easy to go back to being king of the demons. To live there in safety. However, he has to become emperor—even if he can't remember why.

"...I need allies of my own. Keith, are these guards you mentioned human?"

"Barely, but yes."

"I really don't have any human allies, do I? Well, never mind. In that case, call them here to guard me. Bel, you return to the castle and give the demons strict orders not to approach me. I don't want people realizing I can command them."

"Understood, sire."

"Are those your only orders, milord?" Keith glances up, and his eyes are laughing.

Reluctantly, Claude issues a command. "...Bring her to the ball."

"'Her'?"

"Aileen Lauren d'Autriche! There's something I'd like to ask her— Don't laugh! Are you really in my service?!"

Beelzebuth looks a little troubled. *Don't tell me.* Right when he's beginning to have doubts, Keith's laughing lips form a beautiful curve. "Just leave it to me—I'll make your every wish come true, milord."

Paging through the statement of accounts, Aileen looks at the executives of the Oberon Trading Firm. "The cosmetics targeted at aristocrats are selling well. Perhaps the problem is the products meant for the common people. The trial version of the hand cream was well received, wasn't it?"

"Yes. We had maidservants, housewives, and those in occupations where rough hands are a concern try it, and they were all very much in favor of commercializing it. However, they did think the price might be a bit high."

She nods, agreeing with Luc's concern. "True, it is expensive for something meant to be a household staple... Quartz, can't we bring the cost of the materials down any further?"

"...We did all we could. This is the limit."

"What about the packaging budget? Denis."

"If you want it to have an air of luxury, Lady Aileen, we can't really do better than this."

"C'mon, we don't need luxury here. If we want them to make it a staple, convenience should be our top priority."

"But women will be the ones using it, Isaac. It can't be gawky or graceless. Can it, Rachel?"

Rachel, who's passing out tea in the meeting room, nods in agreement.

"Hmm." Denis, who's been gazing at the ceiling, picks up a pencil. "In that case, what about making it a size they can carry around with them? It could be shaped like a flower, something cute."

"Selling smaller amounts will also bring the unit price down, huh? That's not bad. The customers who'll use a lot of it can just buy the other size."

"Then should we consider making the containers go further as well? Customers who bring their containers in can simply have them refilled at the shop for a lower price."

Aileen's proposal makes Denis's eyes light up. "I like that! I'll design several types of containers that customers will want to collect, then!"

"The cream doesn't keep all that long anyway. I think it's a good idea."

"...Seconded."

"In that case, Denis, send me a new budget proposal. Luc and Quartz, you recalculate how much you can make for different amounts by the release date."

"Yes, that sounds good. I believe that's all for today, isn't it?"

"Hey, are you seriously not going to the ball?"

She thought she'd wrapped things up safely, but Isaac hits her with a surprise attack. The others are all stealing glances at her, weighing her reaction. Aileen sighs. "Do you want me to cut you down?"

"What, it's that bad?"

"No. It doesn't bother me anymore. If I accept the dissolution of my engagement without going to the ball, I won't be executed, and it doesn't matter if the d'Autriche family disowns me. I shall live for my work!" She huffs, holding her head high.

Looking down, Luc murmurs, "...True, he's human now."

"...Yeah. Now."

"Huh? But Bel and the other demons keep begging me to do something... Umm... Isaac, what do you think?"

"In the first place, the fact that she hasn't relocated our conference room means she's already losing."

"W-well, I mean, Almond and the others implored me! They performed a *Please don't leave* dance for me, all right?!"

"They'll keep you here forever like that. And anyway, can you really abandon the demons?"

"If the situation grows truly desperate, I shall become the demon king myself!" Aileen declares, one hand over her heart.

The others offer nothing but dubious reactions. However, she is fairly serious. "If I marry Beelzebuth or James, I believe it will work. What do you think?"

"Don't make the situation more complicated than it already is. When the demon king gets his memories back, the world will be doomed if you do something like that."

"But there's no point in dragging the past behind me forever." Aileen is no longer loved. She's accepted that once, so she's sure she'll be fine the second time as well. She should be able to come to terms with it properly. "I'll give some good, solid thought to the future. If Master Claude chooses another woman at the ball..."

There are only two days left until then. Is that a long time, or a short one?

"...At this point, he'll suffer, writhe in agony, and die. A spoonful is all it will take. At this point."

"He's the crown prince now. Can you slip it to him that easily?"

"Oh, I think I could make it happen somehow."

"Don't make it happen, Denis. Just leave him be. You know they'll have His Highness the crown prince assassinated soon, once they're done using him."

Her head whips up. Isaac looks back at her coldly. "Hey, why not just forget him? The guy wasn't worth any more than that, was he?"

"Wh-what do you mean by that? It's not as if Master Claude is to blame—"

"Miss! Is Miss Aileen here?!"

There's a commotion in the corridor, and a moment later,

Jasper bursts into the conference room. He's panting for breath. Something is obviously up, and Aileen frowns. "Calm down, please. Rachel, get him some water."

"Forget that! The demon king—poisoned—his attendant! To be guards...!"

She didn't understand a word of that. However, she grasps that something has happened to Claude. As she starts to rise to her feet, a cheery voice rings out behind the journalist.

"You can always count on Jasper to be the first to know."

"Master Keith and Beelzebuth... What happened? If this is about the ball, I won't listen."

When she prompts them to go on—adding a reminder, just in case—Keith holds out a box. He's smiling. "Lady Aileen. You have a delivery."

She's dubious, but she signals Rachel with a glance. Her excellent lady-in-waiting accepts the box, placing it on the meeting room's long table. Its rectangular shape gives her a bad feeling. She waits for a description of its contents, but Keith just smiles. Resigning herself, Aileen tells Rachel to open it.

Rachel nods and gently lifts the lid.

The contents are a dress. The red and black gown has a plunging neckline, and it's practically the opposite of what a dainty noble lady would wear. However, its design incorporates delicate lace and graceful embroidery, and it projects the elegance of a rose in bloom. The luster of the silk is also exquisite.

But what does it mean that she's been given a dress at this juncture? Aileen scowls. "What is this gown for, exactly?"

"For the ball the day after tomorrow, of course."

"I told you I refused to hear any talk of the ball. Return it, if you would."

"That's not possible. That dress is a present, and an order, from Master Claude."

She turns around. Keith is wearing his usual smile. He looks just the way he did when Claude was here. Jasper, who's finally gotten his breathing calmed down, leans in. "Hey, Adviser, what's this about?! I know the one about the demon king nearly getting lethally poisoned and having new guards assigned to him, but those guards are Walt and Kyle, and the attendant is you!"

"What's going on?! It can't be— Have Master Claude's memories...?"

"Unfortunately, no. However, Milord said to bring you to the ball in that gown."

Why, when he still hasn't regained any of his memories? What can it mean? Aileen is confused. Somewhere in there, the demons have appeared, and they're lined up, gazing at her. Beelzebuth just watches Aileen as well.

Claude really has ordered it. That much is clear from the demons' reactions, and Aileen shrieks, "I—I won't go!"

"I'm sorry. He ordered us to bring you even if you cried or screamed or risked execution. To put it bluntly, Lady Aileen, you have no right to refuse."

"W-wait just a moment! You know Master Claude's personality isn't like that now!"

Unlike when he was his old self, the current Claude should have been sweet, purehearted, and awkward enough with women that he'd pull back when she did. Understanding what Aileen is trying to say, Keith gives a wry smile. "Sadly, with or without memories, Milord doesn't change. It's just that he's very shy with strangers. In addition, when he's taken with something, he refuses to let go even if it kills him."

He can't be implying that this version of Claude is taken with Aileen, can he?

When?! Where?! Even though I slapped him?!

As Aileen wrestles with her confusion, Luc and Quartz step in front of her. "No matter how you look at it, this is tyranny. Does he intend to make enemies of us in earnest?"

"...I can't condone using methods like this when he hasn't even apologized."

"I believe Master Claude intends to apologize in person later. Although, it will probably only be lip service."

Insincere, right from the start. Denis clasps his hands behind his head. "I think it's fine. It means the demon king's fallen for Lady Aileen again, right?"

"As if I could believe a thing like that now, this late... I—I absolutely refuse to go!"

"Come now, don't say that."

Aileen has taken a step back, and Keith steps forward. *I have to pull myself together*, she thinks, but her voice trembles. "I-if I see Master Claude again—I may cut him down on the spot, you know!"

"By all means, be my guest. If you can manage it without letting that face of his get to you first."

"Aileen, come. The demon king is calling! Dance!" At Almond's encouraging shout, the demons begin to dance. How could she fail to be moved by their desperate efforts to change her mind?

Aileen turns to Isaac, her final lifeline. "Isaac!"

"Maybe just give up?"

He's summarily betrayed her. Aileen covers her face with both hands. Heartlessly, Isaac tells her, "It's a waste of time," and shrugs.

★ ★ ★

When she did her best to tempt him, he'd been brusque with her, and now that she's trying to give up, he chases her. She thinks perhaps it's because of the idea that men are hunters—that may very well be the case here, but it's absolutely unforgivable.

In the first place, I can't accept that Master Claude has allowed Master Keith, Walt, and Kyle to stay with him so easily! He rejected me, his fiancée! What's brought this sudden about-face?!

As Aileen fumes in frustration, everyone tells her, "You took the wrong approach." She can't even begin to fathom what they're talking about. Her mind refuses to work.

In sharp contrast to Aileen's emotions, Almond is ecstatic. He checked with Aileen again and again, making sure she'd attend the ball, then flew away gleefully, saying that the demon king would be happy. If the demons are acting like this, it must be true that Claude wants her to attend.

That said, Aileen has her own pride to consider.

Picking up on that, Rachel helps her get ready. Aileen's father, who will be escorting her into the ballroom, also accepts her choice with a smile. When this father of hers smiles, it tends to be a bad sign, but in any case, Aileen reaches the imperial castle without besmirching her pride.

When she passes Auguste, who's on guard duty in the gallery, he's so dumbfounded that he drops his sword and immediately gets yelled at by a senior guardsman. In a corner of the resplendent ballroom, Isaac and James choke and spit out their drinks, but it serves them right. Walt and Kyle, who've brazenly taken up positions behind Claude, are wearing despairing expressions, and she's actually quite proud of that achievement. However, she's rather irked by Cedric's contemptuous gaze and the fact that Lilia's fighting back such incredible fits of laughter that there are tears in her eyes.

Even so, there are some things she cannot yield.

All right, Master Claude! Rue the invitation you sent me.

On the marble floor, with her hand still in her father's, she raises her head in a dignified way.

Aileen Lauren d'Autriche is the daughter of a duke, brought up to become empress. She's always embodied that upbringing perfectly, but right now, she has flung her rank aside. She doesn't regret its loss in the slightest.

The conductor fumbles his baton, and the elegant strains of the violins fall silent.

"...Why are you a duck?"

In the middle of the hushed ballroom, Claude's brows are knitted as tightly as they'll go.

"You ordered me to wear this dress, but you gave no specific instructions regarding my face." Aileen, who paired the gown with the head of the duck costume, proudly throws out her chest.

Tonight is the grand ball where the crown prince will meet his bride for the first time. This travesty would normally be more than enough to get her ejected immediately. In fact, it's a miracle she made it this far to begin with.

There is no man who would want to dance with a young lady like this, much less make her his fiancée. Especially not Claude, who's currently trying to fulfill the expectations of those around him as crown prince. Of this, Aileen is certain. As she's gloating to herself inside the duck, Claude turns his face to the ceiling, then sighs. "...Prime Minister d'Autriche. Can you assure me that it is indeed your daughter in that duck?"

"Well, I haven't seen her face, so it might be someone else." Rudolph dissembles, smirking.

Claude glares at him. Then he stalks over to the duck and grabs the headpiece firmly. Aileen holds it down so he can't remove it. "Why are you resisting? Do you want to be a duck that badly?!"

"The duck look is in fashion."

"No one is buying that! You'll destroy the mood in more ways than one, so take it off!"

"I refuse! I have no face to show you, Master Claude!"

With a disgusted *tsk*, Claude lets go. She feels relieved, but in that same instant, the world flips. Claude has put an arm around Aileen's waist, picked her up, and slung her over his shoulder.

"Wha...? Master Claude! This behavior is clearly outrageous!"

"I don't want to hear it from a woman who comes to a ball wearing a duck's head. Clear the way."

Possibly because they'd really rather not look too closely at the duck, the crowd promptly parts for them. Claude strides down that path. At this point, she has nothing left to cast aside.

"Don't do this! Unhand me! —Walt, Kyle!"

They both make the sign of the church in unison. She'd like to ship them back to their precious house of worship.

"James, Isaac... They ran for it! Elefas, then?!"

There's no response. Everyone's very quick to flee. In frustration, she calls names whose owners aren't even present.

"Auguste! Luc, Quartz, Denis, Jasper!"

"How many do you have...?"

"That's all of them! I'm terribly sorry there are so few!"

"That's plenty... I only want to check on something. Hold still—Aileen."

He's said her name. It's the first time since the night when he called her his love.

The moment she realizes that, Aileen stops fighting.

This isn't fair.

The next thing she knows, they've left the terrace of the radiant ballroom and are heading out onto the grounds. Down a little path through dense trees, there's a small summerhouse. It's a perfect place for lovers' trysts, away from prying eyes. There, finally, Claude sets her down.

As one would expect, Aileen's head has cooled, and she puts some distance between Claude and herself. "What exactly do you want to check—? Oh!"

"First things first. This duck is in the way."

He strips the duck head off her, tossing it aside. Then long fingers slide across her cheeks. He seems to be confirming something.

"...You aren't crying?"

"Why should I have to?"

"I see... That's a pity. May I embrace you?"

"What?"

Before she can react, he's holding her close. Instantly, anger flares inside her. "Don't toy with me, or I really will be angry with you!!"

She tries to shove him away, but although she pushes at his chest with all her might, he doesn't budge. The arms he's put around her aren't hurting her, but she soon discovers that she can't shake them off, either. If this is how things stand, she'll have to stomp on his foot with her high heel or thrust an elbow into a vulnerable spot.

"...I do know exactly how tightly I should hold you."

When she hears that murmur above her head, Aileen stops

moving. Her cheeks grow hot, this time in a different way. "Wha—
Wh-wha— Wha-wha-wha...? Was that what you w-wanted to
confirm—?"

"Keith told me to put my face up close to you and call your
name."

"What ideas is he putting into your head?! What on earth
could that possibly tell yo—?"

He peeks into her face, and she stops breathing. As if teasing
her for her nervousness, Claude reveals a slow, melting smile—
even though his eyes are still black.

"Aileen."

As he runs his mouth over the syllables of the name he's just
learned, the sweet sound makes her legs give out. Aileen crumples, and Claude supports her, sitting her down on a bench in the
summerhouse. However, it seems to have tripped an odd sort of
switch inside him. He puts his lips close to her earlobe and whispers again.

"Aileen."

A little shriek escapes her. Claude gives a captivating laugh,
deep in his throat. "I see. So you're not as accustomed to men as
you pretend to be, hmm? You tricked me."

"Tha— ...That's not true, there's no way...I would be like—"

"In that case, perhaps I'll experiment a bit more."

"R-refrain from speaking next to my ear, if you would! It's
shameless! We aren't yet married, so this is— You were the one
who said so, Master Claude!"

"After everything you tried on me, I don't want to hear that
from you."

It can't be. Is this payback? She evades desperately, shifting to
the side, but Claude slowly pursues her into a corner. He looks as

if he's enjoying himself enormously; she really hopes that's just her imagination.

"Yes, there are things my body remembers."

She doesn't know what he's recalled, but it can't have been anything decent. As she turns pale, Claude slowly nibbles his way along the curve of her cheek. "Doing this with you is very soothing."

"—I shall slap you again! You intend to break off your engagement with me, don't you?!"

"Oh... Of course. I'm getting the order all wrong."

Coming to himself with a jolt, Claude straightens up. He very nearly pushed Aileen down, and he pulls her upright again. He even smooths her disheveled hair back into place.

"Aileen."

It's a bright night, with a full moon. In the moonlight, she can see his face clearly.

"I love you."

He's said the words a little bashfully.

Wide-eyed, Aileen echoes him like a simpleton. "You...love me?"

"Yes, I love you. I want to make you cry and spoil you rotten."

"Even without your memories, that's still the direction you choose?!"

"Apparently, whether I have memories or not, it doesn't change my love for you. This must be fate."

Claude is blushing shyly, but it isn't cute. Aileen refuses to think that way. More than anything, his new position is terribly arbitrary and far too unfair. A dry smile comes to her lips. "It's too late... Do you think you'll be forgiven if you say that now?"

"I'm fairly sure of it," he tells her, straight-faced.

Aileen slams a fist into the stone wall of the summerhouse. "I...I want...to cut you down!"

"Even if you are my fiancée, you're very bold."

"I'm serious! Do you have any idea how I've felt all this time...?!"

"If you say you can't forgive me as is, then I have an idea, Aileen."

He takes her hands, guiding them to the perfect contours of his cheeks. Under the moonlight, the fierce beauty in her hands whispers, "You may do as you like to me until you're satisfied—to my face, and..."

To his body.

"As if I cooooooooould!!" Smacking his hands away, she screams from the bottom of her heart.

Claude's cheeks flush, and he lowers his long eyelashes. "I see. That's a pity. Wondering what you'd do was making my heart race."

"That's the exact opposite of what you've been saying up till now! Are you aware of that?!"

"Love changes people."

"Do you think I'll forgive you if you make it sound suave like— You're far too fickle!"

"If you can't forgive me, then I'd like you to break me with your own two hands."

"Enough!! You'll stop if I forgive you, yes?!"

Just hearing him whisper dubious lines with that face is draining her. Between the wretchedness and the embarrassment, she buries her face in her hands.

Claude stands up. "Let's head back. Unless I dance with you, no one else will get the message."

In other words, Aileen is still Claude's fiancée.

My engagement won't be broken...

It only really sinks in when Claude holds out his hand to her. When she doesn't take it, he looks perplexed. "What's the matter?"

"Oh... G-go on ahead, please. I—I—I need to fix my makeup first! My clothes as well."

She technically is made up already, but she'd intended to go home as the duck, so she wasn't very careful about it. She hasn't made sure the dress will complement her appearance, either. Due to the duck's head, her hair is also a mess.

Claude pulls her to her feet, puts an arm around her waist, and whispers, "You're quite lovely enough as it is. I don't want to let you go now."

"Th-the crown prince's fiancée has to do better than this. If I'm forced to dance with you looking like I am now, I'll revert to the duck!"

At the word *duck*, Claude grimaces. Drawing Aileen by the hand, he leaves the summerhouse, then releases her in a brighter spot a little way down the path. "All right. If you swear you won't turn into a duck, I can wait. I'll go back to the ball for now."

"Very well. I won't keep you waiting long!"

Hastily turning on her heel, she looks for Rachel. Sure enough, her brilliant lady-in-waiting quietly appears from a side path, surely reliably standing-by all along. She must have been keeping an eye on the summerhouse from a distance. Even if they are engaged to be married, making sure a young lady and gentleman aren't left entirely alone is one of her basic duties.

"Rachel. You've brought my cosmetics kit, haven't you?"

"Yes, of course."

"Then hurry and fix me up, please... I'm to dance with M—Master Claude."

Since she's just said she wouldn't attend the ball and was more than ready for her second engagement to be broken, the embarrassment makes her voice fade a bit at the end.

However, Rachel smiles softly. "I expected nothing less, Lady Aileen. You slapped him, and he fell for you just like that!"

"...Huh? Was that it? Was that what did it?!" Aileen is aghast, but Rachel's nerves have grown steadier since she became a lady-in-waiting, and she only smiles back at her.

Briskly shown into a waiting room, Aileen seats herself at a dressing table.

"I'll go and fetch the brushes and things. Wait just a moment."

She nods, and Rachel leaves. The ball has only begun, so there's no one in the room. Perhaps since she's all alone, her face softens into a smile.

Master Claude said he loves me...

There has been no second time. Even when his memories are missing, Claude has chosen her.

"—You look radiant, Lady Aileen."

Suddenly, a blade gleams at her throat. Her assailant has approached from behind without betraying his presence, but he's reflected in the mirror. Aileen's eyes widen. Slowly, she calls his name. "...Elefas. What is this about?"

"You really did win the love of the demon king. I don't believe in the power of love, so I assumed it was impossible, but..."

"All according to plan, correct? Is there a problem?"

"If this goes on, the demon king may even reclaim his memories. That would be troublesome."

She frowns. Elefas's character should be trying to make Claude the demon king again. Reality has deviated from the game's plot before, but it's rare to see something flip completely... *This was my blunder. I was distracted by precedent, and I misread Elefas.*

Even if she'd been beside herself over Claude, a mistake is a mistake.

Elefas takes up a lock of Aileen's golden hair and kisses it, as if paying his respects. Then he gazes at her in the mirror. His eyes are cold. "You were a very appealing master. I wish I'd met you before I met her."

"My, who might that be? This true master of yours, a lady so attractive you'd jilt me for her."

"A dreadful, monstrous woman."

"Then I must release you from your captivity." With a dauntless smile, Aileen manifests the sacred sword, thrusting its point toward Elefas's throat. The sword negates all magic. Even if Elefas is an outstanding mage, in the face of power that could defeat the demon king, he'll be helpless. He seems to understand this; he doesn't move.

He only turns his hand over, and a birdcage appears on his palm.

"!!"

Before the tip reaches him, she makes the sword vanish.

The silver cage holds a crow with a red bow tie around his neck. His chest rises and falls, but he's lying there limply, as if his usual clamor was a mirage.

"Your friend is still alive, of course. For now."

Elefas answers her question before she can ask it, then makes the birdcage vanish again. It's probably still there, invisible. It's a very obvious threat.

"The demon king's subjects really are innocent, foolish creatures. They didn't even doubt me."

Elefas takes a small bottle from his jacket. "Excuse me," he says and splashes the immobile Aileen with its contents.

A stain spreads over her dress, and a familiar, cloying scent rises. It's diluted demon snuff.

"...Master Claude gave me this gown. I'll make you regret ruining it."

"Please don't say that. This is a very valuable substance. Even the church can't get it anymore."

"And? What will I be required to do?" Aileen raises her head resolutely.

Elefas smiles back at her gently. "My place is behind the scenes. The assembled players will make sure everything goes smoothly from this point on—Master Lester, in here! It's just as you said. Aileen Lauren d'Autriche has scattered demon snuff all around!"

In response to his call, the door to the waiting room opens, and guards burst in. From behind them, the bespectacled pawn appears. "What a shame, Miss Aileen Lauren d'Autriche. It's just as I predicted."

It's the start of a pathetic excuse for a play. Aileen meets the group of ham actors with a villainess's smile.

She wondered where they were going to drag her off to, and it proves to be the ballroom. If this is the stage, then the matter probably won't end as a farce in which she's simply falsely accused.

Someone shoves her back. She almost staggers, but she manages to keep her head raised.

The abrupt, ostentatious uproar has thrown the ball into confusion. The emperor and the rest of the imperial family are seated on the dais. The emperor is looking at her, stern-faced. The empress dowager is hiding her lips with her fan, but her eyes are laughing. As always, she looks like a beautiful young girl, and there isn't a single wrinkle on her face.

A dreadful, monstrous woman. True, considering her real age, she is rather monstrous...

However, since Elefas is a character who appears in the game, her suspicions should be directed elsewhere.

"What is all this commotion? Why have you apprehended Lady Aileen, Lester?!"

The second prince's fiancée—a girl rumored to be kind to a fault—opens her eyes wide, signaling the start of the performance.

The man who responds is a pitiful clown who isn't aware he's her pawn.

"She was strewing demon snuff in the waiting room. Hence the arrest."

"Demon snuff?" someone in the crowd asks dubiously.

Lester pushes his glasses up, sounding self-important. "I can't reveal the details. I'll say only that it is an incense that attracts demons. In short, she intended to summon demons to attack this place. Just as she did during Prince Claude's failed abduction."

A confused murmur spreads through the assembly.

Claude, whose name has been brought up, is watching the crowd calmly. He knows it wouldn't be wise to say or do anything when he doesn't understand what's going on. She's always found his levelheadedness reassuring.

"It's just as I said, Lilia. This woman masterminded the kidnapping."

"No! But Lady Aileen saved me from the demons! I told you she did, remember?!"

"...I understand that you are kind and wish to believe the best of everyone. However, she couldn't deceive my eyes." Like a stalwart defender of justice conveying a painful truth, Lester pauses for the space of a breath. "That kidnapping was a self-orchestrated affair. She did it in order to gain your trust, Prince Claude."

"...What do you mean?"

"She drove a demon mad with demon snuff, compelled it to abduct you, then rescued you from a crisis of her own making. She slipped in among the apprentice knights, risking her life; no doubt that gesture touched your heart. It's a simple thing, really. You didn't know it was a trap."

Claude is frowning. She can't tell whether he believes these charges or not.

Lester pivots to face Aileen. "By rescuing the crown prince, I imagine you thought you'd be able to get away with violating an imperial edict. Unfortunately for you, we've already found that the carriage was also treated with demon snuff."

"...That's the first I've heard of it. I think you may be reading too much into the situation." It would seem strange if she didn't argue at all, so she tells the truth, letting it double as a warning.

However, Lester only smiles coldly. "The demons' movements were very orderly. They couldn't possibly have pulled off that maneuver if it hadn't been an act. Even I couldn't manage it."

"That's only because you're incompetent. Unlike you, my retainers are brilliant."

Isaac was the one who'd proposed an operation that used Almond and the others, then trained them. Denis, Luc, and Quartz helped with the drills, since they were particularly close to the demons. Provided it didn't violate the demon king's orders, as long as they won the demons' trust, it was possible.

Her taunt makes Lester's lips twitch, but he doesn't rise to the bait. "You've just admitted that you've put the demons through military training."

"...Yes, I did train them."

"You also managed to source demon snuff. You were seen making a deal at an underground auction."

Lester is probably the type who puts together a hypothesis first, then collects proof that supports his theory. By unconsciously collecting only evidence that's convenient for him, he skews his findings. It's a common error.

"In short, you are attempting to turn His Highness the crown prince back into the demon king and use the demons to control this empire!"

The scale of the story has grown rather expansive. Is that all right? Doesn't it risk collapsing the scenario?

As she arbitrarily worries about this, the empress dowager speaks up, getting things back on track. "In other words, driven by a lust for power, this woman pretended to save my darling grandson and incited the demons? Gracious, how horrible. Let us execute her at once, Pierre."

The really horrible thing is the way she brings up execution so casually, with a girlish smile.

However, in this land, the emperor's decision is the one that carries the most weight. The rather kind—or timid—emperor turns to the prime minster, Aileen's father, who's waiting below him. "What say you, Rudolph? She is your daughter. Did the girl save our son, or did she lead him astray? Depending on your answer, you may not emerge from this unscathed, either."

"Do you mean suspicion will fall on the d'Autriche family as well, Your Majesty? If so, I must defend my daughter's honor with all my might."

"I've heard you are also troubled by the young lady's unprecedented behavior. Is it true?"

If you abandon your daughter, we'll let your family off the hook. That's what the empress dowager is implying.

"Actually, yes, we are."

Aileen vows to tell her brothers and mother about this. Absolutely.

"Even so, she is my daughter. I want to hear her side of this."

On top of that, the slippery way he's avoided the decision and is watching to see how things play out is utterly exasperating. The empress dowager probably thinks so as well, but she doesn't let it show. Her vibrant lips move. "Do you mean to say that being caught red-handed in the act of scattering demon snuff isn't enough?"

"Of course it isn't. If she's trained the demons, she could have them attack this place without resorting to demon snuff. The story is inconsistent. Scenarios like these need to be laid out with care, lad." As the final flourish, he takes a dig at Lester. Of course, Aileen is the one who gets hit by the recoil.

"There are other problems. Crown Prince, I believe you intend to name her as your fiancée again, but that would be a mistake. She isn't suitable for you."

"...What are you implying?" Claude sounds a little put out.

Smiling in a way that doesn't go past his lips, Lester insults Aileen. "During her time as the crown prince's fiancée, she is suspected of having relationships with multiple men."

In that moment, Aileen realizes exactly what role she's been assigned. As proof, although Elefas has only waited behind her all this time, he softly approaches.

Claude sounds irritated. "I was told they're merely her retainers."

"The most timeworn of overused excuses. Don't tell me you took her at her word."

"...Prince Claude. Please believe me. You're the only one I love." Brazenly, she simply tells him the truth.

Behind her, Elefas murmurs, "I'll let that one go. After all, it would look extremely contrived if you acknowledged this out of nowhere."

Claude looks at Aileen, then at Lester. With no memories of his own, it's only natural that he'd hesitate.

"Go on, deceive Prince Claude...if you value that demon's life."

"That said, I understand why you would want to believe her. Prince Claude, you're familiar with this man, aren't you? He accompanied Lady Aileen."

Elefas steps forward to stand beside Aileen, then bows to Claude. Claude's only response is silence, but that means he does know.

Wearing a warped smile, Lester takes a step to the side, away from them.

"These accusations are all based on information we obtained from him. He claims that he and Lady Aileen spend every night on the most intimate of terms."

"Wha—?"

"Prince Claude, I'm terribly sorry!" Elefas falls to his knees, prostrating himself on the floor. Claude stares at him, wide-eyed.

"I won't make excuses by telling you I was seduced. I am but a man. However, I— No, *we* betrayed you."

"...'We'?"

"Wait just a minute! What are you—?!" James starts to speak up, but Isaac restrains him. It's just like the time he hung back and watched Cedric break off his engagement to her. Walt and Kyle also try to step forward, but Keith stops them.

They suspect there's something more to this whole charade. Her retainers are outstanding, and she's truly proud of them.

"I thought I could just keep silent. However, I've reached my limit. If you were still the demon king, it might be different, but now that you are merely human, I feel terribly guilty. No, the one I really can't forgive is myself. Falling in love with my lord's betrothed and going so far as to have relations with her—it is something only the lowest of beasts would do."

The abrupt confession has left Claude stunned. While his face suggests otherwise, Claude is unexpectedly pure of heart. She's learned as much through this uproar over his lost memories. She's sure he won't forgive infidelity.

"But please, I beg you, don't put Lady Aileen to death! I don't care what happens to me, but she was simply lonely and—!"

She hates to do it while he's still talking, but she kicks him, hard and in earnest. Her voice is cold. "I'm amazed you can lie like that. Don't listen to him, Prince Claude."

For that last bit, she plasters onto her face an artificial smile she's copied from Lilia. Has she managed to do it well?

Claude has seen Aileen's brutal kick, and his eyes begin to waver. That's fine. She snorts disdainfully, like a villainous young noblewoman.

"I was a fool. If only I hadn't taken pity on the Levi tribe, the dregs of humanity."

"...He's trying to save you. You think nothing of that?"

"I am the victim here. How could you say such a thing?" She behaves in a way that's bound to disillusion Claude. It doesn't hurt her at all.

Not if the alternative is losing Almond.

"At any rate, cease casting untoward suspicions on me. I'm—"

"No, Lady Aileen! You said you were lonely, and you wanted me to comfort you— You said I was the only one you could trust. Was that a lie?!"

"—Enough!"

Claude interrupts loudly, rising to his feet. There's contempt in his black eyes. However, his gaze is focused directly on Aileen. "Tell me you love me. If you do, I'll believe you. No matter what anyone else says."

Aileen's eyes widen, and it isn't an act. Then unusually, she feels regret. *I wish I'd told him* I love you, too *earlier.* Right now, she needs to tell him the polar opposite. Elefas has thrown himself at her feet, and he's looking up at her with eloquent, crescent moon–shaped eyes. *I know.* Aileen smiles thinly.

"...You fool."

"What?"

"—I mean, it's true, isn't it? Wouldn't you know, ordinarily? Why would I, a human, genuinely love the demon king of all things?!"

Oh, this is awful. Because she loves him, she's able to choose the words that will hurt him the most. They're efficient and precise.

"I bore it in silence all this time. After all, you are the crown prince. The ability to command demons was convenient as well, but I've had enough! Being loved by you makes my skin crawl!"

"...What do you mean?"

"You don't know your own true form, do you?"

Claude's eyes are wavering. Even so, she has to wield this blade.

Master Claude, Master Claude.

The wound inflicted when humans shunned him, calling him a demon. Aileen will do the same thing. She's sure she won't be forgiven for this.

Even if Claude forgives her, she won't forgive herself.

"You monst—"

"**No!**"

There's a sound like breaking glass, and something black darts across the room. Aileen's eyes widen.

"**This is wrong, Demon King! Aileen lies—!**"

It happens in an instant.

A bullet of magic pierces Almond's body.

Black feathers flutter, and there's a spray of red.

"...That was uncalled for."

Elefas is sitting up now, his fingers paused at the end of a flicking motion. He clicks his tongue in irritation.

I have to move. The thought is there, but she can't do it. She gazes at the shape on the marble floor.

It's not true.

A single fierce spasm runs through the crow, and then the noisy demon falls still.

The puddle of blood is slowly expanding, swallowing the red bow tie.

It can't be true.

"It's a demon!" someone yells.

She clenches her fists, and screams a name in a voice filled with fury. "Elefas!!" She focuses power in her right hand, calling the sacred sword to her, but just then—

—a violent blast of wind whips through the space. The table-cloths flip back, and silver dishes fly this way and that. Chairs are smashed, the glass blasted out of the windows. No one can even scream, and so the one voice that calls out sounds unnaturally loud.

"...Al...mond...?" Claude murmurs. He's dazed, his eyes fixed on empty space. However, in the next instant, his face twists with pain, and he buries it in his hands.

"Aah...... Aah, ah, AAAAaaaaaaaAAAH!!"

As he screams, the wind rises, buffeting everything and every-one even more violently. Down on her hands and knees, trying desperately to keep from being flung away, Aileen shouts, "Master Claude!"

The wind stops so abruptly, it's as if it never blew. Claude looks at her, and the sight of his face makes her gasp. His right eye is still black. However, his left is—red.

"...Aileen?"

It's the same, kind way he always says her name.

Aileen feels dazed. "...Master Claude. It can't be... Have your memories...?"

"—Kill that girl at once! She is a traitor! She'll ruin our son and turn him into the demon king!!" Before anyone else, the emperor rises to his feet, shouting. He looks frightened. "Put down the demons in the forest as well, immediately! Summon the Holy Knights! Mobilize the army!"

Claude starts to say something, but he crumples, doubling

over. His face is twisted in pain. Aileen tries to run to him, but someone grabs her from behind. "Let me go, Isaac! Master Claude is—!"

"No way, you heard the emperor! We have to get out of here!"

"But—!"

"Run... Aileen, help the demons...! I'm still not— Keith, Walt, Kyle!" Covering his face with his right hand, Claude cries out, pleading. "The demons, hurry...! Until I *return*!"

"Elefas, the emperor has commanded you! Put the girl to death right this minute!" the empress dowager shrieks.

Elefas turns toward her, his face expressionless. Magic leaps from his palm, but James bars the way, canceling it out. As if they've come to their senses, the guards begin to move, but Walt and Kyle send them flying with powerful kicks. Together with Keith, who has drawn his short sword, they take the lead, opening a path. Isaac drags Aileen away, but she tries to turn around. "Master Claude...!"

In that moment, the world around them changes.

"Aileen!"

She blinks; Beelzebuth has called her name. She's in Claude's office, in the castle in the forest. When she looks around, everyone who attended the ball is present.

Claude has forcibly teleported them. Stunned, Aileen falls to her hands and knees.

The floor on which Almond had lain in a pool of blood is gone.

"Just now! Just for a moment, I sensed the king's presence! It's strange, though. I can't sense Almond anymore. Did something happen?"

Beelzebuth crouches down, putting himself at eye level with

Aileen. She can't bear to look him in the face. She can't bring herself to say, *I couldn't save him.*

"Almond is with Master Claude," Keith answers mildly. Aileen looks up, and he nods once, as if he's speaking directly to her. "That means it's all right. More importantly, we have things to do. Don't we, Lady Aileen?"

"—Hey, if we just stand around, we're gonna get boxed in by the Holy Knights and the army."

Isaac had gone straight out to the terrace and taken a look at the area around the castle; he comes back shaking his head, which is now soaking wet. Rachel hastily offers him a towel. James sighs. "Rain, hmm? Let's hope it delays our pursuers…"

"Pull yourself together. You're gonna be the demon king's wife one day, right?"

After that remark, she has no choice but to focus on the future. Biting her lip, Aileen gets to her feet.

Claude has asked her to take care of the demons.

"…Isaac. Is there a way for all of us to escape together?"

"Technically, today was the delivery date. If he made it in time, we can use that."

"Oh, Isaac, there you are! I finished it!" Denis flings open the door with a *bang*, completely failing to consider the mood. He's covered in mud, but his eyes are practically shining. He's so excited that he starts talking before anyone can ask him anything. "Now we'll be able to move between this castle and the outskirts of the capital anytime we want! We brought the supplies in, too; I bet we could hole up in here for half a year… Also, I set all the traps I could think of in a big circle around the castle! I still have to test them, though."

"Yeah, don't worry about that. I'm pretty sure some thoughtful Holy Knights will help us test them in a minute or two."

"Ah, Denis! It's finally finished, is it? The giant moles must be thrilled!"

"Yes! We made it really ominous, Bel, just like you asked! Since everyone's here, I thought we could drink a toast while I showed it to you, but..." All that talking seems to have calmed Denis down a bit. Looking around at the others, he cocks his head. "Huh? Come to think of it, didn't you people have a ball to go to? What about the demon king?"

"Denis, before we get into that...what on earth did you make?"

"What did I make?! An underground labyrinth!"

Incredibly, the newly completed project is the demon king's final dungeon.

Aileen's expression freezes up for a moment, but then she smiles dauntlessly. Her retainers really are brilliant. "And it's already functional?"

"Yes! —Oh, do you want to go see it right now?"

"Yes, show us to it, please. We'll evacuate all the demons in the capital!"

Having shaken off all the hands that attempted to care for him, Claude is on his knees in a vast gallery. It's in the imperial family's residential wing, lined with the portraits of past emperors. Now that he's come this far, there aren't many people who can follow him.

The ball has ended early, but abrupt torrential rains have kept the guests from leaving. The Holy Knights and the army are probably having trouble moving out for the same reason. He hopes it will buy at least a little time. Is that hope what's behind this sudden change in the weather?

Rain runs down the large windows like a waterfall. His face is reflected in them; his left eye has turned red. It's the mark of the demon king. He understands that barely, but nothing else. He only caught fleeting glimpses of his memories, and nothing's come back. He hugs the still body of the crow demon to himself.

Aileen.

Is she all right? Just as he thinks that, his black right eye twinges, and he covers his face. The moment his hand hides his right eye, the floor of the gallery changes.

"...What is this?"

Aileen and the others are running through a gloomy, underground space. It doesn't take him long to realize he's able to see them thanks to magic.

Oh, good. They're safe...

When he looks closer, Aileen's group is being pursued by an enormous round boulder. He hears *"We took the wrong route"* and *"If you wouldn't randomly press things, Jasper"*— Is it possible he's hallucinating the words? He starts to worry that they may not actually be safe. Then he sees Beelzebuth pulverize the boulder with a single fist, and he closes his eyes, relieved.

When he opens them again, he sees his grandmother rampaging around as if she's lost her mind.

"My skin! My face! What if they grow ugly?!

"You good-for-nothing! Who do you think has allowed your tribe to survive?

"Grab that girl and drag her here right this minute. If you don't, I'll have all the hostages killed!!"

"Oh, Prince Claude. Peeping? You mustn't do that."

As though a connection's been broken, his vision reverts to the world in front of him. Someone is approaching from the depths of the gallery, footsteps echoing hollowly. It's his half brother's fiancée. The former Maid of the Sacred Sword. She flirted with him once, and then— His head throbs sharply.

As Claude's face twists in agony, Lilia speaks to him gently. "It hurts, doesn't it? You shouldn't push yourself. You've had an awful lot of magic stolen from you, and then you went and changed its flow by brute force. Besides, you're not allowed to break the rules. Lady Aileen is the protagonist, you know? You're a supporting character. Becoming the demon king again now would put everything out of order."

What is she talking about? Leaning back against the wall, Claude looks at the girl.

"Still, that was a surprise. I tripped that event flag properly, but you still chose Lady Aileen."

He can see nothing of his sweet future sister-in-law in her now. What he does see is the sort of innocence that amuses itself by squishing bugs one at a time. Either that, or the cruelty of a victor who makes full use of her pawns on the game board, then discards them.

"A character I can't romance. My opinion of you has risen a bit. No wonder Lady Aileen chose you. It is an *otome* game, after all; it may be there simply to make things convenient, but we really can't do anything without the power of love—and so, Prince Claude..."

There's a thunderclap, and a bolt of light streaks from the sky. Backlit, the girl wears a crescent smile. Something's shining in her hands. The sacred sword.

"...I'll make you the heroine."

Impulsively, Claude makes the crow demon vanish. In the same moment, the sacred sword pierces his shoulder. The magic is rapidly draining out of him. Because the blade has pinned his shoulder to the wall, he can't even collapse.

"Don't worry. I'm just taking away your magic so the demon snuff will work better; you won't die right away. After all, we must have Lady Aileen come to your rescue. The protagonist rushes in to save the heroine who's being gradually consumed by demon snuff—doesn't that sound amazing?"

He and this girl will never see eye to eye. Certain of that one thing, Claude peers up at the little bottle in her hand. He knows what's about to happen to him. What she's going to make him do.

"...Was it you who stole my memories?"

"Ha-ha! That's a secret. The protagonist has to be the one to unmask the culprit, then deal with them."

"Do you not love Cedric?"

The abrupt question makes the girl look at him blankly. That's enough to tell him the answer.

Is that why Cedric's struggling against this?

His foolish, precious little half brother. His brilliant fiancée had made him feel inferior, so he discarded her. In doing so, all he gained was the role of an unloved pawn, controlled by that very inferiority complex. The fact that a life like that is the one that suits him must be hard to accept.

"...Remember this. I—we are not your pawns."

"Hee-hee. Just the sort of line you'd expect from a losing character."

"But you are the one who can't win against the power of love. A mere pawn."

Crossly, Lilia uncaps the bottle. Claude slowly closes his eyes.

When they finally reach the exit, faint light is beginning to steal into the sky.

"I...I never dreamed we'd be forced to actually clear a dungeon..."

Not only that, but since the exit is also disguised as a fireplace, they're coated in ash. Limply, Aileen leans back against a wall, then slides down to the ground. She's truly grateful that she took off her ball gown at the castle.

"Was that the end of it? Are there more traps? Shouldn't there have been more?"

"Hmm, you have a point. Maybe I should have made it a bit more elaborate."

Beelzebuth—who's been extremely useful in this surprisingly dangerous place—and Denis both seem to have plenty of energy left. Luc and Quartz have washed their hands in a bucket of rainwater, and now they're checking to see if anyone's hurt. The old mansion looks as if it might come crashing down around them at any moment. It's dusty, and the floor creaks with every step they take.

"That final illusion of the demon king, the one you said you'd gathered everyone's magic to make. Wasn't that overdoing it?"

"Ailey's sacred sword sent it flying, but it was pretty tough."

"That was bad for my heart... Whose idea was it?"

The next ones to emerge are Walt, Auguste, and Kyle; they're all grumbling.

James responds curtly, brushing ashes off himself. "Elefas set that up. Apparently, it uses a magic item."

At the sound of that name, everyone looks uncomfortable. Aileen sighs. "I'm to blame for the matter of Elefas. For now, though, let's focus on making our escape. Keith and the others went on ahead; I wonder how they're doing..."

"They'll be fine. After all, it's the demon king's order. That adviser is seriously scary."

"Of course he is. The king chose that human." Beelzebuth throws out his chest proudly.

At the very, very end, Keith had shown them his trump card: He's the demon king's deputy. During Claude's absence, just once, Keith can give and enforce an order that carries the same weight as the king's. Apparently, it's authority Claude bestowed upon him in advance. Since he could only use it once, he'd been watching and waiting for the right moment. However, thanks to that, every demon has complied with the order to flee the capital. When a whole flock of fire drakes flew to them, Aileen had been awed by the demon king's power all over again.

"In the future, I would also like authority, just in case Master Claude is ever absent again."

"The demon king's not gonna go for that. You'd countermand his orders without even blinking," Isaac points out, and everyone nods in agreement.

"Your uncle Jasper thinks so, too. The best one is that adviser, and the runner-up is James, wouldn't you say?"

"...Let's table that as an issue for next time. A dragon is coming here as well, correct? We have a lot to carry. Will that be all right?" James glances over his shoulder. A group of fenrirs is sitting obediently behind him, looking sharp. The cyclops who tried to abduct Claude the other day is there, too. All of them are carrying untold amounts of food, with the fenrirs holding some on their backs while the cyclops holds an armful.

Aileen and the others went into the labyrinth because while they were tied up with sealing the castle and loading the incoming demons onto the backs of dragons and whatnot and sending them off, the army had surrounded them. Flying would have been an effective way to go, but they didn't want to take off from the castle and show their enemy where they were heading. Since it was on their way, they brought out the food and coins that had been stored in the labyrinth. Those resources would be absolutely vital later on.

"As far as cargo is concerned, the demons take priority. They'll stand out no matter what we do. I want everyone to carry small amounts of food, water, and gold in case of an emergency. Everyone knows where the rendezvous point is, correct? If anything happens, make your way there—"

In the middle of her explanation, a ferocious blast of wind blows the roof off. A dragon peeks in from above. It's a rather flashy entrance, but she's grateful for the early arrival.

"Ribbon, you and the others get on first. Go on," James orders, and the fenrirs walk up the dragon's tail in single file. This seems to tickle the reclining dragon, but the grand creature endures the minor ordeal. The cyclops is quite large, but that doesn't seem to pose a problem, either. The world of demons is wonderous and profound.

Casually, she circles around to the side of the dragon's head. The demon stays low, chin to the ground, while swiveling one big eye to look at her. This dragon's face alone is taller than she is. A demon like this willingly obeys Claude's every order. If Claude felt like it, he could probably take over the world. That isn't what he wants, though.

"...Thank you for your help."

The dragon looks away, peering at the sky. Aileen looks up, too, wondering if something's there, and sees a white crow flying straight at them. It's Sugar, the leader of the second unit of the demon king's air force.

"Alert, alert! Cavalry approaches! To arms! To arms!"

Sugar circles overhead, delivering the message in that quaint, old-fashioned speech. James *tsk*s. "Soldiers are one thing, but horses are bad news. They'll overtake us if we're not careful."

"Can't we just fly really, really high?" Auguste points at the sky.

Walt shakes his head. "If we climb too far, the humans won't last. I'm not even sure how the demons would handle it."

"So we have no choice but to fight? It will become a battle of attrition."

"...We'll send out a decoy and confuse them." Isaac is looking straight at Rachel.

Before Aileen can catch his meaning and speak up, Rachel steps forward. "All right. Then I shall pass myself off as Lady Aileen."

"Rachel!"

"It's all right. Our heights are similar; they won't figure it out easily. I thought this might happen, which is why... Here! I've brought a wig as well!"

"You know that isn't the problem! You have it backward! I'll stay and draw their attention. If you don't run, you'll be in danger! I have the sacred sword, so I can handle—"

"You have to rendezvous with the demons, Lady Aileen. Isaac, please…" As Rachel looks at Isaac, her eyes are kind.

Conversely, Isaac's are cold, and he shows no emotion whatsoever. "Thanks for your help."

Rachel smiles happily. Isaac's taking advantage of her affection, and Aileen feels a flash of anger. "Isaac! Listen, you…!"

"Um, in that case, I'll guard Rachel. It won't look right if she's alone." Auguste raises his hand.

Kyle volunteers next. "I'll go, too. Having a few people will make for a more effective decoy."

"If I'm not with you, they'll get suspicious since we're always together, so count me in as well. James, what about you?"

"…Since I can communicate with the demons, it would be better to have me there. We can lay low somewhere and collect information about the capital. I'm also concerned about Master Claude. How does that sound?"

Folding his arms, James prompts Isaac for his decision. Isaac looks down for a brief moment, then nods. "Yeah, let's go with that… You know where the rendezvous point is, right?"

"Of course. I'll take full command of the decoy maneuver, then."

"Wait just a moment. Rachel, you're all right with this?"

"Yes, it's fine. You're more important to me than Isaac is, Lady Aileen." Behind her, Aileen hears a hollow *clunk*, as though someone has run into something. "So please entrust me with this duty."

Aileen doesn't turn around to see what's happened, or whom it's happened to. She looks Rachel in the eye, then heaves a deep sigh. "I trust you."

"All right."

"Hey, Luc, Young Master Isaac's hurt; better take a look at it. At times like this, he sure is young, huh?"

"Let me see that, Master Isaac. Oh, yes, that's a cut. Quartz."

"...This stuff stings a whole lot, but that's what the doctor ordered."

"Whoa, time-out— Ghk! Owww, ow, ow, geez, are you sure that's normal ointment?!"

"Rachel. Here, take this! If you hold this bit to your opponent's body and press this button like so, a current of magic will run through it and knock them out! It can only be used five times, so be careful! You can test it on Isaac if you want; he won't die!" Denis hands Rachel a dangerous-looking weapon, and she flashes a wry smile.

Aileen looks around at the group that's volunteered to guard Rachel. "Auguste, James, Walt, Kyle. Thank you for your help. However, your safety and Rachel's takes top priority. You understand that, don't you?"

Everyone nods. Walt looks up at the sky.

"Okay, let's get going. Sugar, show us the way. Here, I've got one of those sugar cookies you love so... Oh."

"All crumbs! Incompetent human louts...!"

"Sugar, please. We need your help."

At Kyle's earnest request, Sugar turns away in a huff, then flaps dramatically. "Follow me! I will lead the charge! Humans, follow me!"

"Yip!"

"No, Ribbon. I've got work to do." Stopping the young fenrir, who's threatening to leap off the dragon's back, James transforms into a demon. Then he hauls Auguste up by the scruff of his neck, tucks Rachel under his other arm, and takes flight. Rachel hastily pulls on the blond wig. From a distance, it looks as though a demon is carrying a blond woman. If the pair who are famous for guarding the demon king leads the way, and a flying demon holding a woman with golden hair follows, the cavalry will probably focus their attention on them.

"...Aileen, let's go." As Aileen watches their receding figures, Quartz gently taps her on the shoulder. She nods. Luc and the others have already climbed onto the dragon, and they pull her up on its back. Without anyone giving an order, the dragon spreads their wings.

The ground falls away. She would have preferred to hide their escape somehow, but inconveniently, there isn't a cloud in the sky, and the morning sun has already begun to rise, illuminating their surroundings.

"Is it all right to head straight for the rendezvous poi—?"

Gravity tugs them in a precarious direction, nearly making them fall. The dragon has listed abruptly, and magic that looks like a flash of lightning streaks past their wing. It's coming from above them. Aileen looks up, then screams, "Elefas! How did you know where we...?"

"You used the sacred sword to break the magic item I gave you, correct? Adding a detection ability to it seems to have been a wise decision." Far up in the sky, his cloak streaming in the wind, Elefas looks down at Aileen and the others. "Now. Would you come with me, Lady Aileen?"

Magic crackles like sparks, forming multiple arrows. Aileen's eyes are grim. She brings the sacred sword out in front of her with both hands, transforming it into a defensive wall. The thin wall deflects the magic arrows that rain down on their heads.

"Did you get him?!"

"I only blocked it. The sacred sword doesn't work on huma—!"

Someone grabs her neck from below, and her feet dangle in empty space. Elefas has slipped through the sacred sword's wall.

"No one move, please. Not unless you'd like to take a very final tumble." Elefas is holding Aileen by the neck with his right hand, while his left is pointed ostentatiously at the dragon's back. Ribbon growls, but no one's able to do anything. "Lady Aileen. If you come with me quietly, I'll let the rest go."

"...How kind...of you. Is it all right to...let the demons go?"

"Yes. Now that Prince Claude is ours, we'll be able to do whatever we like with the demons. However, since you have the sacred sword, there's no telling what you'll try."

Her vision warps. She's being teleported.

"Come back to the imperial castle with me. Prince Claude is waiting."

The others' shouts grow distant.

If I go back to the castle now, it won't solve anything. I need some sort of clue at least—!!

Light flares inside her, overflowing. For the first time, Elefas's face twists. "The sacred sword?! Dammit—!"

She grabs the hand Elefas has been choking her with. The world warps and begins spinning backward.

The ground is muddy from the previous night's heavy rains. Rachel stumbles, and Auguste keeps her upright.

"Sorry about this. It's only a little farther. Oh, do you want me to carry you piggyback?"

"N-no, it's fine. Do you suppose James and the others are all right?"

"Oh, I'm sure they're fine. Those three are tough. Still, the security in the capital is really tight, huh?" Peeking out at a major street from the shadows of a building, Auguste sighs. They've managed to enter the fifth layer, but the Holy Knights are everywhere, so they haven't been able to make much progress for a while.

"It does means they haven't yet found Lady Aileen's group, but..."

"Still, there's no way they don't know James and the others have started fighting outside town."

"...Although, I guess if those three wiped out that first group, then maybe not."

"Yes, Nameless Priests are human weapons, while that other one is a powerful humanoid demon, even if he is a cambion. I doubt a mounted patrol unit will be any match for them."

The voice has spoken abruptly from behind them. By the time Rachel turns around, Auguste has already knocked his opponent's short sword away, then twisted her arm up. Rachel is startled. "Lady Serena."

"Ouch— Ow! Let go, you ruffian!"

"Be quiet," Auguste tells her in a low voice. He's holding the point of the short sword he's taken from her up to her throat. There isn't a hint of his usual charm anywhere to be found. Overawed, Serena gulps as he says, "We don't have time to play right now. If you resist, I'll show you no mercy."

"…Even if I said I'll help you?"

Auguste narrows his eyes. Rachel gives a smile that doesn't go past her lips.

"While I'm at it, I'll tell you where the demon king is, too. What do you say? It isn't a bad deal."

"Why would you do that? The empress dowager dotes on Prince Cedric and Lady Lilia. I can't think he'd have any reason to help his brother Prince Claude now."

"He does, though. When the demon king's memories return, he'll let Prince Cedric off without any serious punishment."

In other words— Involuntarily, Rachel and Auguste exchange looks.

"Since I'm going to be Prince Cedric's mistress, I need him to maintain *sufficient* rank. That means I'm in a hurry. Well? What will you do? I don't mind turning you over to the emperor's men if you'd prefer that. Just so you're aware, I'm doing this out of kindness. Be grateful."

"Why would you be that kind, Serena?"

With the sword still pointed at her throat, Serena examines Rachel seriously. Then she sighs.

"…From the way you look, he's made you that woman's stand-in, hasn't he? Used you as a decoy."

"……"

"I'd write him off if I were you."

"……"

"Huh? Rachel, come on, why did you go quiet?! I-Isaac completely didn't ask you to do this because he wanted to! It hurt him inside; there was just nothing else to do. You know that, right?!"

"More men who assume that women who've fallen for them

will forgive them no matter what they do—who do they think they are?"

"Who indeed...?"

"Why are you looking at me like that—? Wait, that's not even what we're talking about now!"

As Auguste shouts, they hear a voice asking if somebody's there. Serena *tsks*. "If you weren't noisy, these things wouldn't happen."

"What, it's my fault?!"

"Well, what will you do? Will you come with me or not?"

"...Help us meet up with James and the others. You could sell us out to the empress dowager and escape trouble that way as well. If you can't do at least that much for us, we can't trust you." Rachel smiles at her.

Serena looks taken aback. Then she sighs. "That's a decent answer, I suppose. All right, this way. Follow me."

"—Hey, there he is! The Holy Kni—"

The knights step into the narrow alley, but before they can raise the alarm, Auguste deftly knocks them out. At times like this, there's absolutely no hesitation in the way he uses his sword, and he doesn't leave any openings for them to exploit. Serena has dashed off, leading the way, and she glances at Auguste, who's acting as the rearguard. "To think you actually made it into the Holy Knights only to be treated as a traitor. Your future is ruined."

"Why would I be a traitor? The Holy Knights are under the direct command of the emperor." Once Claude Jean Ellmeyer becomes emperor, Auguste wouldn't be a traitor or anything of the sort. Even under the current circumstances, he believes this without question. Serena clicks her tongue in irritation. "Wh-why do you always treat me like that when I'm helping you?"

"Auguste. For now, escaping takes priority."

In a weird way, Rachel understands how Serena feels, so she tries to cover for her diplomatically. Auguste looks unconvinced. As they run, he checks with Rachel. "You won't hate Isaac over this, will you?"

"Don't worry. I'll pay him back properly."

"Oh, so you are going hold it against him…"

"Of course she is," Serena calls back to them loudly. Auguste looks like he has mixed feelings about it. *So will you, Lady Serena,* Rachel thinks, but she leaves it unspoken.

Someone is speaking. She's dazed, and her mind is cloudy.

"Release me. If I don't return, Her Majesty the empress dowager will consider me a traitor, and she'll raze the village."

"'Her Majesty' the empress dowager, huh? It sounds like you've gotten pretty used to living over there."

"So all our fates rest on your shoulders, hmm? That's real impressive."

"That's not what I meant…! I just want to save the village, so—"

"Yeah, that's why we're resurrecting the demon king. And who got in our way? That would be you, Elefas!"

Demon king. Elefas.

Aileen opens her eyes. She isn't able to sit up, however. Both her hands and her feet are bound with chains. The stone floor is cold. In front of her, she sees iron bars and the shapes of several men. There's another cell on the opposite side of the corridor, and some sort of argument is taking place through its bars.

"We know you rewrote the secret art for awakening the demon king! How long are you going to spend fence-sitting like this?! If we'd turned the demon king into a dragon, the capital would be in ruins right now!"

"As long as they have the sacred sword, we can't use the demon king as our trump card even if he awakens! Besides, they're holding dozens of our women and children hostage in the capital. How could we abandon them?!"

"A few sacrifices are inevitable! I'm sure they'd prefer that to being held by the imperial family until the day they die!"

"That's ridiculous! In any case, now isn't the time to fight. Calm down and—"

"Then when, Elefas? In ten years? Twenty?" At the sound of the old man's hoarse voice, silence falls. Aileen holds very still, listening in on the conversation from the other cell.

"Since they keep taking our women and children as hostages, our population of mages has dwindled. I doubt we'll ever be more capable of fighting than we are now."

"That's... I'm well aware of that. But for that very reason, we need to think of another way to resolve this."

"Says the traitor who wags his tail when the empress dowager calls! I bet you don't care what happens as long as you're fine."

"Currying favor. That's all your family ever thinks about."

"Enough. This guy's old man, rest his soul, begged the empire for his life. Even if we're captives, we're alive because of him... Not that anybody's happy about it."

The speaker practically spits out that last remark. It paints an eloquent picture of Elefas's position.

"We're through talking. Our spell to awaken the demon king is working. Now we just have to control him and attack the capital once it's fallen into confusion. The fact that we haven't sent your head to the empress dowager is all the mercy we can show you. We'll take the woman you brought in with us as an example. She's an aristocrat from somewhere, right? Those are some fine clothes she's wearing."

"We'll take our time with her later."

"...even..."

"Huh?"

"—I wondered what mages who can't even compete with me were planning to do by banding together, and the answer is *inflict harm on an unresisting woman?*"

She hears glass shatter. Someone's struck the bars with a wine bottle. Shards fly all the way to the bars of the cell where Aileen is lying.

"Just because your magic's halfway decent, don't go talking like you're better than us!"

"Hey, right now, his magic's all tapped out. We could drag him out of that cell and thrash some manners into him inste—"

"U–um, I—! I brought food."

The impending fight is broken up by the voice of a small child. Apparently, even this crowd doesn't intend to get violent in front of a kid; the men *tsk* and make for the stairs at the back of the room. A child with a tray runs up to the bars of the cell opposite hers, taking their place. "Mister Elefas, are you okay?"

"...Yes, I'm fine. Never mind that, what are you doing here?"

"Sis said to bring you a meal... Hey, you really are all out of magic. What happened?"

"Oh. A certain someone made me push myself too hard."

The child sounds amazed. "They cleaned out all *your* magic?! What kind of monster were you fighting?"

"—Forget about that. Is what they were saying about attacking the capital true?"

Elefas approaches the bars to accept his meal, and she finally gets a look at him. It may be due to the darkness, but he looks terribly exhausted. His tone is missing its usual easy composure, too.

"Yeah, it sounds like it. Since yesterday, those guys have been saying everybody who disagrees with them is a traitor and locking them up or taking their families hostage, so nobody can go against them. We couldn't stop them, Elefas; I'm sorry."

"You don't need to apologize... So it was what happened yesterday that started it, hmm?"

"Yeah... The demon king got his magic back, didn't he? Lots of people said our spell had activated, and then they got all excited. They said we'd be able to control the demon king, and now was the time to fight..."

By awakening, did they mean the fact that Claude's eye had reverted to red at the ball? If so, they'd really jumped to conclusions.

In an odd coincidence, Elefas sighs and explains why. "I neglected to keep them informed about my situation, and it's worked against me. I explained that the demon king hadn't awakened, but none of them believed me."

"Sis and I believe you, and so do the other people you saved! In the first place, it's thanks to you that those guys get to stay in the village at all! You negotiated with the empress dowager and said you'd do the work by yourself, so now everybody except the hostages gets to live in the village. But those guys keep saying they'll save the village, like they're big shots or something!"

"Some things can't be helped; the situation's complicated... Listen, if it comes down to it, run and save yourself."

"...I mean, you can say that, but... We don't have any place to run to."

"I'll handle it somehow. I haven't been the imperial family's slave this long for nothing."

The child gives him a worried look. Does Elefas realize it isn't unease about an uncertain future, but concern for Elefas himself?

Once he's finished his meal, he bids the child to hurry back, and the kid climbs the stairs, glancing at him several times on the way. Finally, when it's so quiet that they can hear the sizzle of the burning candles, Elefas exhales deeply.

They're alone. Thinking it's probably about time, Aileen sits up. "What do you intend to do now?"

"...Lady Aileen. You're awake? When did you...?"

In the cell across the way, Elefas blinks. Without answering him, Aileen goes on. "If you don't stop them, the Levi tribe really will be destroyed this time. They can probably mount a surprise attack, but..."

"Yes, just looking at the material disadvantage, it's obvious they'll lose. In the end, Lady Lilia's prophecy was correct."

Aileen's eyes turn cold. "So she's your master, then? Not the empress dowager?"

"No, you were right: My master is the empress dowager. Lady Lilia is someone I arbitrarily... Why are you looking at me as if I'm filth? That hurts a bit."

"I'll do what I can about my expression. Keep going. Depending on what you tell me, though, I may abandon you."

"You mean you hadn't already? That's a surprise."

Elefas smiles, joking with her. Then haltingly, he begins his tale.

I first spoke with Lady Lilia six months ago. It was at an aristocratic tea party that I visited on an errand from the empress dowager. She was surrounded by young noblewomen who were bullying her, and they poured tea over her head. It seemed unwise to ignore the second prince's fiancée, so I used magic to tidy her up. Since I was a mage, I thought she would treat me like some eldritch being; however, she was delighted by it and said magic was wonderful. She apparently found it quite novel.

"I don't suppose you'd skip over this bit? I know the general outline already. It's just the standard buildup, correct?"

......

Lady Lilia knew my name. She said Prince Cedric had told her. She also knew of my circumstances. People said that while she might be a baron's daughter, she was really nothing more than an upstart commoner, and neither her education nor her manners were adequate. However, I saw that she must have been studying quite assiduously, and my opinion of her rose.

"Of course she'd research the individual she was targeting; that's only natural. By the way, that includes the part where she intentionally says something wrong and accepts your correction when you point it out to her, demonstrating how agreeable and mindful she can be. You aren't going to tell me you thought her sweet because of that, are you?"

......

At the time, I was tired.

"So it was the perfect opportunity. A little kindness, and you'd be hers in a heartbeat. That's why she went after you, you know."

...Th-the empress dowager had taken a liking to me, and I'd grown

able to work toward improving the village's lot, as meager as it was. An increasing number of villagers were displeased with this.

"She understood that people were hard on you even though you were doing your best, and it made your heart skip a beat. Really, you're too easy. And then? For both her sake and to save the village, you felt compelled to do something about the rebellion, and to that end, and so on, and so forth— Is that how it went? But I imagine she stuck her oar in, telling you she couldn't let you fight alone. And besides, she had a problem of her own, correct? All right, you can continue now."

Elefas is on his hands and knees on the floor of his cell, his head drooping. "Er... Lady Aileen. I don't suppose you could stop interjecting repeatedly and mercilessly breaking a certain precious something of mine, could you...?"

"If that something can be broken by a little push like this, then let it break and never look back. In any case, although you're sugarcoating it nicely, what you've really been doing is falling for someone else's spouse. No doubt your enthusiasm grew while you were harboring the secret in your heart. There is an age where that sort of guilty pleasure is particularly appealing, isn't there? *As long as she is happy, I'm...* That's the one."

"Um... Really, could you please stop? It's embarrassing, and I'm beginning to want to die..."

"And then? Although she couldn't have known anything, she said something along the lines of *If nothing changes, the Levi tribe will be destroyed.* Am I right?"

Since Elefas, who was plotting to restore the demon king, is positioned as the final boss, it's hard to imagine an outcome where the Levi tribe is spared a terrible fate. At best, like the villainous Aileen, they'll have been wiped out by one of the demon king's light rays or killed off without any fanfare in the narration.

It was just a guess, but from Elefas's startled expression, she knows she's correct.

"...She said she saw strange dreams. That was what she'd originally come to me to discuss. She seems to see the future. A girl with no magic, even if she is the former Maid of the Sacred Sword... At first, I thought they were simply dreams, but they really are accurate."

"For example?"

"At first, she foretold an incidence of corruption at Lester's workplace. It was tax embezzlement, and there was a plot to pin the crime on Lester. He was dubious, but when he investigated, it shockingly proved to be true."

This was an event on Lester's route. Aileen narrows her eyes, and Elefas continues, "That isn't all. She knew the culprit behind Prince Cedric's attempted assassination, and—in terms of small things—what would be on the menu at a dinner party. When the empress dowager lost a jewel, she knew where it could be found. She also predicted that the demons would rebel in Mirchetta."

The girl remembers the contents of the game in great detail. Lilia orchestrated the Mirchetta incident herself, but Aileen is impressed by the way she's used her knowledge to her advantage. It's an achievement based in very thorough gameplay.

"And so when she said the Levi tribe would be destroyed, you believed her."

"It really didn't seem as if it could be a lie. The village actually had developed a secret spell in an attempt to awaken the demon king. If that was discovered, no matter what form it took, we would never escape unscathed. Besides—she had retaken the lost sacred sword."

As one would expect, this makes her look up, startled. Elefas gazes back at Aileen through the bars.

"I don't know how she did it. However, to me, it seemed to be no less than an omen that the demon king would awaken as a dragon, as her dream had foretold."

"...Then you never really intended to ally yourself with us, did you?"

"No. That foresight of hers is terrifying. She even did the seemingly impossible and recovered the sacred sword. Ultimately, I did not think the demon king could win. Even if he awakened as a dragon, I thought he would probably fall to Lady Lilia's sacred sword... Although, I was startled when Prince Claude nearly regained his memories while still human."

Elefas gives one significant sigh, hanging his head. "If this went on, as she prophesied, the tribe would meet its doom. With that in mind, I made a proposal to the empress dowager. In order to make the Levi tribe's efforts benefit her instead, I tampered with the secret art, borrowed the power of the sacred sword, and... It was I who stabbed Prince Claude that night and brought him to the castle."

His confession comes out easily. There's probably little point in hiding it any longer.

"The spell I cast on him broke the magic connections that run all through his body, diverting his power into the empress dowager's magic item... In the end, as Lady Lilia had said, stealing Prince Claude's magic resulted in the loss of his memories. It made me shudder."

"Then did you stay with us after that because Lady Lilia ordered it?"

"That order came from the empress dowager. Lady Lilia has been absorbed in caring for Prince Claude, and I haven't seen her since. When she stepped in to stop us at the ball, I was worried, but she didn't even glance at me. I was grateful for that, of course, but...I suspect she has no more use for me."

"Well, she probably doesn't."

If Elefas was romanced, then he wouldn't become the final boss and resurrect the demon king. In other words, Claude would end up living as a human, without his magic or his memories. That's what Lilia has been after all along.

She got one over us. To think she'd make him do the exact opposite of what he did in the game by romancing him...

And on top of that, she's tried to romance Claude. The woman really has no morals.

Elefas slumps his shoulders. "I expect you're right about that."

"My, you acknowledged that very easily. Weren't you writhing in heartrending agony?"

"Please don't put it that way. In any case, I was too busy keeping an eye on you to be concerned about such things. You dress as a man and barge into the enemy's camp without turning a hair, you pursue the reluctant demon king every which way, you attempt to capture a demon. And besides..."

Elefas breaks off abruptly and looks at Aileen. His gaze is intense, and the two sets of bars between them do nothing to block it. Aileen looks perplexed.

"What?"

"Nothing... In the end, it comes down to the same thing. I wanted to save my tribe, and so I did not ally myself with you."

He seems to be implying that he has no regrets.

"For all that, you've spoken quite freely. Don't tell me you've given up."

"...Frankly, I have. My magic is drained dry, and I can't leave this cell, while in another hour, they'll teleport to the capital and invade it. I have no time to wait for my magic to recover."

"By the way, why exactly is your magic drained?"

"Because you ripped every bit of it out of me with the sacred sword. As a result, my teleportation failed, and we landed in my hometown of all places."

"I see. The sacred sword took your magic... Perhaps that's why I feel so energized."

"Huh?"

The moment she summons the sacred sword, the chains on her arms and legs split with a metallic *clink*.

The sacred sword doesn't work on humans. It does work on objects, though, and it can destroy magic all day long. The sword is sparkling in an odd way, as if it's been waiting for its turn to take center stage, and when she uses it to cut the iron bars, it positively pulverizes them. Apparently, it's a magic-reinforced cell.

"Now then, it looks as if I'll be able to save your hometown. Is there anything you'd like to say to me?" Aileen, who's marched right out of her cell, folds her arms and looks down through the bars at Elefas. "Unlike Lady Lilia, I am not kind. I don't tactfully nudge men in the right directions and preserve their pride for them. Naturally, I won't tell you *Life has been hard for you* and extend a helping hand, either."

"...But, Lady Aileen. I—"

"Nor have I any need for masochism. If you mean Almond, I will never forgive you... However, I'm sure Master Claude will.

That is just the sort of person he is. That is the sort of man I love. I want to be a suitable match for him… And so." Aileen grabs the bars firmly. "Debase yourself and beg, Elefas. Crawl wretchedly and implore me to forgive you. Abandon your pride and everything else and beg for your village to be saved. If you do that, I'll be able to excuse myself to Almond!"

Aileen bites her lip. Elefas looks up at her with clear, steady eyes. They're a gentle orange, mixed with the reddish hue that shows he possesses magic. He looks down again—and in the next moment, he's plunged his finger into his own left eye.

"What are you doing?!"

"I used my right eye as the vessel to catch the demon king's magic. The eyes of a mage with strong magic can become powerful magic items. That eye has been incorporated into the empress dowager's magic item. Just in case, I made it so that someone in possession of my left eye could undo the spell I cast on the demon king."

His left eyeball has fallen onto his palm. With a light cracking noise, it transforms into a red crystal. Elefas holds it out to her, then kneels, bowing his head. "If you use that, it should restore both Prince Claude's memories and his magic. That is the greatest act of loyalty I can demonstrate right now…although I know it can't make up for Almond's life."

"……"

"Oh, I won't be a burden. I can augment my vision with the magic within me. Once my stores of power have recovered, I'll create a natural-looking prosthetic, as I've done with my right eye. It's just that it isn't pleasant to look at right now, so I will keep my eyes lowered."

"…You're a fool, aren't you?"

Eyes still closed, Elefas raises his face toward Aileen. There are
no traces of blood on his cheek. No doubt even they have become
part of this red crystal.

"...As I suspected, though, you aren't crying."

"Why should I?"

"When Lady Lilia learned that I had given up my right eye,
she cried. She apologized for not being able to do anything. I told
her I hadn't wanted her to save me...but that's a lie. I wanted to
save my village, and I wanted to be saved. By someone, at any
rate—and right now, I wish to be saved by you."

I was jealous of Prince Claude.

More jealous of the man who had your love than of Prince Cedric,
who had Lady Lilia's.

She pretends she hasn't heard those words. What he's offered
her is his loyalty. Not his love.

"We are a foolish tribe. Deceived, oppressed, in possession
of no hope except in acts of vengeance. Stop us, please. When
Prince Claude regains his memories, I'll accept any punishment.
So please, I beg you." Elefas bows his head, pleading fervently.
Aileen tips her head back, looking up at the ceiling.

It's all right if I save them, isn't it, Almond?

He had always been a strong, straightforward demon. She
could just take the red crystal and abandon these people, but if
she does it, Almond will despise her. He might never speak to her
again.

When she touches the iron bars, the cell shatters like ice and
vanishes. Even then, Elefas doesn't move. Aileen turns her back
on him. "You keep that crystal. If I accidentally touch it with the
sacred sword, it will probably crumble to dust."

"That's… But are you sure you don't mind leaving it in my possession?"

"It's fine. I won't ever let you dream of defying me again."

She draws a deep breath, then smashes through the prison's wall with the sacred sword. It turns out they're in an underground dungeon, and so the ground is gouged away, and a set of stairs forms, leading up to the surface. The sacred sword is feeling rather thoughtful today.

"All right. Shall we?"

"Um… Do save the tribe, won't you? Please don't destroy them."

Pretending she has no idea what he's talking about, Aileen climbs the dirt stairs. Apparently, the explosion hasn't gone unnoticed; she can hear screams in the distance. It won't be long before the group that was raging about storming the capital shows up again. Aileen folds her arms, waiting. Elefas stands quietly behind her, a little to the side.

"By the way, what is the empress dowager's magic item? The one you poured Master Claude's magic into."

"Oh… Didn't her youth ever strike you as odd?" *It can't be.* Aileen's expression goes stiff, and Elefas nods. "That is the product of magic. A spell that restores youth. There is a magic item that creates a crystal that stops your time when one pours magic into it. Swallowing that crystal will keep your body eternally young. Of course, if the crystal's magic runs out, the effect vanishes. That means she can't maintain that form unless she harvests crystals on a regular basis, and creating the crystals requires a tremendous amount of magic. More than what a single mage possesses."

"…Do you mean to tell me that's what the Levi tribe's hostages are used for?!"

"Very astute. Yes, they are hostages, and also convenient sources of magic. I'm told the measure was initially taken because it was considered dangerous to let them keep their magic, but..."

"What a waste of a mage! She's squandering them! It makes no sense!" She rakes her hand through her hair in exasperation. "I understand that it wouldn't be good to rely on them overmuch, but surely, there are scores of effective ways to use them! As disaster countermeasures, for example. And yet she uses them to make herself look young?! Is she stupid?!"

"Is... Is that what concerns you?"

"Not only that, but from the direction the conversation was heading...she's using Master Claude's magic now, isn't she?"

"...His magic is vast, after all. It does mean she's stopped draining the hostages of their magic and killing them. I'm sure you aren't satisfied with the situation, Lady Aileen, but—"

"Over here!" yells a voice she recognizes. It belongs to one of the men who was in front of her cell earlier.

"However, the empress dowager's age is considerable. The hostages can no longer provide her with enough magic. That is most likely why she accepted my proposal when I suggested taking the demon king's magic."

"I see. Master Claude really is a problem, isn't he? Popular with literally everyone..." Sighing, Aileen turns to face the crowd that's assembled. She checks with Elefas. "That manor over there. No one seems to be maintaining it. Is it abandoned?"

"? Yes, it hasn't been used in yea—"

She swings the sacred sword, and the shock wave blows the mansion away. In the midst of a cloud of dust, Aileen smiles elegantly, sword in one hand. "It's a pleasure to meet you. I am Aileen Lauren d'Autriche."

Even when the dust has cleared away, Elefas stands frozen with a smile on his face.

"Thank you for rescuing me when I was unconscious. By the way, I'm told you intend to invade the capital. I would like to discuss it with you. Who is your leader?"

"—Everyone, prepare to attack. Use fire! Burn her to death!"

"Ah, so it's you! You're the one who proposed making an example of me!"

"Um... Lady Aileen... Please do keep it peaceful... I'll apologize on behalf of the others, so..."

Elefas pleads with her in a small voice, but it doesn't matter. A volley of magic arrows flies at her, but she knocks every one of them away, and her graceful smile never wavers. "You didn't want Elefas to save you, correct?"

"Eep..."

"Not only that, but you're also attempting to do all sorts of things to my Master Claude. You must show me this self-confidence of yours. Fight like men, won't you? To the death, of course."

That is what it means to go to war.

With a dauntless smile, Aileen launches herself into action, bringing the sacred sword hurtling down.

"—Lady Aileen, do you intend to attempt world domination?"

"Mm, well... Master Claude would probably manage it. So you see, I feel that I should be able to do at least that much on my own, and I'm constantly working to improve myself."

"...Are you actually the last two people in the world who should be allowed to marry?"

"Gracious, you'd speak of my relationship with Master Claude that way? I'll drop you." She glares at him from beneath half-lowered eyelids. Elefas shakes his head emphatically. Behind him, in a distant mountain valley, she can see the Levi tribe's village. The wind is carrying them along nicely, so the view is good.

A pleasant journey through the sky. In a seemingly impossible display, they're in a balloon buoyed by nothing but magic.

"How long will it take us to reach the demons this way?"

"Perhaps until nightfall."

"I see. Well, it's far faster than walking."

"That's true. However, if you hadn't blown away the magic circle for the teleportation spell, Lady Aileen, we'd already be rendezvousing with—"

"You mean if your magic recovers quickly, don't you? Do you want me to drop you?"

"I'm sorry." Elefas shifts the direction of a device that's emitting a gas-like magic. Below him, Aileen is relaxing on a carpet in the basket, leaning back against a cushion the women of the Levi tribe brought her. *Now that I've taught them a lesson, they should stay quiet for a while.*

According to Elefas, the mages were merely armchair warriors with no practical combat experience. The demons were probably more capable of coordinated maneuvers than they were. Even though the fight had been one against many, since they had so little in the way of any practical combat skill, Aileen completely dominated the battle. After that, those who'd been against sending out soldiers helped her restrain the ringleaders and throw them into the dungeon. Everything following that worked out quite nicely.

Magicless as he was, Elefas hadn't been any help in the fight. However, the fact that Aileen had been accepted so easily was due in large part to his popularity. All he'd done was explain that this was the master he served now and that she was acting to improve the Levi tribe's lives, and they promptly loaned them this balloon.

"You must be cold, Lady Aileen. Have a blanket."

"My, thank you."

Even after he's draped the blanket over her, Elefas's hands linger on her shoulders. Aileen looks back at him, wondering what this is about. His face is a little too close. After a short silence, he speaks.

"...You leave yourself surprisingly vulnerable. I wonder why your retainers are content to stay as they— As I said, please don't look at me as if I'm garbage. You'll wound me."

"Then quit saying foolish things and keep watch. If you betray me again or try anything funny, I really will cut you down."

"I know that... Although, if I betrayed you here, it would immediately end as a double suicide."

"What are you talking about? I'd survive. If you intend to die, do it by yourself."

"I would have preferred it if you'd said something along the lines of *Let's die together*— Lady Aileen, look there."

As Aileen had ordered, Elefas had risen to his feet and begun scanning their surroundings, and now he points at something. Aileen also stands, with the blanket still around her shoulders. Then she leans forward.

"A horde of demons?! Why...? Elefas, take the balloon closer!"

The demons are charging over the vast desert, kicking up clouds of dust. They're making a beeline for something, running single-mindedly. When she looks in that direction, her face goes pale. *It can't be— Are they heading toward the capital?!*

"Lady Aileen, isn't that Isaac following them on horseback?"

"Yes, Isaac and Master Keith... Beelzebuth?!" When she sees his figure cutting across the sky, Aileen's eyes widen. Beelzebuth seems to register her presence; just for a moment, he glances at her. He doesn't veer from his course, though, and after a moment, he's gone.

Something's happened to the demons. They descend until they're able to identify the tiny human figures in the distance. Aileen shouts at the ones pursuing the demons on horseback. "Isaac! Master Keith!"

"Lady Aileen?! Ah, I knew you'd be all right."

"Hey, what's that mage doing there?! Didn't he kidnap you?!" Isaac yells, clinging to his galloping horse.

Buffeted by the wind, Aileen yells back, "Don't let it concern you. I've broken him!"

"Lady Aileen, could you phrase that some other...?"

"Never mind that, what's going on?! We were supposed to get the demons away from the capital, remember?"

"They say something's happened to Master Claude!" Keith tells her. Aileen turns to look at the hoard of racing demons.

Isaac picks up the explanation. "We did make it to the rendezvous point, but they suddenly started yelling about saving the demon king and immediately turned around!"

"If Milord is in danger, my proxy authority is worthless. Even Beelzebuth won't listen to me."

"—We're going to stop them. Elefas, you must have recovered some of your magic by now. Soften my landing!"

"Wha—? Lady Aileen?!"

Setting a foot on the rim of the basket, she leaps out. She doesn't even consider the possibility that she'll fall to her death or be trampled by the demons. She only uses the sacred sword, creating a wall in front of her, so that the demons will stop.

"Halt!"

Beelzebuth is the one who's shouted. The horde of demons screeches to a standstill. They glare wordlessly at Aileen, who's barring their way.

"Move, Aileen."

Beelzebuth has stepped out in front. Uncharacteristically, his gaze is terribly cold. "We must go save the king."

"No, you must not. Master Claude asked me to lead you all to safety."

"Enough nonsense, out of the way! What if we arrive too late? The king is screaming!"

"Calm yourselves. Master Claude isn't calling for you, is he?"

"Then you're saying we shouldn't save him?! Do you think the humans are more precious than the king as well?!" As Beelzebuth howls, a sandstorm whips up around him. There's murder in his red eyes. Behind him, the demons make no attempt to hide their hostility. They seem ready to charge at her, sacred sword or not. Keith has caught up, and he leaps off his horse, spreading his arms wide.

"Calm down, Bel...!"

"Keith, move! Why do humans always treat the king with contempt?!" With audible cracking noises, fissures open in the ground. It's as if they're responding to the demons' rage. "Even if it's you two, if you stand in our way, we'll kill you. Who cares about the sacred sword?! Nothing is more important than the king's orders!"

"Bel— Lady Aileen!"

Beelzebuth has charged straight at the sacred sword's wall. And so Aileen makes the sword vanish.

With nothing barring their way, Beelzebuth's long claws bear down on her. However, she doesn't avert her eyes, and they stop just shy of her throat.

"...Why did you get rid of the sword?"

It would be easy to force them to submit with that blade. If she takes that approach, though, the only way to stop the demons will be to kill them all. Aileen looks straight into Beelzebuth's eyes.

"—Beelzebuth. Stand down."

"I'm asking you why you got rid of the sword!"

"And I am telling you to stand down. What exactly do you think you're pointing at your king's consort?!"

Keith and Isaac, who's finally caught up, and Elefas beside her—all of them hold their breath as they watch the scene unfold. Behind them, the demons go silent.

"*I* will go save Master Claude. You protect the demons."

If she looks away, she's likely to be killed. Neither reason nor bargaining will work on the demons, and she can't just bluff her way through this impasse. As a matter of fact, she's impressed they've held back this long. They've believed in Aileen and the others—in humans—and toughed it out so far.

"...It's only a little longer, Beelzebuth. Elefas has told me how to restore Master Claude's memories and magic."

"Is that true, Lady Aileen?!"

"Yes. That's why... Beelzebuth."

Wordlessly, Beelzebuth lowers his claws. He speaks briefly, and his eyes are still cold. "One hour." He's taken out his pocket watch, and he dangles it in front of her eyes. "I will wait no longer. I will take those who are drawn here by the king's screams, and we will all go to save him—if anything happens to him, we will torture all the humans to death. Including you."

"Very well. One hour, then."

"Hey, it's gonna take an hour just to get from here to the capital! Give it a little longer—"

"That's not my concern. We've already spent long enough trusting you and waiting."

Overawed, Isaac shuts up. Beelzebuth turns his back on them and rejoins the other demons.

Keith puts a hand to his forehead, exhaling deeply. "At this point...I wonder if I chose the wrong time to use that authority."

"No, that's not true. One could say that we've bought ourselves time, since we've come a good way from the capital—Isaac. Just so you're aware, I reject any plan that involves abandoning the demons."

Isaac scratches his head at a loss. "You can say that, but we've only got one hour. Including the time it'll take the demons to get to the capital, that's two hours tops."

"...I think I could teleport myself and one other person to the capital."

Everyone looks at Elefas. He sets a finger against his lips, thinking hard. "That's where the trouble begins, though. In order to restore Master Claude, we'll need to set the crystal I gave you in the magic item the empress dowager has, and I don't know where it is."

"You don't know?"

"I've seen the actual object, but I don't know where she keeps it. It is the empress dowager's greatest weakness, after all. She'll move it periodically. It is an enormous grandfather clock of a peculiar design, so it should stand out, but... If we narrow our objective to simply stopping the demons, there is another way. We can secure the demon king himself and return him to them. Even if those screams the demons are hearing don't stop, it's very likely that that would stave off the crisis temporarily, at least."

However, only Elefas and one other will be able to reach the capital immediately. Not only that, but since he'll also use up his magic again teleporting them, they won't be able to count on him for much more. In other words, they won't be able to split up.

"It felt as if I'd collected quite a few people, but it seems I'm still shorthanded…"

"Nah, don't collect any more than this. Even the demon king's gotta be at his limit."

"We should focus our efforts on the option with the greatest odds of success. Recapturing milord's personage seems to be the easiest path… Oh, but we don't know where he is, either, do we?"

"Hey, what do you suppose James and the others are up to? If he's the guy I think he is, he's probably in the capital already. We've got no way to contact him, though… I guess I've been leaning on the demons too much as well."

"Yes, up until now, our environment allowed us to summon them—" On a whim, Aileen looks down. The sun is directly overhead, and there's a shadow at her feet. "…Elefas. Has Master Claude's magic returned?"

"Pardon? Only very slightly, but yes. No doubt that's how his screams are reaching the demons."

"What a fool I am! …James! James, if you can hear me, respond!"

James is a cambion. Even under these wild circumstances, he's very likely to have retained his reason, and although there isn't enough magic for him to pass through her shadow, her voice may reach him. *I'm begging you… Master Claude!*

Understanding what Aileen is trying to do, the others all stare at her shadow...but there's no change. *It's no good, then.* Just as she lets her shoulders fall, it happens.

"...*Aileen?*"

"James!"

That's the final boss of Game 2, all right. His reception is magnificent. She falls to her hands and knees, looking down at her shadow. She doesn't know if there's any point in it, but she speaks loudly. "Where are you now?! The capital?!"

"*Yes, but we're busy! Not only that, but Master Claude's screams are making it hard to hear you.*"

"If you can hear his screams, can you tell where he is?! We can't restrain the demons any longer. We have to help Master Claude somehow, or else...!"

"*He's right here! He's been heavily drugged with demon snuff, though, and he won't wake up.*"

"Master Claude." Keith crouches down, too, gazing at the shadow.

"*We've been surrounded, and we can't leave this building. All because Auguste trusted that woman... Shut up, no one needs your excuses! At any rate, the demon king's screams are because of the demon snuff. It's eating away at him.*"

"...What should we do? Is there a way to get the demon snuff out of his system?"

"*Restore the king's magic. That will disperse the taint in an instant.*"

Now she knows what they need to do—returning Claude's magic to him will resolve everything. Aileen looks up, and Isaac mutters, "Now we just need to figure out where the empress dowager's magic item is."

"James. The woman you mentioned earlier is Serena, isn't it?"

"Yes. She claimed she'd tell us where Master Claude was, and she did, but then the woman promptly sounded the alarm and ran! First, we're used as a decoy, then we're surrounded by the enemy. What a disaster...!"

"Did she say anything else? Anything about where the empress dowager might hide something important, for example."

"No, only Master Claude's location... What? Quiet, Auguste! You have no right to spea... The north tower of the castle? ...This idiot says she was headed there."

"Oh, well done, Auguste! Let Serena keep fooling you forever!"

"Hey, come on, that's mean."

"And? Rachel's all right, isn't she?"

Isaac flinches, falling unnaturally still. James sighs. *"She's fine... Can we wrap this up? I can't afford to stay on the sidelines for long."*

"Yes, that's fine, thank you. Elefas and I will return to the capital now."

"Elefas? That mage? Why?"

"I've broken him."

"...I see. Fine by me, then."

"Um, why does everyone seem to be convinced that phrasing is accurate?" Elefas apparently finds it disturbing, but the others ignore him.

"We've already found a way to restore Master Claude's magic. I swear to you I'll save him, so please hold on until I do. Protect him."

"...Understood. However, keep yourself safe as well... If you don't, Master Claude will be sad."

"I won't make him sad."

"I'd imagine not," he mutters quietly, and then her shadow falls silent.

Rising to her feet, Aileen pivots to face Elefas. "All right, let's go."

"Yes, of course."

"...You're awfully docile." Isaac glares at him.

Elefas responds with a smile. "I'm the type who gets more enthusiastic the more rivals he has."

"Oh, I see."

"That doesn't matter, just hurry. We're going to save Master Claude!"

This time, for sure. With her own hands.

She's going to launch that so-called player's scheme into the stratosphere and leap into his arms.

✦ Sixth Act ✦
I'm the Villainess, So I Fought the
Maid of the Sacred Sword

In the blink of an eye, the scenery changes, and they're high in the air. Elefas grips Aileen's hand; he's wearing a wry smile.

"I'm sorry, my magic's run out—we're going to fall."

"Wha...?"

After she's landed in the bushes, Aileen praises herself for managing not to shriek. Any ordinary young noblewoman would have screamed or fainted.

Of course, it isn't as if the demon king's future wife can afford to be ordinary.

"Are you all right, Lady Aileen?"

"Yes. You're not injured, are you, Elefas?"

Brushing the leaves out of her hair, she looks up at him. He's caught on a tree branch.

"Not injured, but...I can't get down. My magic..."

"You aren't that far up. You could simply jump."

"To tell the truth, I tend to lean on my magic. I'm altogether hopeless at any kind of genuine physical activity."

"Is that the sort of thing you should be confessing with a straight face? Hold that branch with both hands. Yes, that's right. And then—"

Before Elefas can jump, the branch snaps and drops him. He isn't able to break his fall properly, and he hits the ground with a *thump*. She looks down at him from under half-lowered eyelids...

Of all the final bosses so far, he's definitely the weakest. Well, he is human, and it was a fan disc, so maybe that's just how it goes.

He was an intellectual type of final boss, deeply knowledgeable about magic in all its forms. Probably.

"Lady Aileen, you look as if you're exasperated with me, but I am average for a human, all right? Isaac and the others are the same. In the first place, too many of the people around you are inhuman."

"Once this matter has been dealt with, you're going to study self-defense. Ask Auguste or Master Keith to help you."

"...Both Auguste and Keith seem rather inhuman, so I suspect I won't be able to keep up..."

"You're rather inhuman yourself, you know. As long as you have magic—"

Partway through, he claps a hand over her mouth and drags her back into the bushes. Before she can ask what's going on, guards run down the path right in front of them.

"It's the southern imperial villa! Bring every soldier you can get! They've holed up with His Highness the crown prince as a hostage...!"

"Dammit, there's only four of them! How is this happening?!"

"The new Holy Knight is there, too. Can we get the knights to send reinforcements?!"

From the remarks she overhears, she gathers this is about James and the others. When the footsteps have receded, Elefas removes his hand from her mouth.

"Apparently, we have them to thank our friends for the fact that there are no soldiers standing guard."

"Let's go. James and the others have limits as well—the north tower is in that direction, correct?"

"Lady Aileen, if you wish to enter the north tower, you must enter the castle first. The tower's only entrance is a connecting corridor on the fourth floor."

On the other side of the path, Elefas opens one of the castle's service doors. It appears to be a guardroom. No one is inside, and they pass straight through it, then climb a staircase.

"You seem to know it well."

"As far as the Levi tribe is concerned, this tower is infamous. The magic item that guards the connecting corridor— I should call it a monster, really. It's a troublesome thing that devours any magic it sees."

"Do you mean that the north tower is where the Levi tribe's hostages are held?"

"Yes. Many have fallen victim to it. Both those who tried to save them, and children who tried to run away." His cloak flares out, and she sees that his hand is balled into a fist. Aileen frowns, but Elefas turns back slightly, smiling at her. "It's all right. I beat it when I was ten or so."

"You won?!"

"I slammed more magic into it than it could take, and it burst... But I wasn't able to save everyone in the tower. Even if we got away temporarily using magic, once our magic dried up, our pursuers would win by brute force and capture us again. We had too few allies. That's why I decided to go back and sell my services to the empress dowager."

I'll do the work alone, so don't use anyone else. Had that been his bargaining chip?

Aileen thumps him lightly on the back. "The choice you made then has led us here now. Take pride in it."

"...Thank you very much."

"Besides, that means the monster or whatever has already been vanquished, yes? This should be easy, then."

"No, the empress dowager had it repaired, and it's fully restored. It is a tool, after all; it can be fixed." Aileen gives a dissatisfied frown, and Elefas laughs a little. "It's fine. It's only made of magic. Nothing we need to worry about when you have the sacred sword."

"...What on earth is the empress dowager anyway? She isn't a mage, is she?"

"I hear her ancestors hail from a distant land in the east, and she brought a variety of things with her through those connections. Their magic operates differently from ours..."

As they're talking, she hears an explosion from a passage that branches off to the right, and the blast wind rushes past them. After that, there's a sound like a beast's howl that makes her cover her ears. "What was that noise?!"

"It came from the northern tower. Thanks to that monster, no one can get near it, so what could have...?"

Abruptly, Aileen puts a hand to her chest. It's hot.

Sacred sword?

A second blast and the screams of something dying echo up the long corridor. There's smoke in the wind that buffets her cheeks. Aileen's long, golden hair streams loose, and she laughs. "...Oh, but there is someone. Another besides me who has no fear of monsters."

"Huh?"

"Come with me, Elefas." Footsteps clicking on the floor, she walks down the long, broad corridor. Every possible surface has been painted flat white, and it's disorienting. It was probably intended to be.

However, right now, what hits her senses the hardest is a vile scorched smell. That, and the sound of her heart, which beats in rhythm with resonance of the sacred swords.

Before long, she sees a figure in the depths of the blindly white corridor. A girl turns toward them; she's just pulled her sword free of a corpse that's an unsettling color somewhere between red and green. Behind Aileen, Elefas gasps. "Lady Lilia..."

"Oh? Elefas, why are you still alive?" Innocently blinking those large eyes of hers, Lilia tilts her head prettily. "You should have been executed in the village, shouldn't you? The most pathetic route, in which you try to stop the demon king's resurrection and your village treats you as a traitor. I like that one quite a bit. It's just so heartbreaking. I did adjust the affection levels properly."

"...Was that your prophecy?"

"Prophecy? Oh, don't worry about that. It isn't something a character would understand—isn't that right, Lady Aileen?" Lilia turns to face her, and her lips curve into a smirk. "What did you think this time? I learned from my previous attempt and worked very hard."

"...I would say you focused your efforts in an entirely wrong direction."

"Really? It's quite difficult to produce the sacred sword on Lester's route, you know."

The sword Aileen took from her is the one from Cedric's route. Internally, she *tsks*. *So she got another sacred sword by romancing a character from Game 1. Don't tell me there's a spare for each of them...*

As if she's read her mind, Lilia laughs.

Aileen draws a deep breath. As she does so, the sacred sword materializes in her right hand. "And? What are you doing over there?"

"This is where the empress dowager's magic item is. On the Claude route in the fan disc, if you break that magic item, Claude will be severed from his past as the demon king and go on living as a human for the rest of his days... But, Lady Aileen, it looks as if you might use it to restore his memories, doesn't it?"

"Elefas," Aileen calls softly. Keeping her eyes on Lilia, she whispers into his ear. "I'll draw her attention. While I do, you get that door open and lift the spell on Master Claude."

"...Lady Lilia is an ordinary human. The sacred sword won't work on humans, so as the man, I should—"

"Elefas. Does that woman look like an ordinary human to you?" Elefas falls silent, and the silence is his answer. "I'm counting on you," she presses him. Then Aileen levels the sacred sword at Lilia. "And so you've come to get in my way?"

"Well, Lady Aileen, I'm the only one who can actually fight you." Setting her left hand against her chest, Lilia gives a sweet smile. "Besides, *this* is the best seat in the house; I'll get to see you at your most dashing." In her right hand, she holds the sacred sword. She's the true Maid of the Sacred Sword.

"Don't suffer a humiliating defeat, Lady Aileen. After all, you are the protagonist."

With an insincere smile that only reaches part of her face, Lilia lunges at her.

As the sacred swords clash, light bursts and a blast wind whips up.

Beelzebuth gazes at the watch hand as it ticks forward. His irritation has fallen silent, but even so, waiting is hard. Still, a promise is a promise.

"Beelzebuth."

Keith comes toward him, parting the demons' ranks. The fact that the man has managed to approach through a crowd of murderous demons as if it doesn't bother him at all is impressive, but among humans, Keith is a special case. Keith is fully aware of this. It's precisely why they call him the demon king's left-hand man.

"Have you cooled your head?"

"...Because the king's screams have nearly died away, yes."

"That's... No, let's not get into that. Lady Aileen has already gone ahead anyway."

"If anything happens to the king, I won't forgive you. I will stop knowing what forgiveness even means."

"I imagine so." Keith nods mildly. "That's fine. If it happens, feel free to devour me headfirst. Most of my deeds have been bad ones. I wouldn't mind being killed by demons; I couldn't ask for a more fitting fate."

"What's that supposed to mean?"

"Well, I was jealous of you. All of you... If the king is screaming, it means Master Claude is in pain, doesn't it? I can't tell. I'm always the only one who doesn't know." Beelzebuth is sitting with his arms around his knees. Keith sits down beside him, looking in the direction of the capital. "But you see, right now, just a little bit, I think it's a good thing I couldn't."

"Hey, if you can talk, let's get moving." Another figure approaches through the path Keith cleared. It's Isaac, the human Aileen keeps giving important jobs to.

"Get moving? Where to?"

"To the capital. A crowd this massive hanging around in the middle of the desert makes for an amazing target."

"You people are the ones who told us to wait here." Beelzebuth scowls.

Isaac shrugs. "We need insurance, just in case the worst happens and Aileen loses. We know where the demon king is. In that case, take him back with you." Without thinking, Beelzebuth gets up, and Isaac steps back as if he's afraid. Even so, he continues, "If we can at least rescue him physically, there's still hope. Besides, the confusion may make it easier for us to move."

"...Are you sure about this? Don't you want to help Aileen?"

Isaac winces as if that one hurt. "Aileen's the one who said we're not cutting you loose. So I've got no choice, okay? I'll think of the best possible move. Anyway, you've helped me a whole bunch of times."

Humans are curious beings. They have all sorts of things they want to save.

"You still have to wait that hour you promised, though. And then...if possible, I want you to help us out. Break the wall around the capital so that James and the others can get away."

"......"

"If you do, they'll be able to run to us. In other words, it'll be easier to recover the demon king. Understand?"

"Yes, we do. Don't we, Beelzebuth?"

Prompted by Keith, Beelzebuth gives a stiff nod. Isaac looks relieved. "Great. Okay, then."

"Isaaaaac, Beelzebuth! We caught up!"

Someone shouts behind them, and they turn around. A cart drawn by two horses is racing toward them, canvas cover flapping in the wind. Denis leaps down from it. "Boy, that startled me! Everyone got excited and ran off; I had no idea what was happening."

"…Are there any injured demons?"

"So what's going on? I went for broke and brought all sorts of things! Powder that temporarily makes it impossible to stop crying when you spread it around, and even a gas that makes you hallucinate and lose your mind!"

"That gas sounds like real bad news! Argh, my aching bones. Don't push old folks so hard…" Jasper pounds the small of his back with a fist.

Isaac narrows his eyes at him. "The only thing you did was ride in a cart, man. Every muscle I've got is going to be screaming tomorrow, count on it."

"Ha-ha! You really were clinging to that horse, weren't you?"

"Shut up! I do all my work with my brain. Anyway, demons, what do you want to do? Wait here for an hour, then charge in without a plan, or work with us and raise our odds of saving everybody?"

Isaac turns to Beelzebuth, and he's not sure what to do about it. He doesn't really understand the things humans think.

"Why would you save the king? If you love Aileen, then the king is just an obstacle."

The air freezes up with an audible *crack*, but Beelzebuth doesn't notice.

"Of course, even if you fragile humans worked together, you'd be no match for him. Your very existence can't compete with his. However, right now, you're— Mmmph!"

"Bel, a little tact, all right?! Learn about the complicated male heart!"

Keith reaches around from behind, covering his mouth. As Beelzebuth keeps making muffled, unintelligible noises, Jasper bursts out laughing.

Isaac gives him a cold look. "What's so funny, guy?"

"Nah, I just thought he was completely right. Why save him? It's simple, my fair demons—humans are dumb. Way dumber than any of you. We think if we put our minds to it, we can make friends with anybody."

"...Anybody?"

"Right, even with you lot." Raising his beret slightly, Jasper winks.

Beelzebuth is taken aback. The tension in his shoulders fades. "I see. That's very human. Arrogant and self-centered to the bone... All right."

"Yes, we're just trying to score some points and make ourselves look good."

"Luc... Let your elders look impressive once in a while."

"Well, if we're done talking this over, let's go. If we don't, we'll fall behind Lady Aileen and James's group." Keith claps his hands for attention, taking charge. It's strange how it makes Beelzebuth begin to feel as though everything's back to how it used to be.

"Let the invasion of the demon army begin, then. That's all right, isn't it, Isaac?"

With a long sigh, the human turns his back. Then he says it.

"Yeah. Let's go rescue the demon king."

None of them say, *Let's go rescue Aileen*, and although Beelzebuth doesn't know why, it makes them seem very strong.

The demon king's screams wake him.

Startled, he's fully alert in an instant. Apparently, he's been injured. His body refuses to obey his mind. As he screeches inarticulately, a condescending blond guy tells him to settle down. Then he tosses him into a weirdly sturdy iron box.

He's worried about the demon king, but he can't move. As he's lying there, he realizes that none of the places that are supposed to be wounded actually hurt. On the contrary, something that's buried inside him is toasty warm, and just holding still for a while is making him feel better and better. It has to be some sort of recovery spell. And so no matter how badly the demon king's screams hurt, he waits quietly, enduring them.

Then eventually, the box's heavy lid opens.

Someone asks if he can tell that help is here, and he gets a look at his face. He knows that face. It's the guy who did awful things to Aileen. However, he's also the only human who watched as the demon king left long ago. As he gazes back steadily, the guy goes off somewhere. The window is unlocked.

When he carefully tries to move his wings, they oblige. Once he's sure of that, he can't stand it any longer, and he flies straight toward the demon king's screams. However, when he sees that the building is surrounded by lots of people with weapons, he thinks for a little while. As the captain, he's not allowed to charge in carelessly under any circumstances. He needs a strategy. Besides, he can sense that there's a demon inside the building as well. When he peeks in through the skylight in the roof, he sees the half demon who's a human most of the time, and with him is the demon king.

The demon king is lying on top of a stone casket. Around him, his guards are hard at work. Sugar is protecting the demon king's casket, too, trembling all the while. Aileen's lady-in-waiting, whom he thought was demure, is swinging a frying pan around and spattered with her enemies' blood. The sight makes him decide not to write her off as weak anymore.

The demon king doesn't stir. He's like the sleeping beauty in the picture book he read the other day. That's annoying. Aileen's not here. A terrible time like this, and she isn't here—what a naughty wife.

Just as he thinks this, there's a bright flash in the sky in the opposite direction.

What he's seen is the power that burns demons to death. In other words, it's Aileen. Even as he shudders, he takes to the air.

Really, his body feels awfully light. He's in fantastic shape. It's almost as if all the bad places have been healed—but this isn't the demon king's magic.

At that point, he finally remembers he was shot. However, the spell that entered his body seems to have absorbed all his magic, amplified it, and given it back. What a nice guy. But why did he do a thing like that? Humans never make any sense.

He doesn't hate them, though.

When he's partway to his destination, the shock wave from the sacred sword almost sends him flying. Rubble from the long corridor that links the castle and the tower flies right past him. It won't be safe to go near this. He has to push ahead, though. Even the demon king has to be concerned about this. After all, the king always asks him how Aileen is doing.

Still, is it really okay for him to take such a scary woman as his wife?

That thought crosses his mind briefly as he watches the

corridor get gradually blasted apart until it's barely more than a scaffold. He's trembling.

During the tenth clash, she started to see the sky. When she pushes her back, Lilia does a midair flip, coming to rest on rubble from the caved-in ceiling. Her physical abilities border on superhuman.

"First, Serena, and now this—are you trying to become an assassin?! There is no such route in Game 1!"

"Oh, but the Marcus route has a 'female knight' ending. The strongest female knight, who possesses the sacred sword."

Curse you, heroine bonuses. Inwardly, Aileen grinds her teeth. The developers really should rethink game-design concepts that keeps players from getting stressed, right this minute.

Lilia tilts her head, flashing her cute little smile. "Goodness, Lady Aileen, don't get mad! You know how this works. The heroine's efforts are always rewarded; that's the best part of *otome* games."

"In that case, go grow your etiquette parameters as well. You're the second prince's fiancée, remember?"

"That's not really conducive to exercise, is it? But I do think you're also benefiting from the game's blessings, Lady Aileen. Villainesses usually have high basic specs, don't they? When there are multiple rivals for each potential love interest, the abilities get dispersed among them, but Aileen is the only strong player in Game 1."

Athletic abilities, brains, etiquette, and knowledge. Enemy characters are created to be worthy opponents for the protagonist to defeat someday. If they were too weak, they wouldn't be much of an enemy in the first place.

"The only bad part is your personality, I think."

"I wouldn't deign to call it good, but I don't want to hear that from you, either!"

Aileen has backed away, and Lilia springs at her again. Out of the corner of her eye, she sees Elefas moving. So does Lilia. She laughs. "It's no use."

With an electric *snap*, Elefas is blasted away from the door. He collapses on the floor, writhing.

"Elefas!"

"It's a wall I made with the sacred sword. Lady Aileen and I are having fun right now. Don't get in our way, all right?"

Lilia turns, slashing at Elefas in the same motion, but Aileen gets there a moment sooner and stops her. Lilia's eyes widen; she's thrown off-balance, and Aileen spots an opening.

First things first: I'll relieve her of the sacred sword!

She swings her own sword at its blade. At that angle, she should have sent it flying...but Lilia thrusts her palm out toward its point.

"Wha—?!"

"Ha! Ha-ha-ha-ha, owwwwww, oh, this really does hurt, doesn't it...?!" Lilia's laughing. Her palm is absorbing the sacred sword.

It's the reverse of what happened before. Wide-eyed, Aileen yanks on the hilt, but Lilia's latched on to the blade and won't let go.

"Hee-hee-hee, Lady Aileen. You say this is reality, not a game, but scenarios are important. For example, the sacred sword grows along with its owner, and Auguste *borrows* it, remember? In other words, it's possible to put the sword back where it came from... and also to make it stronger."

"—Do you intend to assimilate my sacred sword?!"

"I'm repossessing it. Didn't I tell you? I've learned from my mistakes."

Aileen braces herself, resisting with all her might. Light bursts, and wind whips up from below them. However, Lilia doesn't let go; she continues absorbing that power. Just as Aileen once did.

"I've been thinking about how I could beat you, Lady Aileen. Just having the sacred sword won't be enough. I have to reclaim yours as well. If I do that, I can destroy both the demons and their king."

She's right. Even the demon king is no match for the sacred sword. If Lilia is the only one who has it...

"Ha-ha. Ha-ha-ha-ha! That means you'll play this game with me all the time, won't you, Lady Aileen? Say, aren't you curious? About why the demon king was born into the imperial family, for example, when they're supposed to be descended from the Maid of the Sacred Sword."

Aileen closes her eyes. *Sacred sword*, she says, moving her lips silently.

You are the sword of the woman who will marry the demon king.

"Or about what the Maid of the Sacred Sword is."

The sacred sword *stole* Elefas's magic. At her feet is the shadow made from Claude's magic.

The demon king's wife should be able to do at least that much.

"Or about what the regalia of saints, demons, and maidens is!"

"That would be the power of love, obviously!!"

Black light races forward, knocking Lilia's hand away from the sacred sword it's trying to swallow. Her shocked face tells Aileen that her plan is working, and she flashes a thin smile.

Magic like black lightning coils around the sacred, shining sword. It's Claude's magic. The sword has absorbed it from the shadow at her feet.

This is Aileen's regalia of saints, demons, and maidens.

If she wants to defeat the real Maid of the Sacred Sword, she has no choice but to bet on this gambit.

"Are you insane?! Your demon king is at death's door! He's been able to resist the demon snuff only because he has faint traces of magic left, and yet you've absorbed that magic and used it to boost the sacred sword?!"

Aileen is aware of all that. However, with no hesitation, she swings the sword down. Lilia catches it on her own sword, but sparks fly, and the blade begins to dissolve. Staring, Lilia shrinks back, but of course Aileen isn't going to let her escape. She gives chase immediately.

"D-do you mean to kill the demon king?!"

"You know Master Claude would never die and leave me behind!! Besides—"

Light flares, and both Lilia's sacred sword and its magic continue to gradually disintegrate. Just then, there's a sound like breaking glass. The wall the sacred sword created across the door at the back has vanished.

"—I simply have to rescue him before that happens!"

Elefas breaks into a run. He already understands Aileen's intentions. However, as soon as he touches the door, he stops. "It's no good, Lady Aileen! The door is sealed with magic. I can't open it!"

"Wha—?!"

"Ha...ha-ha...ha-ha-ha-ha-ha, aaaaah-ha-ha-ha-ha, tooooo bad!" Lilia grabs Aileen's wrist. Glaring at her, nose to nose, she shouts, "What will you do now, Lady Aileen? Elefas doesn't have enough magic to break the seal on that door! You'll have to do something about the door before you erase my sacred sword. Or do you want to keep going and see which disappears first—my sword or the demon king's life?!"

"............!"

"But even if this sacred sword disappears, I'll just produce another one! I win!" Lilia shrieks with laughter.

What can I do?! Isn't there anything?!

Every time their sacred swords clash, Lilia scatters more sparks. Little by little, it's disappearing. Meanwhile, the black lightning that coils around Aileen's sacred sword is visibly dimming as well.

Claude's magic is running out. In other words, he's dying.

Even so, when she scans her surroundings, she sees Elefas standing in front of the door.

He's smiling.

"It was only for a little while, but I am in your debt."

When nasty developments happen at times like this, the nature of the content is pretty much a given.

"It's all right. I made sure what I gave you will remain even after I've destroyed myself."

"Wait, no, Elefa—"

Her scream sticks in her throat. She thinks it's all over, and this is the dream that comes after.

But.

"...Is it my turn?"

She could never mistake the face that's peeking in through the broken ceiling, or that red bow tie, or his voice, for anyone else's.

Crying will have to wait. Facing forward again, Aileen screams, "—Almond! Go, break that door, save Master Claude!"

"Leave it to me!!"

"Wha—?!"

In the moment Lilia's distracted, her sacred sword scatters its last light, expiring along with Claude's magic. Now, as Almond makes a beeline for the door, she has no way to stop him.

Beating his great wings, the crow demon blows the door away.

"I am cool!"

As Almond boasts, Elefas scrambles in through the broken door. A large clock stands eerily right in the room's center. He fits the red crystal into an impression, then turns it.

With a rusty creaking noise, the clock begins to spin backward—and finally, the clear peal of a bell sounds in the sky over the capital.

It rings once more, and then again, as though urging someone to rise from their slumber.

"Did that...do it...?" Aileen murmurs as the bell keeps ringing.

Lilia staggers, slumping back against the wall. Uneasily, Elefas looks up at the sky from the crumbling corridor. "That should have broken the spell... But if the demon snuff has gotten to him first..."

"—Stop right there, Aileen."

Multiple sets of loud footsteps sound on the corridor floor, falling into rows. Marcus steps out in front. The sight of the rubble-strewn corridor makes him frown. However, as he issues his declaration, he stands tall. "This is an order from the empress dowager. Aileen Lauren d'Autriche, you and your companions are under arrest for violating an imperial edict. The punishment is execution!"

Come to think of it, they haven't dealt with that problem yet. Even as Elefas turns pale, he and Almond step in front, shielding her. Marcus glances at them, then looks at Lilia. "You too, Lilia. After an uproar like this, I'm afraid you'll...have to be questioned."

Lilia, who's still leaning against the wall, looks up. "No, no." She shakes her head, sweetly entreating, "It's your job, isn't it? This is how it had to play out. If I explain properly, you'll understand. I was only trying to protect something that's precious to the empress dowager."

"Why you brazen little..." Aileen's exasperation knows no bounds.

"Well, it's true, isn't it? Hee-hee, how sad. To think you'll die by execution, Lady Aileen."

Lilia hides behind Marcus. Marcus frowns, but in a manner that befits the young ace of the chivalric order, he fixes his eyes on Aileen. "Seize her. By imperial command, it doesn't matter if you kill the demons now."

"Lady Aileen. Take Almond and flee. I'll be able to hold them here for a little while."

"No! If we don't do something about that woman right now, she'll get her hands on another sacred sword!"

"But the sacred sword alone won't work on humans! The shadow spell is gone, too," Elefas points out, and Aileen clenches her fists. Just after she'd erased Lilia's sacred sword, Claude's magic faltered, vanishing from both her sword and the shadow under her feet. She refuses to let herself think that she may not have made it in time. However, without the shadow spell, she can't

borrow the aid of the other demons, and the enemy's numbers are too great for her to fight without help. She won't stand much of a chance.

The knights draw their swords, leveling them at her. Should she run, or steel herself to die in battle and charge at them? While she's hesitating, there's a streak of light, and the knights' swords fall to pieces. It's as if some invisible creature has sliced them apart.

"Who are you pointing your weapons at?"

The speaker is floating in the sky, his glossy black hair streaming in the wind. His suspicious gaze is as cold as ice, and even with rather disgruntled-looking arched eyebrows, he's breathtaking. Standing in full sunlight doesn't impair his perfect beauty; on the contrary, he's dazzling. A diabolically alluring king, who causes all who see him to kneel.

The relief makes the sacred sword vanish from Aileen's hands. "Master Claude...!"

His eyes are both red, and they glare down contemptuously over everything below him.

Alighting in front of Aileen and the others, Claude speaks quietly. "What are you doing to my fiancée? Stand down, all of you."

"Your Highness, Crown Prince Claude... But His Majesty ordered us to—"

"I am in a very bad mood right now. I feel like venting it on everyone I see." With a crackling noise, something like magic rises from Claude's back. Almond shrieks and clings to Aileen, trembling. "Can you understand this anger? An anger with no outlet, since when I awakened, everything was nearly resolved... And here you are, saying you refuse to heed my orders. There could be no better prey. I'd prefer not to create the mistaken impression that the demon king is cruel—but that won't be a problem as long as there's no trace of you left."

"Y...your memories are back?" As the other knights cower, huddling together, Marcus bravely speaks up. No doubt he doesn't want to look pathetic when Lilia's taking shelter behind him. That attitude alone is admirable.

However, the word *memories* seems to fan Claude's anger even further, and a blast of wind whips up. "Memories? Oh, yes, that's right. How dare you make light of me, then humiliate me. What would you have done if you'd made Aileen hate me? I believe you owe me an apology."

In the next instant, Marcus and the other knights all sink to the floor as though something heavy has pushed them down. Without the sacred sword, even Lilia isn't immune.

"Oh, so you are capable of listening. That's a pleasant sight. I feel a bit calmer now. Is it possible that you are my allies?"

"M-Master Claude... I sympathize completely, but that's probably enough..." The difference in strength is so overwhelming that Aileen's begun to feel sorry for them.

On his hands and knees, Marcus looks up, his expression desperate. There are beads of greasy sweat on his forehead. "Y-Your Highness... Th-this is...an imperial edict... We have to...carry it out."

"Ah. An imperial edict. I see. This was my fault as well. Maintaining composure is oh so important—everyone stand at ease and listen to me: The imperial edict has been repealed."

"...Wha...?"

"His Imperial Majesty's health is poor. He is about to depart for rest and recuperation. Therefore, as crown prince, I will be acting in the emperor's stead—isn't that right, Cedric?"

At the sound of that name, Marcus turns to look into the corridor's depths. The pressure Claude was exerting upon them seems to have vanished; Lilia also rises, moving sluggishly.

Frowning, Cedric looks at the prostrated knights and sighs. "If my brother says so, that's probably how it's going to be. All of you, stand down."

"Cedric! What are you playing at? Lester's plan was—"

"Lester? Oh, you mean the fellow who received a false report that the empress dowager's ball would be attacked by demons, believed it without verifying anything, and caused a scene?"

Although Marcus has made a grab for Cedric's shirtfront, he makes a strangled noise and falls back a step. Lilia gets to her feet, turning a puzzled face toward him. "Cedric? What do you mean?"

"Even Julian and Gilbert. Who'd have thought they'd been up to so much mischief, and on Lester's orders? Commissioning assassinations from the church, underground auctions, and a litany of illegal transactions... I expect that vast sum of money from an unknown source was a bribe."

"W-wait just a second. What are you talking about? ... Marcus?"

"You were too honest, and you don't seem to have been involved in those plots. Even so, you're attempting to arrest an innocent individual on trumped-up charges. You've been used. Very neatly, I might add."

"Wh-what...?" Marcus seems stunned; he just stands there.

Lilia shakes his arm, pleading with him. "Marcus! Something's gone wrong with Cedric. How could he doubt our friends?!"

"Don't worry, Lilia. They all say you had nothing to do with it...even though they were all doing it for your sake. What a terrifying woman. We can't just leave you to your own devices. Isn't that right, Brother?" Shifting position slightly, Cedric looks at Claude.

Claude sighs. "...You're right. However, from the sound of it, she doesn't seem to have done anything personally."

"If Lester and the others have gone off the rails, the fault is mine. I am their lord. As my fiancée, she shares my crimes. Pass judgment on us."

Voluntarily, Cedric kneels in front of Claude. Marcus and Lilia look dumbfounded. Aileen also blinks at them.

"Brother. I can be useful to you. I can let those who are opposed to your rule set me up as the central figure of a rebellion. Then in the end, I'll take all the responsibility and be executed for it. I'm the only one who can play that role."

Looking down at his half brother's bowed head, Claude narrows his eyes. "Then I will give a fitting punishment to you both. Confinement comes first, and you'll need to be placed under guard as well."

"Yes. If you do that, then unsavory types are bound to seek me out."

"Wha—? Cedric, you must be joking! What is all this?!"

"Just what it sounds like, Lilia. All because I'm spineless... I'm sorry."

Cedric is smiling, but his eyes are very dark. The intensity in them makes Lilia shudder and involuntarily take a step back. Her fear probably isn't an act.

The scene is starkly real, and when Aileen sees it, she finally understands Cedric's incomprehensible actions. He wanted to betray Lilia, in order to show her he wasn't a character who could be puppeted at will. He wanted her to see him as a living human being.

"However, my love for you won't change as long as I live."

Lilia looks as if half her soul has left her. Bewildered, Marcus arrests her, then he pulls her through the corridor, accompanied by Cedric. Cedric has said he'll voluntarily go to the west prison tower to be confined with Lilia until he's officially sentenced. He walks away so merrily that they don't even bother putting a guard on him. However, on Claude's orders, Almond goes with him.

"…So even half-siblings can resemble each other a great deal, then?"

"Why, I have no idea what you're talking about, Elefas." Elefas has tried to bring something inconvenient to her attention, and she glares at him but receives a worried look in return. She refuses to take his meaning. No cell of ice ever existed.

As she brushes the dust off, the tension leaving her shoulders, Claude turns around. "Aileen."

Her body responds first, reflexively, and she turns her back on him. Her heart is racing because of nerves. She only saw his eyes for a moment, but they were definitely red.

Still, right now, she doesn't have the courage to look him in the face properly.

"Are you angry?"

"N-no, not at all. It's only, you know… I'm not emotionally prepared for…" She laces her fingers together in front of her uselessly, biting her lip. She feels as if she knows what she wants, and yet she doesn't.

"I'm sorry."

"A-as I said, I'm not angry. It's just that I—"

"You were frightened, weren't you?"

Her chest constricts. Something wells up inside her, and she swallows it back down with an audible gulp. *I wasn't frightened.*

After all, I'm the woman who will be your wife. She'd taken pride in that and raced all this way at full tilt. She didn't have the time to bother with unease or fear. The demons had been afraid in their king's absence. She had companions to help her. When did she have time to cry? What reason had she to hesitate? She fixed her eyes firmly on the future, and she never wavered. That had been her role, her mission, and her pride.

But the truth is...

"You did very well. It's all right now. Come here, Aileen."

There's just one person who always says the words she wants to hear.

Biting back a sob, Aileen flies into Claude's arms, and he holds her close. He's the only one she'll ever confess to how very scared she was.

"I-is everyone...all right?"

"They're safe. James, Walt, and Kyle were wounded, but I sent them to Luc and the others. Rachel wasn't hurt."

"Um, listen, Elefas is..."

"Yes, I know." The familiar sound of snapping fingers echoes, and behind them, the floor of the north tower explodes. "The hostages are being held down there. Go and save them."

Relieved, Aileen closes her eyes, resting her forehead against Claude's chest.

"I'll heal your eyes as well; come by later. I understand about Almond, so don't run. There's something I need to ask you."

"Yes, Prince Claude. I will tell you everything about who I served, and what I did—"

"I don't care about that. What I want to know about is this relationship you claim to have with Aileen." Claude's tone acquires a rather dangerous edge. She can tell Elefas has frozen up, but her head feels heavy. "I want to hear about that in detail. It won't just be you; I'll be interviewing everyone separately."

"Huh...? No, that was, er—"

"The matter is settled."

"Pl-please wait. Lady Aileen! Explain it to him... Lady Aileen?"

Her feet rise lightly into the air. Claude has picked her up. With great effort, she opens her eyes. His kind face is all she can see. "Sleep. Leave the rest to me."

A kiss lands on her eyelid. The last thing Aileen hears before she releases her grip on consciousness is a sweet, whispered "I love you."

The time he feels most at ease is when he's seated on his throne, looking out over the deserted audience chamber. With a little sigh, Emperor Pierre Jean Ellmeyer sets his elbow on the arm, resting his chin in his hand. "This is too much for us to handle. You do something about it, Rudolph."

"Could you specify what you mean by *something*?"

"We mean *something*! Your daughter is the one who started it! Mother warned her that she mustn't meet with our son, but she ignored that and caused a massive commotion. And on top of all that, she's trying to turn him back into the demon king."

"When you put it that way, the only thing I can do is agree with you, Your Majesty. Ha-ha-ha." His prime minister's laugh echoes hollowly.

Pierre gives another long, deep sigh. "How did it come to this? Even though we don't have what it takes to be emperor..."

"What are you saying? You were the one who ordered to have my daughter executed and the demons subjugated, Your Majesty."

"How could we do anything else? Without you and Mother, just about all we are capable of is being a father."

"A father, hmm? ...Unless His Highness the crown prince becomes the demon king again, your order was a wise decision, Your Majesty. Ever since the title of crown prince was restored to Prince Claude, the surrounding countries have been restless. Some have even begun acting in disquieting ways. I myself feel that having the demon king as emperor may prove problematic."

Come to think of it, ever since Cedric's assault on the duke's daughter, it's been one headache after another. He would have preferred to hush the whole thing up, but they'd presented terribly detailed proof. The only way to protect Cedric's position was to yield to their demands and restore Claude's right to inherit the throne. Meanwhile, from a political standpoint, having Duke d'Autriche's daughter engaged to a member of the imperial family was a boon. The only problem was the fact that Claude was the demon king.

He thought his son's ongoing amnesia would resolve that issue, too, and that everything would go well, and yet...

"However, Your Majesty. Children must eventually let go of their parents' hands and grow on their own."

"Quite true. If they stayed children forever, even we would be troubled by it."

"Thanks to you, something entertaining happened...and so I'll gladly help you with the cleanup."

"? What are you saying—?"

With a ponderous *creak*, the heavy floor-to-ceiling double doors swing open. A shaft of light lances into the dim throne room, seemingly conveying two shadows into the grand space.

There's a soft footfall, and the rustle of fabric on marble. "Ouch," a woman wails—it's his mother. Someone is holding her by the head and dragging her across the floor, one-handed.

"Mother! Claude, wh-what are you doing?! Release her!"

"Pierre! Pierre, stop this boy, please, ouch, it hurts!"

Claude hurls his girlish grandmother all the way to the throne on the dais. He's treating her like a piece of laden cargo.

Cold sweat trickles down Pierre's back. Fearfully, he looks at his son's eyes. They're both red.

"Father, Aileen may not look it, but she has a surprisingly romantic side." Wearing a gentle smile, the demon king approaches the throne step-by-step. "She wants to marry with the full approval of her family, and she's also concerned that my human relationships are lacking. I wanted to make her wish come true." Claude stops right before the great stairway that leads up to the throne. "But to that end, I let you do as you wished, and this was the result."

"Pierre! Pierre, what are you doing?! Summon the guards! Somebody—" His mother's shriek turns into a breathless wheeze.

An object has appeared next to Claude—an enormous grand-father clock, with an oddly large number of gears. It's the magic item his mother cherishes.

Softly, Claude sets his hand against the clock, and it begins to glow. The light seems to explode from inside it, and his mother stares. Shaking her head so hard that her hair comes undone, she screams, "Don't! Stop, no, anything but thaaaaat!"

However, her pleas are in vain. The clock bursts. It falls to pieces, burning until only a mound of ash remains.

Stunned, his mother sinks weakly to the floor. However, her eyes promptly blaze with anger, and she claws at the marble with her red-lacquered nails. "How...dare you...! How dare you, you monster!"

"That's a nasty thing to say. Especially when I can make what you need, every day." Something that looks like a blue candy drop materializes on Claude's palm.

His mother tumbles down the stairs, reaching out frantically for the blue object his son is holding. "Give it to me, give me that! Hurry, give it here... Hurry!"

Claude shakes his hand once, and the object vanishes as if he's performed a conjuring trick. With a scream, the woman clings to his feet. "Wh-what is it you want? That girl's life? Or do you want the order to subjugate the demons repealed?"

"...M-Mother."

For the first time, Pierre sees his mother beg. She always behaves as if the world belongs to her in its entirety, but there's not a trace of that strength or dignity left now. For some reason, this shakes him more than he imagined it would.

Swallowing hard, he looks at his son. No, he can't think of him as his son any longer.

"Please... We implore you, Claude!"

"Father, Grandmother, it seems to me as if you need a long rest. You do, don't you?" Ignoring his grandmother's entreaties, Claude sets a foot on the first step. "You tried to execute my fiancée, and you attempted to put down the demons. If you issued an imperial edict that ridiculous, you're clearly tired and in need of a break. You've forgotten why I gave up my right to the throne, and why I reclaimed it."

"That's, um."

"Go recuperate at your leisure. Somewhere near the northern lands of exile, with the empress dowager. Take your time. It's all right, I'll call you to the coronation. When I do, I'll give you that blue candy."

"No, it has to be now! Tomorrow, my face will— My skin's going to—"

"Y-you— Do you intend to exile your father and your grandmother from the imperial capital?" he asks, his voice trembling. Step-by-step, a smile so beautiful that it doesn't seem human is drawing ever closer as his son climbs the stairs.

"If people say I usurped the throne, it will cause Aileen undue hardship. Let's see. The emperor went away to convalesce; however, it proved impossible to predict how long his recovery would take. The real power had passed into the hands of the crown prince, and after a year, it was decided that his official coronation would be held—how does that sound, Prime Minister d'Autriche?"

"...Good, I believe. If you have an heir by the coronation, nothing could be better."

"Rudolph, even you? What are you sayin—?"

"Your Majesty. Prince Claude is suggesting that you take a holiday... If you do, he will tolerate what you've done."

"*Tolerate?* What's that supposed to mean—? Who do you think you are?! Y-you are speaking to your father!"

Claude chuckles, deep in his throat. He's already reached the throne. "Cedric has made himself more valuable by choosing to live a limited life in order to lure those who are dissatisfied with me out into the open. He's a splendid half brother. You're different, though. I don't consider you my father. I doubt Cedric does, either."

"Wha...?"

"After all, you aren't a father. You're that woman's child."

The statement is only natural, but the idea had never even crossed his mind. *Even if we weren't capable of being a great emperor, we at least tried to be a good father.* He grips the armrests with shaking hands.

Quietly, Rudolph lowers his eyes. "...I assume it's all right if I make arrangements for His Majesty's residence?"

"I'll leave it to you. After all, no doubt you'll have a lot of time on your hands as well someday soon."

"I'm aware of that. However, please, *Emperor* Claude. Even as he is, this man is your father, despite everything."

Just once, Claude blinks. Pierre looks up.

He hasn't seen his son up close in quite some time. The young man is taller than he is. When did he surpass him? He didn't even notice. That's all the "father" he was.

"You don't have to sit in that heavy chair anymore. Please take care—Father."

However, he is father enough to understand that those brief words are the greatest kindness his son can muster.

It's a very rainy season. However, no one is worried that it may rain on the promised day. The demon king's emotions control the weather. The light, lingering scatter of raindrops on the stained-glass ceiling reflects the sunlight, and it pours down over the lovers' vows in a rainbow of colors. The ring on the bride's finger gleams in a curious hue that could be either gold or silver.

"And now, you may kiss the bride."

Aileen's lowered eyelids rise as her thin veil is lifted. The figure standing before her is, without exaggeration, the most beautiful bridegroom in the world. In the tranquil rays of sunlight filling the church, she could easily be convinced that he's an angel or a god come to earth. Even though he's actually the demon king.

As she's thinking these things, he softly grasps her shoulders, pulling her to him, and kisses her on the forehead. Then he gives her a smile more innocent than a bride's. His beauty is like ice, and yet the expression he shows her is charming, brimming over with happiness. Aileen, who's let her thoughts skip forward to what lay ahead, blushes in spite of herself.

Preparations for this wedding would ordinarily have taken a year, but they'd been rammed through in a stomachache-inducing two months. She feared the ultra-condensed bride training might make her spit up blood, but this face makes her think the whole ordeal was worth it, and it just isn't fair. Still, no matter what things were like before, starting today, she mustn't let that face trick her into spoiling him. A wife is responsible for training her husband.

When they leave the cathedral, the bride and groom are greeted with cheers. White doves and black crows take flight all at once, and flower petals shower down. The rainbow that seems to surround the cathedral is probably the groom's doing.

"Now you are my wife," Claude murmurs, looking like the happiest man in the whole world. He sweeps Aileen into his arms. As the groom carries his bride down the stairs, confetti flutters around them.

Without letting her smile falter, Aileen whispers back quietly, "Master Claude. Hurry, if you would; the parade is next. We absolutely must not be late."

"......"

He looks back at her wordlessly, as if he'd really like to complain. However, she's just decided not to spoil him. "After that comes the ball. And you have a conference before the dancing starts, Master Claude, so make haste."

"I know, but why not be a little more, um...? We've just had our wedding ceremony, but the atmosphere is rather lacking."

"You mean the ceremony that was held because we threatened the church?"

"The church congratulated us from the bottom of its heart. They sent us a mountain of gifts."

"Those are called bribes. No matter how you try to ignore it, it won't change the fact that because you rushed the wedding, the schedule is jam-packed. So packed, actually, that I haven't been able to make room for that day where I do nothing but gaze at you, as promised." He sighs. Mercilessly, she finds fault with that reaction as well. "You mustn't knit your brow like that; smile gently. Go on, smile at those young ladies who are waving at us over there. I'll wave in this direction."

"Are we a show?"

"Yes, the best show in existence."

This is the crown prince's wedding. A wedding ceremony held at taxpayer expense is an auspicious occasion, a public performance in every sense of the phrase, and certainly not for Aileen and Claude's personal benefit.

Claude probably understands this as well. He may be reluctant on the inside, but as Aileen has instructed, he turns a blissful smile on the people gathered at the cathedral. Shrieks go up, and some of the younger women topple over like dominoes. Noticing this, Aileen discreetly cautions him. "Hold back a bit. Right now, Master Claude, you're three times as handsome as usual."

"Even though your heart doesn't seem to be fluttering at all?"

"I'm more worried than anything else. This wedding dress is as heavy as armor, isn't it?"

They'd told Denis he could use as much as he liked of whatever he wanted, and he threw the whole of the empire's prestige behind the design of this wedding gown. Layer upon layer of delicate lace, miles of ribbon, a spreading train, and a fine scattering of jewels. The pure-white wedding dress is bound to go down in history. It's both a first-class article filled with maidens' dreams, and a heavy piece of equipment that permits no retreat.

Claude, who is carrying both Aileen and that dress, has nearly reached the bottom of the long stairway. He responds with a straight face, "Actually, my arms are starting to tremble a bit."

"...G-give it your best, please! You're almost there! Perhaps use magic to cheat a bit!"

"No, that won't do. I'll carry you myself."

This can't be that "male pride" people speak of, can it? Simultaneously appalled and rather pleased, Aileen hugs him, flinging her arms around his neck with deliberate force. Claude nearly stumbles, but he manages to stay on his feet.

"I intend to marry Aileen."

Claude made a public declaration to that effect immediately after the emperor and empress dowager had departed for their mending in seclusion.

If their goal was a coronation one year from now, marriage

was an effective stepping stone. They'd be able to use the joyous event to lessen unease at the emperor's absence and divert attention from exactly how Claude had abruptly come into power. As a matter of fact, the citizens saw Claude's wedding as part of his preparations for becoming emperor. His marriage would also serve to advertise the fact that he was human to other nations, since marriage was a system created and observed by humans. If people thought the demon king had taken control of the Ellmeyer Empire, foreign lands blazing with an inconvenient sense of justice were bound to come out of the woodwork.

...And so Aileen readily agreed to the marriage. Or rather, when told *"I want you to marry me"* by a face and voice as sweet as honey drizzled on top of a pile of sugar, the only possible response was *"Yes."*

Perhaps the empire's citizens had also been busy preparing for this auspicious wedding; there hadn't been as much domestic backlash as they'd feared. This was thanks to the fact that Claude had always been very popular with the lower classes. The proof of the nobles' corruption that Serena had collected on Cedric's orders hadn't hurt either.

There were still mountains of problems, of course—but that was precisely what made the wedding so important.

They had to show the empire who would lead it to its future happiness.

"Master Claude, just use magic to change, please! Walt and Kyle, take this to the venue! I'll go check on the ball with Beelzebuth and come right back. While I'm gone, James, you take care of this!"

"...Understood. Master Claude, Jasper's given me the topics you'll be taking questions on during the conference. Look them over while you walk. Elefas, you guard Aileen."

"Aileen, step it up! You're running out of time to change!"

Isaac is beckoning from an intersecting corridor. Claude, who's been referred to as "this" by Keith, turns his back before she even has time to speak to him. Luc, who's been lying in wait for her down the hall, holds out a medicinal tea. Aileen doesn't even slow down; she gulps it without coming up for air, then hands the cup to Quartz, who's waiting up ahead. They're so short-staffed that they've even drafted these two into the operation, even though they don't belong to the aristocracy. It's an all-hands-on-deck ceremony.

When Elefas suddenly appears behind Aileen, there's fatigue in his face as well.

"Even though it's your wedding, it's terribly hectic, isn't it?"

"Yes. I haven't even had time to see the 'Demon King Love-Love' dance you learned from Almond."

"You don't need to see that."

"Elefas, while Aileen is changing, send Quartz and Luc to the forest castle, all right? We've left Denis in charge of all the demons on his own."

They've reached the changing-room door when Isaac brings this up, and Elefas agrees. Luc's eyes promptly gleam. "Elefas, before we go to the forest castle, can I have you take us by the clinic?"

"That's fine, but if I teleport too much, my magic won't..."

"...Elefas. There's a flower that's purported to have magic. Would you try eating one, just to see?"

"Huh? Eat a flower...? That isn't really..."

"I'd like your opinion on it. Does it help restore magic? I want to know more about it."

"The thing is, with the demon king, it wouldn't even be an

experiment. You and your tribe are excellent guinea pigs, though, and it's a huge boon."

"...Um, for now, let's go."

Luc is beaming, Quartz is restless, and Elefas has given up trying to persuade them. Still smiling, he teleports himself and the worrisome pair. Aileen, who was behind them listening to their exchange, turns back slightly in front of the changing-room door. "Will that be all right? We can't have him betraying us again."

"It's probably fine. It's better than the demon king's personal interviews."

"What sort of interviews were they? ...No, never mind. I won't ask, so get back to work."

When she brings up that subject, everyone except Denis instantly goes expressionless. Isaac is no exception. She notices that the light has vanished from his eyes, so Aileen retracts her question and enters the changing room.

All Denis will say on the matter is that it was fun... I wonder what Master Claude did.

There are other things that concern her. The way Rachel and Isaac don't make eye contact when Rachel comes to meet her in the changing room, for example. Apparently, her time as Aileen's body double has had lingering aftereffects. However, since it hasn't interfered with their work, nobody's been able to mention it. All Aileen and the others can do is restrain the demon king, who keeps volunteering to play Cupid.

With Rachel's help, she changes into her ball gown. It's pure white as well.

"Lady Aileen, you have a little window of time. Would you like to rest?"

"Yes, I think I will. I never dreamed a wedding dress could be so heavy..."

She lowers herself onto a wide couch slowly, being careful not to get her pearl-studded gown dirty. Just then, though, there's a knock at the door. Before Aileen prematurely gives up on her rest, Rachel goes to see who it is. She frowns. "Lady Aileen, Prince Cedric and Lady Lilia are here to greet you. What shall I tell them?"

"At a time when there's no time to spare... It's guaranteed to be harassment. Let them in, Rachel."

With Aileen's permission, Cedric and Lilia enter, accompanied by Auguste and Serena. At a glance, they look like a guard, a servant, and their masters, but that isn't actually the case. Auguste is watching Cedric and Lilia on Claude's orders, while Serena has been employed until the wedding is safely over, not by Cedric, but by Aileen.

However, Serena still hasn't given up on becoming Cedric's favorite mistress. She's undertaken her current guard duties in exchange for a guarantee of his status and position in court. Auguste seems to be working hard to talk her out of her current plan, even though she calls him names or ignores him in turns.

I wonder what will happen with these two... It doesn't look as if there are absolutely no prospects. Just the other day, possibly because Auguste had worn her down, Serena apparently told him, *"If you make something of yourself in the Holy Knights, I could be convinced to abandon the idea of becoming a mistress."* According to Walt, that meant *"The morning after they decide he's being promoted, she'll be in bed with him naked and force him to take responsibility."* The only one who hasn't realized this is Auguste, who's cheerfully devoting himself to his job advancement.

Cedric—Serena's current target—and Lilia are living under strict guard, and they aren't allowed to set foot outside their prison tower without Claude's permission. However, as far as the public is concerned, they are still the second prince and his fiancée. On the surface, in order to keep others from capitalizing on their estrangement, the members of the imperial family have to act as if they get along well.

They gaze at each other. No one's eyes are even slightly cordial. Then Cedric bows his head; there's a cold smile on his lips. "Congratulations on your marriage, elder sister-in-law."

"Hoh-hoh. Goodness, Prince Cedric. Having you call me 'elder sister' is absolutely revolting."

"It disgusts me, too. Not only that, but the crown princess? You? There's no hope left for this empire."

"My, sour grapes? That's a splendid way to congratulate me. You've made me a very happy bride. Thank you."

"You mustn't, you two! If you get along so well, you'll anger Prince Claude," Lilia cuts in. Her smile is the hardest one to interpret. Even Cedric knows her true colors now, and yet she apparently intends to continue playing the heroine to the bitter end. Aileen turns cold eyes on her, but Lilia takes her hand anyway, artlessly. "Congratulations, Lady Aileen. Your gown is marvelous, and what a lovely wedding ring!"

"Thank you, Lady Lilia."

"Marrying the demon king! I'd expect no less of you, Lady Aileen. It's the ultimate 'bad ending' event flag." Lilia caresses the wedding ring with a fingertip, smiling up at her thinly. Judging by that warped smile, she hasn't learned a single lesson even after everything that's happened.

Aileen snorts, then whispers in her ear, "And you as well.

Sixth Act

243

Congratulations on your 'happy but actually not' ending in prison with Prince Cedric." When she extends her sincere congratulations, for just a moment, Lilia looks put out. Apparently, Cedric's betrayal is the one thing she hasn't come to terms with.

Behind her, Cedric speaks. "Lilia. We can't stay long. Let's go."

"...Oh, very well. Listen, Cedric, it is a ball, you know? I'd at least like to greet everyone."

"No. We can't move without my brother's permission. Even at the ball, don't leave my side, no matter what. Not unless you want to be executed alongside me as a traitor."

Lilia falls silent. Smiling faintly, Cedric puts an arm around her shoulders, and they leave the room. At this point, Cedric won't let Lilia come into contact with other men, particularly the love interests from Game 1. That's going to make it difficult to produce the sacred sword again. Aileen does think it serves her right; however, the way Claude and Cedric sometimes seem terribly similar is more than a little unsettling.

"I'll be all right, won't I...?"

"What do you mean?"

"No, it's nothing. All right, we should go as well. Master Claude is waiting." She draws a deep breath, then rises to her feet with Rachel's help. She mustn't behave in an unbecoming way.

Passing through a corridor where a red velvet carpet has been laid down, they walk through ranks of retainers and servants—all bowing at the same angle—and then she's reached her beloved.

She finds herself gazing at a tall, grand set of double doors.

Having pledged her eternal love, Aileen is no longer the crown prince's fiancée.

She is the crown princess.

"After you two have danced the first dance, you'll need to greet the royals from other countries. You both have their names and faces memorized, correct?"

"Yes. Aileen, what about you?"

"Of course. The one that will require the most caution is the Holy Queendom of Hausel. That's the land of the oracle-princess who gave the sacred sword to the Maid. Since the demon king's wife is in possession of the sword, they may demand that we give it back. Especially if they learn I've added magic to it."

"Oh, speaking of the sacred sword, that reminds me. I've infused that wedding ring with my magic."

She blinks at him. Claude, who's just finished having his clothes straightened and primped by Keith, turns to face her. "If you add magic to the sacred sword, use what I've put in that wedding ring. There's enough for about ten Elefases in it, so it should last a while."

"My...!" Startled, Aileen examines her wedding ring.

Aileen's sacred sword is now able to evolve when it's cloaked with magic. It's a blade that combines the sacred with the demonic, making it a weapon that can affect humans as well. There is nothing that sword can't handle.

In exchange, it requires a vast amount of magic to maintain its form. When she tested it with Elefas, she managed to add magic to it, but it only held for three minutes. Furthermore, Elefas collapsed on the spot. He told her that she mustn't absorb magic from anyone other than Claude, or that person would die.

"I'd expect no less of you, Master Claude. Now I can even defeat the country that provided the sacred sword or its oracle-princess. It's a wedding ring fit for the wife of the demon king!"

"Isn't it?"

"I'll have to be careful not to forget to put it on."

"That's all right. It won't come off."

"In that case, I won't have to worry about losing— Wait, what? It won't come off?" Aileen, who's been gazing at her ring, looks up. Just then, the trumpet that announces the crown prince and princess's entrance begins to sound. She hastily faces forward, and Claude holds out his right hand. Smiling, she sets her left in it, lacing her fingers with his.

From this point on, there's just one vow to make.

"Master Claude. I will make you emperor."

"Yes. And you will be empress."

With a weighty *creak*, the doors slowly open. The light from the ballroom chandeliers, the gleaming marble floor, the silver candlesticks—everything is dazzling.

However, it's best if they can't see what's ahead.

After all, they'll just make any difficulties yield to the power of their love.

After performing a magnificent dance at the grand ball with her husband the crown prince, Aileen accepted the congratulations of the honored guests who presented themselves one after another. Every greeting she and Claude exchanged with the ambassadors and nobility of other countries was an act of diplomacy and negotiation. While she smiled demurely beside Claude, Aileen had to cleverly field the appraising conversations that were directed at her. After parting with Claude, she discussed the latest fashions with young noblewomen and bent an ear to the gossip of chatty middle-aged ladies, gathering information all the while. She kept smiling and talking on and on, unable even to break for a meal. It was midnight before she finally managed to leave the ball.

Once she returned to the crown prince and princess's bedchamber, Rachel helped Aileen undress and change into her nightgown. Now, finally, she's able to rest.

"At last! There's nothing more on the schedule for today."

"That's right. You did a splendid job, Lady Aileen."

Rachel considerately switches out the bedroom's pitcher of water for a fresh one. Serena, the guard, is wearing a maidservant's uniform, but she makes no move to help. Instead, she gives her a warning, sounding distinctly tired. "Your biggest job is still ahead of you, isn't it? It's your first night together."

"I'm all ready. My skin is the loveliest it's ever been. Just look at how silky smooth it is!"

"...You did work hard. I'll give you that, at least."

"If you'll stay on as my guard, I'll provide you with the same cosmetics." Aileen crosses her legs, smiling at her provocatively.

Serena narrows her eyes at her. "I refuse. Our contract ends tomorrow. That was the deal."

"Don't you think you'd do better to ally yourself with me than Prince Cedric?"

"No, I don't. Even after you've given birth to an heir, until the child's grown quite a bit, that second prince is going to be an absolutely vital spare. There's also the issue of whether any child you have with the demon king will be human, and more importantly, there's no way the surrounding countries are just going to stand by and let the demon king become emperor. Most of all, I can't stand you."

Aileen finds being hated this openly and to this extent actually rather refreshing. Besides, it would be a problem if she pulled the girl over to her side against her will and she promptly betrayed them. No doubt the time isn't right yet. She puts a hand to her cheek, sighing. "Well, I suppose it doesn't matter. I'm not against you seeing Auguste, either."

"Huh? What do you mean by that?"

"A little while ago, I heard you had plans to go out to eat together soon."

She and Rachel both smirk at her, and Serena's face stiffens. "That's because he kept pushing...!"

"Now that you mention it, there have been rumors about you and Auguste recently, Lady Serena."

"Yes, and it's a downright nuisance! He has a lot of admirers among the palace's underservants. They keep harassing me in dull ways—not passing along messages intended for me, losing things, etcetera—and I'm fed up with it. I keep warning him not to talk to me, but he insists on telling me I should make friends and checking to make sure I'm not up to any mischief. He's appallingly stubborn!"

"I expect you haven't been very vigorous in your refusals. In any case, you're not the type to suffer harassment in silence."

As befits the heroine of Game 2—a girl who's supposed to be dashing and popular with both genders—Serena is good at navigating relationships with women. Rachel has told Aileen that, under the pretense of helping the weak, she's getting her hands on personal information and vulnerabilities and steadily increasing her number of followers. Since she's also skilled at acting demure and hiding her true nature, her superiors dote on her as well. Her personality is extremely well suited to spying.

"I doubt it's a problem. Auguste will make a success of himself, just as you wanted. *Wife of a Holy Knight* is a highly competitive position. Be careful not to let some other woman kick you down."

"Lady Aileen. Lady Serena is particularly good at kicking people down. Down staircases, for example."

"Oh, that's right. But I think she may attempt to kick someone else down and find herself taking the fall instead, don't you?"

"You people..." As she and Rachel grin together in vulgar curiosity laced with sarcasm, Serena folds her arms, sighing deeply. "I'm only telling you this because you seem to have the wrong idea. We're going to be eating with the entire former student council."

"...Huh? No, it should be just the two of you. How did that happen?"

"I have no idea. At any rate, I fully intend to cancel on him."

"Yes, I imagine you would...," Rachel agrees.

It seems to have made Serena careless, because she goes on, muttering. "He really is a louse. I don't understand. He asked me and asked me, so I agreed, and then he says, 'Great, let's all go together'? Could he make a bigger fool of me if he tried?"

"Most of the people who serve Lady Aileen are a little bit funny."

"Rachel, wait. Don't tell me you're talking about Isaac."

"No, not specifically, but I do think many of them see you as a sacred being of sorts and lose touch with reality."

There's absolutely no reproach in Rachel's voice. However, the direction of the conversation makes Aileen feel oddly responsible. "Why can't everyone fall as deeply in love as Master Claude and I...?"

"......"

And why must her smiling lady-in-waiting and her cold-eyed guard fall silent right there?

Rachel clears her throat pointedly. "Lady Aileen. It's time for Master Claude to arrive."

"Oh, yes, it is... Rachel, do I look all right?"

"Don't worry. You're lovely, Lady Aileen."

"A-am I? W-with things like this, I hear first times are vital. I mustn't make any careless mistakes." The thought that it's almost time makes her restless and fidgety. She straightens the hem of her skirt and takes deep breaths, telling herself there's nothing to be afraid of. On the contrary, she must display enough composure to boldly tempt Claude. To that end, she's made careful preparations so that no matter what he sees, it won't be a problem—

"…Wait a moment. Master Claude will be disrobing as well, won't he?"

At Aileen's eccentric question, Rachel and Serena exchange looks. Then they nod. "That would be the normal thing to do, yes. Although, if the demon king's not normal, then I couldn't tell you with any confidence."

"I really don't think he'd do anything too extreme tonight."

"…I can't."

""What?"" Rachel and Serena say in unison, and she wails.

"Completely naked, with that face?! I won't be able to look straight at him. I'll die! What should I do, Rachel?!"

"I—I really don't know."

"Oh— I wonder if wearing a blindfold would solve the issue!"

"That would be bad in a different direction."

"Would it?! Th-then what should I do…?"

"—Lady Aileen." Smiling firmly, Rachel sets her hands on Aileen's shoulders. "You're going to be fine. Just leave everything to Master Claude, and everything will be fine."

"I—I see— Yes, you're right. Since it's Master Claude, I'm sure he'll… Wait just a minute. This is Master Claude. Will I really be all right if I leave everything to him?"

When she insists on confirming this, both Rachel and Serena avert their eyes.

"Well, I should take my leave soon."

"You haven't answered my question, Rachel!"

"If you'll tell me what happened later, I'll consider being your guard one more time. The demon king is bound to be incredible."

"Incredible? What do you mean, specifically?! I don't know what is considered the average— Wait!"

But Serena has promptly turned on her heel, and Rachel bows elegantly, then leaves the room as well.

What a heartless lady-in-waiting and guard! Left alone on the bed, Aileen clutches her head. "'Incredible'? What was she talking about...? No, don't, don't think! Don't think, don't think... Master Claude is kind, everything will be fine. It's actually what's after that—what comes next is most important! That's the part that will be hard." Trying to persuade herself of this, she rolls over onto her side. The first-class bed cradles her softly. She sighs, realizing just how tired she is. It's only natural after spending the entire day carrying out stiff, formal ceremonies in those heavy dresses.

She looks at her left hand, which she's let fall in front of her face. A ring gleams on the ring finger. A wedding ring, a pledge of eternal love—according to everybody else, a "cursed" wedding ring she can't take off, but that aside...

...*I'm Master Claude's wife now.*

She understood this rationally, but it abruptly hits home. An odd little laugh works its way up from inside her, and the ticklish feeling makes Aileen curl up into a ball on the bed. It's a very roomy bed, but if Claude is there with her, she's sure it won't be cold. Starting tonight, she'll fall asleep in the same bed as he does and greet the morning with him every day for as long as they live.

The coming days will be truly splendid ones.

The wedding ceremony had been the long-cherished wish of the adviser who'd never given up on keeping his demon king human. However, although that adviser closed his eyes and held a hand to his brow in silent consternation during the ceremony, he's been lecturing him constantly today.

"Listen to me, Master Claude. Don't cut loose and ravish Lady Aileen without thought or care."

"I know that."

"Also, don't be so reckless that her minions burst in. Just for tonight, keep it normal."

"Keith, you're being extremely rude. You make it sound as if I'm not normal."

"Stop the falling stars before you say that!" he shouts, pointing out the window.

Claude smiles. "Even the heavens are blessing us. My heart won't stop fluttering."

"Don't give me that! You're giddy, and you're making the stars fall, you walking disaster of a demon king!"

"Hey, there's a meteor shower. Ah-ha-ha-ha..."

"K-Keith. That's about enough, don't you think? It's almost time."

Cautioned by the guards, Keith sighs, giving up. Thanks to those considerate guards, Claude will finally be able to go to his wife's bedchamber. He rises to his feet, then turns to Beelzebuth, who's been waiting beside him. "Beelzebuth. I'll be cutting your connection to my mind tonight, but there's no need to worry. I'm leaving the demons to you and James. You'll be all right?"

"Of course, sire."

"You should hurry and join the festivities, too. I expect James is having a hard time of it alone."

Naturally, Claude's high spirits have affected the demons deeply, and the forest castle has been filled with merrymaking ever since that morning. The gouts of flame shooting into the sky and the flashes of lightning are festive salutes from fire drakes and lightning drakes. The seasons and weather have been warped in the area around the castle, but thanks to the barrier, it isn't affecting anything beyond the forest.

There are lots of demons who are waiting to hear about the wedding as well. Beelzebuth was in attendance, and he's already itching to talk about it. Nodding happily, he spreads his wings and launches himself off the terrace.

"Master Claude. When you said you'd be cutting their connection to your mind, is it because…?"

"I mustn't embarrass Aileen."

That seems to have been enough explanation for Walt, but beside him, Kyle cocks his head. "What do you mean?"

"I mean that tonight, Aileen is mine alone."

"Yes, yes, let's go. You're keeping that precious wife who's yours waiting all by her lonesome." Volunteering to lead the way, Keith opens the door.

Walt and Kyle fall behind Claude on his left and right, and Auguste, who's been waiting outside the door, raises a polished salute. "I'll accompany you to your dressing room, Your Highness."

"You're my guard tonight, hmm? …By the way, did you ask Serena to dinner?"

"Oh, yes, and thank you! I looked up at her through my lashes a little and said 'Can't we?' just as you'd advised me to, and it worked!"

"I'll bet it did. When I do that, Aileen gives me what I want nine times out of ten." He offers a satisfied little smile.

Behind him, Walt is appalled. "What's that advice supposed to be? You're not an innocent young maiden."

"My heart is always innocent."

"Walt, commenting here is a waste of time. Milord is chaste, but indecent."

"Chaste but indecent... Ohhh, I see, yeah that makes sense."

"Th-that aside, you know it's not good to trust Serena too much, Auguste."

"It's fine. We're just going out to eat as a group."

Claude stops in his tracks. It isn't just him. Walt, Kyle, and Keith all look at Auguste. Frowning, Kyle asks a careful question. "...As a group?"

"Oh, I guess I hadn't told you yet. It's next weekend! I've told James already. It'll be the whole former student council! Except Ailey's the crown princess now, so she probably won't be able to make it, huh..."

"...Haaaang on a minute, Auguste. Does Serena know this?"

"Yeah, I told her after she said okay, so she knows for sure. She gave me a kind of blank look, though. And actually, James was really mean about it. He said she was bound to cancel on me."

"Well, yes, that would be the expected reaction." Walt mutters, looking unusually sober. "This is...uh... Should I say I can't make it? I don't really know what to do..."

"I don't mind going, but...are you sure that's okay?"

"Huh? Kyle, yes, absolutely. You're invited and everything. If you don't show up, I'll be sad."

"It sounds entertaining. I'd like to go, too."

"Master Claude, you mustn't. You're currently the acting emperor. A little self-awareness, please."

"So if I'm the acting emperor, I can't go? I see... Then I suppose that's that. Auguste."

When he turns to face him again, the earnest young guy says, "Yes?" and stands up straighter.

"I'll plant a suggestion in Serena's mind so that she'll do what you tell her to for one evening. That's the quickest way."

"Huh? I just want to have a nice, fun meal together. I wasn't trying to..."

"Prince Claude, please don't use your power for something that sinister."

"Kyle. I'm the one who decides how to use my power... That said, if my doing it is the main issue, I'll have Elefas do it instead. You can, can't you, Elefas?"

When he turns his gaze on what appears to be empty air at first, Elefas materializes. He agrees in a noncommittal sort of way, looking troubled. "It's technically possible, but...spells like that eat up quite a lot of magic..."

"Don't worry about that. I'll lend you my magic."

"Oh, in that case, there's no problem at all. Shall I change her personality as well? It may destroy her mind, but..."

"Ugh, no mage that fiendish should have a smile that good!"

"Listen, all I wanted was to have dinner with everybody. How did we get from that to this?"

"Ah, my apologies. Up until now, I've only ever been treated as livestock, so at times, I'm rather lacking in humanity. I mean, I've even mastered the Demon King Love-Love dance."

"Don't worry, Elefas. When you danced that, you were a splendid specimen of humanity."

At Claude's unusual declaration, the others all look as if they'd like to say something, but of course, he ignores them.

"Hey, Demon King. Can I get a minute?"

Isaac appears from the depths of the corridor. They're very near the heart of the imperial castle. He's curious about what strings he pulled to get in here, but he's not surprised. There are any number of secret passages, and anyone Aileen trusts as her right-hand man is bound to be capable of that much. Claude has no doubt that this man will never directly apply for an audience with him.

"Here. Luc and Quartz said to give you this." As casually as ever, Isaac places a small cloth bag on Claude's palm. "They say it's an aphrodisiac."

"I see. Meaning it's a sedative that will put me out of commission for the night. It's nice that they're always so predictable. Tell them I promise to make her happy. *You don't mind, do you?*"

Isaac doesn't miss the emphasis. The young man who's gone out of his way to deliver a thing like this looks straight into Claude's eyes fearlessly. Then sighing, he drops his gaze to the floor. "It's fine. If you don't, they'll get noisy. My parents are on my case to get married already, too..."

"Oh." Everyone's eyes turn lukewarm.

"Rachel, huh? So you still haven't apologized."

"That's completely not it, and in the first place, apologizing would be weird. I made the right call!"

"U-um, I'll do my best, so you give it your best, too, all right?!"

"Why do I have you cheering me on now?! Don't lump us together."

"Would you like me to cast a spell to erase her memories? She might revert to early childhood, though."

"What the heck kind of spell is that?! Don't you dare!"

"—Isaac Lombard. I am grateful to you for that decision." As the rest of the group gulps, Claude speaks to him quietly, as the emperor of the woman he serves. "If the goal was protecting my wife, you made the correct choice. *It was just like you.* A woman who doesn't understand that is not fit to be your wife, and she also disqualifies herself as my wife's lady-in-waiting."

"...Master Claude." Frowning, Keith admonishes him to keep up appearances, but Claude lays his true feelings bare.

"As long as you are like that, I will allow you to stay at my wife's side, as her right-hand man."

"...You just said *my wife* three times. Bragging much?"

"Why not? She is my wife. My wife. My bride. My life's companion. My spouse. My—"

"Argh, yeah, yeah, I get it. That was pretty typical of me, now that you mention it. Man, this is dumb." Scratching the back of his neck, Isaac stares up. His face seems a bit clearer. "Well, there's no point in rushing, is there? Life is long. There's no guarantee that this is gonna work out anyway."

"...You don't have to be that openly defiant about it."

"Never mind, just get over there, Demon King. You're not getting any help from us, all right?" With one final, meaningful smile, Isaac gives a light wave, then turns away.

Claude frowns. "What's that supposed to mean? ...Well, I suppose it's fine."

"Master Claude, didn't you resolve that for yourself a little too quickly?"

"The fact that I'm keeping Aileen waiting is a bigger problem. With these things, the first time is vital."

"Oh, you're right. You are running late." After checking his pocket watch, Keith walks on quickly.

Before long, they reach the very heart of the imperial castle: the residential quarters prepared for the crown prince and princess. First, Walt and Kyle remain in the corridor. Then Auguste stays in the waiting room with Serena, who looks openly disgusted when she realizes she'll have to share guard duty with him. Rachel, the maidservant, tells him, "Lady Aileen is waiting for you," and sees them off. As Claude reaches the door to the bedchamber, Keith takes a step to the side.

"Go ahead, Crown Prince."

"Keith, thank you."

"Hmm? Why so formal all of a sudden?"

"You didn't give up on me. Thanks to everything you've done, I'll be able to have human happiness, and a family." He thumps him lightly on the shoulder. When he's passed him, he hears a sob as if the man is choking something back, but he closes the door without turning around.

My wife, hmm...?

He never dreamed that he would ever have such a thing. As he thinks this, he's aware that he's getting sentimental. He may be feeling a little nervous.

How human of the demon king.

Smiling wryly, he takes a step forward. The lamps are turned down low, and the wide, canopied bed is in shadow. He thinks he sees a shape move on it. "Aileen, I'm sorry. I've kept you wait—"

Claude softly approaches the bed, and then he notices.

His wife is asleep.

A shock as if he's been struck by lightning runs through his entire body, then turns into actual lightning that strikes outside the castle.

The glittering, magical night of falling stars is abruptly transformed into a stormy midnight of torrential rains and unending thunder. The celebrating townspeople hastily retreat into their houses, and both humans and demons turn their concerned attention to the imperial castle—or rather, to their new liege lord, whose emotions literally control the weather.

Although those who serve the crown prince also suspect something unusual from the sudden change in the weather, they can't burst into the newlyweds' bedchamber on their wedding night. When the storm dies down in less than an hour, they're relieved... However, the next morning, their faces turn pale when they discover that the crown prince has spent the night not in bed, but on the couch.

The crown princess, who slept soundly in the bed all night long, turns paler still. Those who serve her simply say, "Once Lady Aileen's asleep, you can try to wake her up, but it's never gonna happen," and roar with laughter.

In the year 666 of Imperial Ellmeyer's calendar, with one year remaining until Claude Jean Ellmeyer becomes the seventeenth emperor...

...the beginning of the newly married life of the unique crown prince and his human crown princess signals a future riddled with difficulties.

Afterword

It's a pleasure to meet you, or perhaps it's good to see you again. My name is Sarasa Nagase.

Thank you very much for picking up my faltering attempt at a novel. Because of you, I've been able to have the further adventures of Aileen, the demon king, and their merry friends published in book form.

This volume covers the third section of the online version. Compared with that version, the epilogue is completely different, and I've written a bit under twenty pages' worth of new story for it. On the other hand, the epilogue for the online version is indeed different, so please feel free to read both and see for yourself how they differ if it strikes your fancy.

The comic version of *I'm the Villainess, So I'm Taming the Final Boss* has started its run in *Monthly Comp Ace*!

Anko Yuzu's versions of Aileen and company are all incredibly lively, and I can't recommend the manga highly enough! I really want you to see the characters moving around on the page with your own eyes, so if you happen to run across it, please do give it your support.

Most of all, I'm truly grateful to Anko Yuzu for creating this brilliant manga. Thank you so much.

And now for the thank-yous.

To Mai Murasaki: Thank you for always drawing beautiful

illustrations for me, even though you're so busy. In particular, I really do feel safe leaving Claude entirely in your hands. Please continue to take care of Aileen and everyone else.

To my supervising editor: It seems like I'm always causing you trouble. Thank you for being so considerate.

I'd also like to thank the proofreaders, the members of the Kadokawa Beans Bunko and Comp Ace editorial departments, the designers and marketing personnel, everyone at the printer, and all the people who were involved in the making of this book. I'm deeply grateful to all of you.

Finally, to everyone who picked up this book: Thank you for staying with me this far. Please continue to give both the novel and manga versions of Aileen and the others your continued support.

Now then, with prayers that we'll meet again...

Sarasa Nagase